TIME TOURS

Duckbills crouched like great frightened lizards in the greenery—huge overgrown iguanas trying to hide amid giant magnolias. The rearmost adults turned, peering back into the dust, keeping a horned eye out for the pursuing tyrannosaur pack.

"Oh, I see them now," Peg hooted in triumph. "Here they come!"

Jake's jaw fell. Under cover of dust and half-light, the tyrannosaurs had wheeled, shifting from line ahead to line abreast, to start another run smack at the middle of the shaken herd.

Peg scrambled out of the wash, lying prone on the cutback, her recorder running. Idiot luck had put her right in their path, between the triceratops herd and the line of oncoming carnivores. Six frenzied tyrannosaurs rushed at her out of the twilight, teeth gleaming, tails straight, clawed feet chewing up the clay pan.

Then a wave of claws, teeth, and muscle swept over her, and her comlink went dead.

Other AvoNova Books by
R. García y Robertson

THE SPIRAL DANCE

THE
VIRGIN
AND THE
DINOSAUR

R. GARCÍA y ROBERTSON

AVON BOOKS • NEW YORK

VISIT OUR WEBSITE AT
http://AvonBooks.com

Portions of this work have appeared in somewhat different form as novellas in *Isaac Asimov's Science Fiction Magazine*: "The Virgin and the Dinosaur" (February 1992) and "Down the River" October 1993.

THE VIRGIN AND THE DINOSAUR is an original publication of Avon Books. This work is a novel. Any similarity to actual persons or events is purely coincidental.

AVON BOOKS
A division of
The Hearst Corporation
1350 Avenue of the Americas
New York, New York 10019

First AvoNova Printing: September 1996

AVONOVA TRADEMARK REG. U.S. PAT. OFF. AND IN OTHER COUNTRIES, MARCA REGISTRADA, HECHO EN U.S.A.

Printed in the U.S.A.

RA   10 9 8 7 6 5 4 3 2 1

WELCOME TO
HELL CREEK, MONTANA
POP: 2

Mosquitoes as big as hummingbirds buzzed in the hot Mesozoic air. The screen of ferns and flowering trees parted, sending toothed and feathered proto-birds scurrying into the upper branches. Jake Bento watched a tall red-haired young woman step naked into the clearing—she moved with a dancer's grace, bare athletic legs bunching then releasing with each step.

At that point-instant Jake had Time by the tail. Five minutes before, he had navigated the Hell Creek portal perfectly, acing the coveted First Run to the Mesozoic with *no nasty shocks*. Microamps beat out an ancient victory anthem, "Light My Fire" by The Doors.

"Isn't it won-der-ful?" Peg rose on her toes, stretching in the steamy Montana air. Beads of sweat ran down between her breasts, across the swell of her belly, to gleam in her red triangle of pubic hair.

Jake had bent down to do a reactor check. When he'd looked up, Peg had shucked blanket coat, buckskins, and moccasins. He grinned in appreciation. "Welcome to the *motherfucking* Mesozoic."

His mix of Universal and English puzzled Peg. Jake tuned down The Doors, reprogramming for full Universal. "Yes, undoubtedly essential. Premium quality."

"You make it sound like a meat substitute. What does *'motherfucking'* mean?" Peg had picked up the awe and

3

reverence Jake packed into the English obscenity.

"A verbal noun, indicating affection." He dodged around the strict definition. "Intense personal affection, so essential it's criminal."

"Well, then this whole *motherfucking* world is ours." Peg swung her arms to indicate the ferns and dogwoods, the pool, the sky, the dry riverbed.

Just like Adam and Eve. Jake thought it, but did not say it. The absolute wonder of hitting that first point-instant in a new place had faded. Even the Mesozoic, the Uppermost Maastrichtian of the Latest Late Cretaceous, did not excite him the way it did Peg. He had lived too long at the leading edge of FTL.

Peg was the neophyte, the first timer, picked for this run because she happened to be young, healthy, ambitious, and overqualified—Biofile rated her as a bona fide dinosaur genius. But only a raw beginner would lay claim to an entire world-era just because humans had finally arrived.

Still, Peg was boss lady on this expedition. Jake's job was to play trusty guide and willing manservant—show *memsahib* the period, haul her gear, bring her back intact. Rendering physical and personal assistance, *as needed*. Easy enough. The sort of assignment Jake could thrive on. Thousands of skilled and dedicated stay-at-homes had worked, sweated, and sacrificed so that he could share this clearing, this whole planet, with a criminally graceful Ph.D. in paleontology. He *owed* it to them to have fun.

She followed his gaze, seeming to notice her body for the first time. "Sorry. My skin needed to breathe. It's so incredibly hot." Fahrenheit surface temperature had tripled since passing the portal. "You don't mind, do you? We are adults."

"Mind? Not in the smallest." Jake was wearing moccasins and fringed leggings, soft as gloves, and a cotton annuity shirt given to him by the River Crow, but he had nothing against nudity. Cretaceous Montana was made for it—mesothermic climate, no rude neighbors, none that cared anyway.

However, he noted an alarming wholesomeness in the way Peg said "adults." As if sex only took place between tipsy teenagers or incurable juveniles. There was no hard, fixed rule that team members had to fuck—but Jake expected it. With Peg, he put a priority on it. And now, barely five minutes into the job, she had already shucked everything but her belly button. Fabulous. But Peg probably just enjoyed the feel of warm air. The blending with nature. Her nudity was not meant for him.

"So, when do we sight dinosaurs?" She swiveled on her toes like a dancer, trying to see over the foliage.

"*Say what*?" Jake slipped back into English, still captivated by smallish breasts and large dark nipples.

"Dinosaurs. Huge archosaurs. Dominant megafauna of this period. Where are they?"

"Give them a moment." Jake was moderately pleased not to have stepped out of the Hell Creek portal into the path of megafauna with big teeth and bad attitudes. A nonsignificant worry—the Mesozoic was a huge place; the very size of dinosaurs meant that they were rare, rarer than elk or rhino in the wild. Navigating the Hell Creek anomaly had been infinitely more chancy than tripping over a tyrannosaur. Jake had a private horror of portal skips—of just vanishing, leaving no clues, no clothes, nothing but the anomaly that ate you. With a dinosaur you at least *knew* you were being devoured.

"Come look." Peg pushed aside a flowering branch. "We could have hit the wrong era—Lower Paleocene instead of the Uppermost Cretaceous. That would be devastating." Hell Creek was the last stop for dinosaurs; in an eye blink of geologic time the huge creatures would be gone.

Never doubting his navigation, Jake took the excuse to stand behind her, making concerned noises, inhaling her odor. Short copper curls tickled the nape of her neck. Sweat beaded at the base of her spine.

He acknowledged that the landscaping *was* dull. Dense vegetation hugged the dry riverbed. The flats beyond were open canopy plains, hotter than a skillet, covered with scrub pines and thorny berry bushes, broken by tall termite mounds. Peg must have made the mistake of trying to explore; Jake noted thin fresh scratches on her creamy hip.

So far Upper Cretaceous Montana resembled precontact Australia. The pool he sat by might have been a South Kimberly billabong in the Dream Time. Little creatures stirring the brush seemed no more dangerous than a goanna or a roo.

A thunderous buzzing shook the air. Streaking from the sand by the billabong, a vicious metal blue insect homed straight for them. Peg leaped backward, twisting and slapping at the whirring horror. Jake's shoulder holster slid his flat neural stunner into his palm.

"Drop," he yelped.

Peg flattened on the sandy bank, and he fanned the air above her. The flying devil fell like a lead slug onto the wet sand.

Peg pounced on the downed insect, prying open the jaws. "See here." She waved the stunned bug beneath Jake's nostrils. "Mandibles meant for dinosaur. Nothing in the Lowest Paleocene would take jaws like that to chew through."

He agreed. The saw-toothed dental work looked ferocious.

Peg tossed the insect aside.

By now, Jake knew the tone to take. Peg had worked herself into a paleontological frenzy just to get here. He had to impress her with his calm professionalism, feigned indifference, and rugged charm. The truly inspirational aspect of this expedition was that things did not have to happen all at once. He and Peg would share a campfire tonight, and breakfast tomorrow, tomorrow, and tomorrow. Sooner or later, they were sure to be wearing out the same sleeping bag. Cheered by that certainty, he hummed through the rest of his equipment check:

> Once a jolly swagman
> Camped by a billabong,
> Under the shade of a koolibah tree;

Jake ticked off each item almost without thinking. He had a fabulous memory, 360K megabytes of RAM tucked in the compweb stretched atop his skull, alongside his navmatrix and music files. A Crazy Dog Blackfoot once tried to lift Jake's hair—not for any personal reasons, just part of the usual hysteria accompanying a Crow attack. One look under Jake's scalp, and the Crazy Dog dropped his knife and ran, spooked by gleaming fiberoptics. At a kill-talk Jake returned the knife. The Crazy Dog thanked him, swearing he would never scalp another Wasichu.

Buckskins, dehydrated rations, shock-rifle, microstove, and lounge chairs were broken down, collapsed, and closest-packed to fit through the portal. The Hell Creek anomaly was newly opened, poorly mapped, generally a tight squeeze. The twelve-megawatt mobile fusion reactor had been the most obstinate piece, harder to get through than everything else combined. People passed easily—too easily, becoming the victims of portal skips or spontaneous transmission. Metals and hardwired electronics were the worst. Only the length of stay and the ground to cover justified bringing the reactor. A herd of pack ponies would have been easier to fit through the portal, but who knew how oatburners would take to Mesozoic Asiamerica. For openers, there was no grass.

Check completed. Jake kicked the reactor, mentally

telling the gray 1.5-meter cube to get into mobile mode.

With a whirr and click, the reactor sprouted four shiny legs, with white rings on the ends. The whirr became a softer hiss. The white rings inflated into four balloon tires. "Mobile" reactors were made to live up to the name.

> And he sang as he sat and
> Waited by that billabong—
> Who'll come a-waltzing Matilda with me?

Jake climbed to a perch atop the pack saddle, reaching down for Peg. "So, will you come a-waltzing Matilda with me?"

"Wat-zing Ma-tilta?" Peg looked up. She was crouched on one knee, squeezing gravelly mud through her fingers—half scientist, half wood nymph. "This *has* to be Hell Creek. Sediment's too dry and rocky for the Tullock formation." She carefully brushed the dirt off her fingers.

Time shock. Jake recognized symptoms of a mild attack. Peg was doubting the period, feeling the air and mud, proving to herself this world was real. Well, it was real. It was Earth. Human population, two. But Home and civilization were sixty-five million years away, thirty times farther than a trip to the Andromeda galaxy at lightspeed.

Jake smiled. "I'll show you dinosaurs. I promise." They were bound to see the big beasts soon, so he might as well claim credit now.

Her eyes lit. "Even sauropods? It's essential I see sauropods." Sauropods were the *big* boys: brontosaurs, titanosaurs, supersaurs, and ultrasaurs. Few had made it to the Upper Cretaceous—none were known in Hell Creek.

"Sure, sauropods." He extended his hand farther. "Don't make 'em wait."

She took his offered hand, vaulting easily onto the saddle beside him.

Jake told the reactor, "Downstream." They lurched into motion, splashing through ponds and puddles, keeping to the lowest part of the bed, feeling for the main channel. Steep banks and tall ginkgos turned the wash into a green canyon topped by a blue ribbon of sky. Pneumatic tires left silent prints in the bare mud.

Upper Cretaceous Montana had a semitropical climate and a swampy coastline; somewhere downstream was the shallow Midwestern Sea separating Asiamerica from Euramerica. Montana was on the east coast of the Asia-american supercontinent, a great arc connecting Mexico to Malaysia—taking in the northern Pacific Rim, China, Siberia, and Mongolia. The Urals were a far western archipelago.

Leaves trapped and reflected back the radiant heat, making the shaded wash into a muggy oven. Greenhouse gases filled the hot air. Jake saw bank soils leached by acid rain. Sort of like the twenty-first century Old Style, without the overpopulation and money collapse.

The young Mesozoic sun sank quickly. Jake unshipped his shock-rifle. Late afternoon was hunting time in hot climates. He boosted his hearing. The microamps in his middle ear turned the rustle of wind and leaves into a roar.

Craning his neck, he switched his corneal lenses from wide-angle to telescopic, searching for fine details. Nothing. No snapped twigs. No three-toed tracks. None of the shed teeth commonly found in Hell Creek rock. The absence of animals was eerie.

"I've seen fossil beds with more life than this," complained Peg, resting a lithe forearm on his shoulder. Her words boomed in his boosted ears.

He finished fitting the shock-rifle together—telescopic vision made each part seem huge as prefab sewer pipe.

Peg eyed the assembled rifle. "Nine out of ten animals in the Hell Creek formation are harmless herbivores. Chances are less than one in a hundred of meeting a really hungry carnivore. You seem overly worried."

"Me? Never." He noted that Peg still talked in terms of sediment formations and fossil ratios, as if this were a bone hunt, not a living, breathing world.

Trundling around a corner, they startled a wee furry fellow drinking from one of the ponds. As it scampered for the undergrowth, Peg leaped to the ground, recorder running. "Why didn't you stun it?"

"Because it was rabbit-sized and scared senseless." The shock-rifle was designed for dinosaurs, and would have blasted the tiny mammal's central nervous system straight out its eyeballs. "I don't expect it was dangerous."

"It was probably a protoungulate—closer to a horse than a rabbit." She fingered prints in the soft mud, and reviewed her recordings—a 3V image of the creature repeated the scurry for safety several times.

"But how am I supposed to know, if I don't get a look at its teeth?"

Jake knew all about the paleontologist's love affair with teeth. Teeth preserved well and told you a lot. Careers had been launched by broken molars—and they were happy as dental hygenists to see a clean, complete set.

"Oh, *great*, some droppings." Peg poked and sniffed through a pile of wet turds squeezed out by the terrified mammal. "A genuine browser; bet he had real grinders."

She climbed back aboard, patting the shock-rifle. "Stow the nuke. Your stunner would be more helpful."

Jake slipped out of his shoulder holster, twisted about, and fit the holster over Peg's bare shoulder. Her skin felt smooth beneath his fingers, with a thin film of sweat— the only outward sign that she was excited. "Here, Annie Oakley, blaze away at the rodents, just don't hit me.''

"Annie Oakley?''

"Friend of Sitting Bull's. I'll tell you about her some-day—maybe introduce you.'' When he was not on the warpath, Sitting Bull had a relaxed and amiable way with women, even Wasichu women, one of the many reasons Jake admired the Medicine Man.

They did not see any more of the tiny horses-to-be. Jake spotted a foot-long tree rat, which Peg thought was a primitive possum. She could not be sure because she was slow with the stunner, not having the bioimplants to control the holster.

The streambed widened into a broad expanse of hardpan, cracked into blocks by the heat, each block as flat and regular as a square of old paving. Jake smelled the oily reek of a jungle river. He halted, spotting a reptilian tail stretching back from the bank. Black fisher-storks stalked about, stepping over the scaly tail.

"That's nothing.'' Peg dismissed the tail with a shake of her head. "An archosaur, but hardly a dinosaur.''

Boosting up, Jake saw a dozen big crocodiles basking in the afternoon sun; five-meter eating machines—jaws, stomach, and a tail. (If you don't believe there are crocs in Montana, just ask the River Crow.) These weren't the gigantic dinosaur-eating crocodiles found in Texas, but *all* crocs were cunning, dangerous cases who would out-live the dinosaurs. The nearest one looked maybe three times as long as Jake and easily ten times as mean.

Peg put down her recorder. "It's so *nonessential*, see-ing everything but dinosaurs.''

"Relax.'' Jake hopped down, keeping an eye on the crocs. He did not expect any to come charging over the hardpan, but it never paid to turn your back on the reptilian brain. Gripping Peg's waist, he swung her to the ground, feeling her skin, smelling her fragrance, forgetting all about the crocs amid the burst of flesh. Strange

how her sweat didn't stink. "I'll show you more dinosaurs than you ever dreamed of," he told her.

She smiled, "Not likely. I've dreamed nothing but
sauropods since being picked for this trip."

Packsaddle and equipment cases followed her onto the
hardpan. Then Jake sent the reactor lumbering down to
the river for a drink, trailing an anchor line.

The crocs looked up. One took a speculative snap at
the big balloon tires. Jake sent it a jarring shock from the
reactor's defense system. After that the crocs ignored the
reactor. Too big to swallow and too tough to chew. They
let the ungainly newcomer waddle into midstream and
toss out a second anchor.

While the reactor drank, Jake laid out sleeping bags
and pink champagne, dragging in dried brush and drift-
wood for a fire, telling his microstove to whip up dinner.
Peg looked fetching in her stunner and shoulder holster,
dashing about recording the sleepy crocs and the flowering trees, radiating megawatts of misplaced energy.

He watched her zoom in on the black fisher-storks,
stalking about the shallows like operatic vampires. The
tall birds spread their wings before them, forming feather
capes to shade out surface glare. Ducking their heads
inside the dark canopies, they would strike at fish, then
step gingerly forward to find a new spot.

It took over two hours for the reactor to extract a half
ton of hydrogen from the river, pumping it into an elastic
gasbag—the reactor opened as needed like an origami
box. When the expanding envelope was sauropod-sized,
fifty meters long and twenty meters tall, Jake told the
reactor to reel itself back to the campsite. The newborn
blimp drifted over to hang above him, blocking out the
setting sun. He sprayed the skin with metallic sealant,
covering everything but the line of vents along the top
and the transparent windows on the cabin space.

Dusk brought more brontosaurian insects. Peg retreated to the campsite, where Jake set up a sonic field

to keep the bugs at bay. He popped the pink champagne, pouring two glasses.

Peg sniffed her drink. "I don't use alcohol at work. There *is* alcohol in this isn't there?"

You betcha, as Sitting Bull would say. Alcohol was an archaic vice; if Peg was an inexperienced drinker, the champagne should go straight to her inhibitions. "But we have a ship to christen." Jake nodded toward the new fifty-meter airship floating above them, gleaming red and gold in the sunset.

"Christen?" Peg was still dubious.

"Sure. In the old days, they launched an airship by having a woman toast the ship with champagne, giving her a name."

"Didn't the woman already have a name?"

"Yes, but she gave the *ship* a name as well—all ships are 'her' or 'she.' " Jake assumed Peg had never been aboard an airship. At Home, ships of any sort were a rarity. A person could work, live, play, even travel from Montana to Pluto, without ever entering a vehicle.

"Well, what shall I call it . . . I mean her?"

"I was thinking of *Challenger*. You know, after Professor Challenger and his Lost World—the great jungle plateau full of dinosaurs." He could see she had not read Conan Doyle.

"Is that fiction?"

"Very much, but *we* are real. So why don't you name our ship?" Be a sport.

She took a deep sip, and smiled up at the dirigible. "I name you *Challenger*."

The little ritual had served its purpose—the bottle was open, Peg had loosened up. He made sure her glass stayed full. Next stop, the cozy fire. Jake was not thigh-struck enough to start his romantic campfire right under thousands of cubic meters of explosive hydrogen. The stressed metal skin was supposed to stop sparks, leaks, lightning, and St. Elmo's fire—but why chance spoiling the moment by being blown clear out of the Uppermost Cretaceous. He told the airship to go up a hundred meters. It hung in the last of the sunset, while Jake served up some simple safari fare, *risotto à la milanese*, with eggplant vinaigrette, and tofu Szechwan in triple pepper sauce.

As they ate, he heard crocs moving about by the river. Night birds cried. Things went thump and crunch in the brush. The Mesozoic night never seemed to get really quiet—too hot.

Jake cut his microamps, telling *Challenger* to watch for movement and illuminate the crocs. Then he settled in, shock-rifle on one side of him, Peg on the other.

Peg lay back against the packsaddle, fed and happy. She had put on a Crow gift shirt for dinner, fancier than Jake's—fringed buckskin, beaded with porcupine quills—but she left off the breechcloth and leather leggings. In the night heat you only needed to be half-dressed. She gave his leg a playful whack, trying out some of his English, "The *motherfucking* Mesozoic. We're here. Aren't you amazed, excited, dumbfounded? Do you even believe it?"

His leg stung from the slap. She was still suffering from time shock, but the champagne had made her frisky. Jake decided he could take a bit of physical abuse from a woman—administered in the right spirit.

He slid an arm around her waist. "Damn well *feels* like we're here."

Seeming not to notice his arm, she stared moodily into the sizzling Mesozoic night. "All except for the dinosaurs."

Right, no damned dinosaurs. He refilled her glass with his free arm, amused by her inebriated swings of mood.

Challenger beeped him. Crocs were moving down by the water. None were coming his way. He went back to admiring Peg's thigh and the dark hollow between her legs.

She smiled over her champagne, "I mean, aren't you disappointed?"

"Not yet." His hand closed on the hem of her shirt, pulling her closer, feeling the warm curve of flesh beneath the buckskin. She had a gymnast's body, taut and muscled.

Peg relaxed into him, saying nothing, wearing a dreamy expectant look. A really *essential* look, one time never touched. Jake had seen that look in the khol-darkened eyes of one of Cleopatra's handmaids, and on the face of a Martian princess aboard a flower petal boat anchored in the Grand Canal. He'd seen it shining across a dung fire in a yurt on the Camelback Steep, beside the Sleeping Sands north of the Gobi. Jake had seen that exact look in a half dozen centuries, on three habitable planets. Thank goodness it always meant the same thing. He and Peg were a millimeter away from foreplay.

Challenger beeped him again.

Jake checked the crocs—no change. Turning back, he found Peg's head resting on his shoulder, eyes wide, lips parted. Her freckled face looked near perfect in the firelight. He leaned in to kiss her, sliding his hand under her hip for leverage.

Peg squealed, leaped up, lost balance, and sat back bare-assed on his hand, breathing hard and muttering, "Oh my, oh my . . ."

Staring at them from across the fire was a great, round yellow eye. The eye was set in a huge bony head, silhouetted by the night—half in shadow, half in light. Above the eye stood a horn as long as Jake was tall.

Triceratops. No 3V imaging, no mounted skeleton, no Feelie stimulation did the dinosaur justice. Imagine a four-legged beast, big as a bull elephant, with an armored head, three tremendous horns, and a terrible cutting beak. Picture this behemoth appearing out of blackness, without warning, when you are sitting by a night fire in a strange place, half-foxed on champagne, your hand stuck under someone else's butt. Jake was paralyzed.

And there were more of them. Immense six-ton bodies appeared on either side of the first, more wicked heads and horns. Hundreds were filling the dark wash, pushing toward the river.

Peg lunged forward to grab a recorder. Her tanned rear eclipsed the triceratops in front of Jake—but all thought of taking advantage of Peg had vanished. He yelled for *Challenger* to reel herself down the anchor line.

The ship did not come half fast enough. Clutching his shock-rifle, Jake watched powerful jaws crunch ginkgo and magnolia like broccoli. Were it not for his campfire, the fleshy avalanche would have trod Peg and him into the hardpan. It could still happen. The dinosaurs being pushed toward the fire acted dangerously agitated. A sneeze could start a stampede.

Challenger's balloon tires touched down atop the anchor grapple. Flames cast dancing shadows on the dirigible's hull. Jake had forgotten the fire. He pictured half a ton of hydrogen gas exploding like a bomb in the midst of a triceratops herd—with him beneath it. The First Mesozoic Expedition would be finished well ahead of schedule.

In a fever to get aloft, he heaved equipment into the cabin atop the reactor. Then he turned to Peg. She was sitting on her haunches, easy-as-you-please, panning the recorder, *totally* absorbed by the milling herd. He grabbed hold of the shoulder fringe on her Crow gift shirt, screaming, "Get aboard."

Peg's eyes shone clear and excited. "We found them."

"Right, and this is too dangerous by half." Unshipping the nylon ladder, he shoved it into her hands.

Reluctantly, she stowed her recorder, climbing the ladder. Armored heads crowded closer. Any moment a horn might puncture the thin plasti-metal gasbag, releasing a torrent of flammable hydrogen. Jake dropped the shock-rifle, planted his hand on Peg's bottom, and shoved. "Put a wiggle in it."

As he pushed Peg into the cabin Jake yelled to *Challenger*, "Up a hundred meters."

They shot skyward. Jake clung to the last rungs of the twisting ladder, watching the campfire shrink to a spark, surrounded by the shadowy backs and heads of the herd. Fumbling above the sea of spikes, he got a foot on the bottom rung, and swung back and forth, full of fright and exhilaration, ninety-odd meters above the hardpan. Perfectly safe as long as he did not let go. Triceratopses soberly watched him swing overhead—"Mama, look at the silly mammal."

"Aren't you coming up?" inquired a sweet intoxicated voice overhead.

Without a word, Jake climbed the swaying ladder, tumbling into the lounge—the middle part of the cabin, with large entrance windows at either end—collapsing on the nonslip floor.

Peg hopped over him, full of alcoholic enthusiasm, trying to record from both ends of the lounge at once. Every so often, she ran over and shook him, with a bit of breathless news. "There are hundreds down there."

A moment later she'd be back. "Make that thousands."

Giggling hysterically, she tugged at him, "Come on, you have to *see* it." She had all the running lights on, illuminating the herd below.

"And juveniles. *Motherfucking* juveniles, moving with the herd." Then she would bound off again to lean out a window, only her legs and bottom in the cabin.

Jake had busted himself to pass the portal, find water, set up camp, get *Challenger* ready, start a fire, serve dinner, and seduce Peg. The moment he had her tipsy and in his arms, he'd been nearly trampled, dangled from a soaring airship, and come closer than he needed to being blown apart. All on a head full of champagne. He decided he hadn't a hope of calming Peg down and sliding her into a double sleeping bag. Finding his bag and kit, he crawled off to the privacy of a barren stateroom, cursing all thousand triceratopses for their pre-*coitus interruptus*.

T. rex

Dawnlight angled in the stateroom window. Jake lay sprawled across his sleeping bag, hammered by a vicious hangover. He had forgotten how deadly sweet champagne was the day after. Groping about, he found his medikit, telling it to take away the misery.

His head cleared, leaving only the happy glow of having made it to the Mesozoic. The first night's prize fiasco faded into a few not unfunny memories. Today had to be near perfect—just to balance the statistics. Cheered by that gambler's fallacy he opened the stateroom door.

Peg was padding back and forth in the ship's central lounge, still wearing the fringed Crow shirt—her tired face full of heartless enthusiasm. Had she slept? Probably not.

"Have you seen them yet?" she demanded. "They are ten times as thrilling by day."

Easing back on the angle of attack, Jake gave her a professional greeting, telling the microstove to conjure up *café au lait*. He took a steaming cup into the cabin's glassed-in nose to gauge the day.

It *was* magnificent. The fore and aft ends of the cabin area were completely transparent. Light poured through the windows and floor. Jake sat amid blue limitless sky filled with towering white anvilheads. Green-brown floodplain snaked beneath him, coiling round islands of red earth. Mountains thrust up in the distance. He had his microamps pound out *Dawn Symphony.*

The triceratops herd was truly awesome. Huge tawny bodies took up both sides of the river; moving, drinking, chewing up the greenery. Crocs had shifted to midstream to keep from being trampled, sunning themselves on sandbars while tickbirds picked their teeth. He told the navcomputer to turn off the running lights, blazing uselessly in daylight.

Peg followed him into the glassed-in nose, constantly recording, shooting through the deck at their feet. Her bright eyes were ringed by dark circles. ''How long before we can get this ship moving?''

''What? Bored here already?'' A day ago she had been dying just to *see* dinosaurs.

Peg waved at where the herd had come from. ''It's essential to see if carnosaurs are trailing the herd.''

He turned down *Dawn Symphony.* Unwashed, circles under her eyes, wearing only a badly wrinkled buckskin shirt—Peg was every bit as stunning as he remembered. Of course, she was the only woman on the planet. The only one in all creation. Which accounted for at least ten percent of her attraction. ''I hate to move ship in this condition.''

''What's wrong with it?'' She glanced about the pristine foredeck.

''Nothing's in place. Everything's piled where I tossed it last night. Lounge looks like a crash site.'' *Challenger*'s cabin was designed to give them breathing room. Lounge, galley, and chart room formed a common area amidships. Twin staterooms aft were enclosed and independent. Fore and aft galleries gave each person a place to be alone with the vast landscape.

Peg bounded to work. Before he could finish his *café au lait*, she had cleared up the litter in the lounge, inflating collapsible furniture, hips bending and swaying as she worked. She was not only a nerveless idiot with no sense of self-preservation, but also a shamelessly cheerful worker, leaving Jake with no good reason to grouse. She finished off with yoga, moving to an inner music that needed no microamps. Her whole body sang. Peg was impossibly supple—chaste and naked at the same time.

Reeling *Challenger* down to the campsite, Jake hopped out for a final visit. Black ashes scarred the dry wash, surrounded by bits and pieces left behind in the panic. The champagne bottle and glasses were ground to fine dust. Next to a shattered case of dehydrated *pâté* he saw the gleaming stock of the shock-rifle, mashed into the hardpan. The rest of the weapon was gone, carried away between some thoughtless triceratops' toes.

An absolutely fine thing to forget! He had set the gun down in order to shove Peg up the ladder. Now they had *nothing* fit to take down a dinosaur. "Shock-rifle—missing," would raise a red flag in his report. Any weapon lost "out of period" was a headache. FTL would want *details*.

He wished he had a more professional explanation than being caught in drunken panic with his hand on his partner's butt. Happily, debriefing was months away. Without a shock-rifle he could easily be killed—then the problem would have solved itself.

Jake returned to the ship, determined to concentrate on piloting, something he fancied he did well. Compweb and navmatrix made *Challenger* an add-on to his central nervous system. Machinery leaped to his least command. Vague curiosity produced immediate data on buoyancy and wind speed. He released the anchor grapple, feeling the snap. *Challenger* rose silently upward. The reactor extended twin propellers. They were off.

Turning west, Jake climbed in huge steps toward the highlands, feeling the ship's balance as though the keel were a giant teeter-totter—anticipating trim changes,

bracing for turns—flying a few tons heavy to maintain
altitude aerodynamically instead of aerostatically. He
relished the sense of control, welcoming the challenge
of translating Peg's instructions into something *Challenger* comprehended.

"Over there."

"Bearing two-nine-zero."

"A little to the left."

"Port five degrees."

"Closer."

"Down twenty meters."

He had Peg so pleased she was running to the microstove to fetch him *croissants* and coffee, though galley work was technically Jake's department. As he
suspected, Peg would put up with almost anything filed
under WORK. Like many people who get good at what
they do, she was eager to learn and not afraid to sweat.
All he needed to do was slip "sex" into her job description, then she would bang away with enthusiastic
efficiency. Coffee and *croissants* were a start.

Steep rolling uplands were drier than a bottle of fine
wine. Carbon lines in Hell Creek rock showed these high
plains suffered from flash fires. Farther west, Jake could
make out the wavy blue wall of the proto-Rockies standing far taller than in his own time. A massive cordillera;
young, vibrant, with gnarled valleys and active
volcanoes.

Mountain chains were the true *terra incognita* of the
Mesozoic, mist-shrouded and mysterious—leaving no
fossil record, they could be home to anything; unsuspected species, outrageous monsters, alien civilizations.
Compared to the Rockies, Hell Creek was comfortably
familiar.

"There it is." Peg pounded his shoulder, stabbing the
air with her finger.

Jake looked down, seeing nothing below but sandhills,
clay pan, and steep gullies, held together by conifer

stands and primitive broadleaf trees. He jacked up the
gain on his corneal lenses. Suddenly, there at the end of
Peg's finger was *T. rex*.

Jake had always pictured the brute striding along,
jaws agape, striking terror among law-abiding dinosaurs—but this one seemed to be asleep, sprawled on its
side. Jake did a low pass and pirouette. Stretched out,
the tyrannosaur was maybe fifteen meters long—nearly
three times as big as the crocs that had worried him
yesterday. The tyrant king did not even look up.

"We have to land." Peg was already half out the
window. He suspected she wouldn't really feel she was
there until she shared the ground with this great beast.

Jake descended, flushing out a flock of yellow-brown
ornithomimids that looked and ran like ostriches. Dropping a grapple and anchor line, he told *Challenger* to
reel herself down, keeping the ship "light," ready for a
fast takeoff. Then he slipped on his stunner holster, following Peg out the window.

Glare off the sandstone kicked in polarizers on his corneal lenses. The sleeping tyrannosaur had stood out like a
small hill from the air, but the ground was a maze of dry
wadis and cutbanks, divided by long lanes of scrub pine.
Twenty meters, and they could no longer see the tyrannosaur, or the dead ground between them and the airship.
If *T. rex* decided to wake and stalk about, the carnosaur
could appear anywhere. Jake's stunner felt like a flyswat-
ter tucked under his armpit.

They came on the beast abruptly. One moment, the tyrannosaur was "somewhere over there." A minute later,
Jake was nose to nose with the napping monster, its enormous bulk half-hidden by a shallow wash. Mottled black-
and-tan coloring broke up the big beast's outline. Jake got
an uncomfortably close view of great shearing jaws and
saw-edged teeth, reeking of half-eaten meat. Tickbirds
flew up to twitter in the nearby trees.

Peg went down on one knee, recording, while Jake

kept nervous watch, shifting from foot to foot. *Challenger* was not near enough to warn him if another huge carnosaur popped out of a neighboring gully.

"Magnificent," she breathed. "Probably female—they're most likely the largest." Jake nodded absently, not about to lift its tail to see.

"Look at the ropes of muscle in those cheek bulges." Peg was clearly in awe of the nasty creature. "I wish it would open its mouth; we'd get a better view of the teeth and interior attachments."

The tyrannosaur opened one evil eye, looking right at Peg.

"She knows we're talking about her," Jake whispered.

"Don't be a worrier. See that blood smeared on the premaxillaries. Probably sleeping off a kill. I doubt if we look much like a meal to her."

"Mere *hors d'oeuvres.*" The ogre could down them like a pair of canapés. Jake found the gore on its fangs in no way reassuring.

Peg smiled, "You *are* the nervous type, aren't you?"

"Not necessarily so." Every epoch had its burdens to bear. The fourteenth century had the Black Death; the twentieth had world wars and commercial TV. The bane of Jake's time and place was that people like Peg were too protected. Home period had no terrors to compare with *T. rex*, an eight-ton carnivore that could run you down and swallow you whole.

"This isn't a 3V or stimulation," he told her tensely. "Everything here is real. Including her. Screw up, and no one's going to drag you out of that gullet."

The bony muscular head lifted up, turning snout and teeth toward them, stretching its powerful neck. Jake nearly jumped out of his leggings.

"Don't startle her." Peg held his stunner holster, keeping the gun from leaping out. Jake held his breath as the beast settled back, resting its giant chin nearer to them. The huge eye shut, shaded by its horny socket.

Just as Jake thought it was all over, Peg put down her recorder. She took two purposeful steps, leaned forward, and touched the horrible toothed head lightly on the snout.

The tyrannosaur snorted, giving Jake a seizure.

Walking back over thorny wadis, under an unblinking sun, Peg explained, "That creature has no natural enemies, nothing to fear or defend against. If you are not afraid, or appetizing, you have nothing to fear from her."

He didn't argue. Maybe Peg was right. Maybe she was merely insane. Either way Jake was not about to run back and pat *T. rex* on the nose. He settled for picking up a shed tooth, notched with wear and larger than his hand. The cutting edges had fine bevels, like a jeweler's saw.

In the scorching air of noon, Hell Creek lived up to its name. Even Peg wound down under the incandescent heat. Shocked at the way Peg wilted, Jake realized she probably had not rested since arriving in the Mesozoic. Feeling a flood of concern and fondness that was less then two-thirds lust, Jake took *Challenger* aloft, so that she could sleep in the swaying air-conditioned cabin.

When they awoke from their noon sleep, the shimmering landscape had cooled. Jake felt fresh enough to tackle tyrannosaurs—exactly what Peg intended. "Can you take us back to the river? Let's see how these carnivores handle the triceratops herd."

The navmatrix in his compweb let Jake retrace his every movement, never allowing him to get lost. Releasing the anchor grapple, he gave *Challenger* full port rudder, flying with up elevator, letting the terrain fall away beneath them.

Peg kept urging him, "Closer." Which meant venting hydrogen to get right down at the cypress tops.

The glassed-in forward gallery looked out on green-

tan countryside, cut by a vast loop of the red mud river
channel. Jake saw bathing triceratopses, big crocs, and
duckbilled hadrosaurs. Farther off, the river branched
out into flat delta country, a collage of blue bayous and
cypress swamps. In the far, far distance, his boosted eye-
sight made out a blue horizon line merging with the
sky—the Middle American Sea, a shallow arm of ocean
filling the Mississippi Valley, connecting the Gulf of
Mexico to Hudson Bay.

"Here come the carnivores." Peg pointed to the right.
Jake applied starboard rudder and down elevator.

Sneaking along a deep creekbed was a smallish, long-
legged tyrannosaurid, about the size of a walking killer
whale. Peg identified the skulker, "*Albertosaurus megagracilis*—a stalker and sprinter. It'll hang about the
herds trying to pick off a straggler or juvenile."

From a secure height, Jake liked the little fellow. *A.
megagracilis* was rust-colored with brown spots, more
compact and graceful than the tyrannosaur Peg had
played tag with, but also faster, hungrier, and a greater
threat to humans.

Peg pulled on the leggings and moccasins that went
with the Crow gift shirt, not bothering with the long,
trailing breechcloth. The result was a short fringed mini-
dress over hip-length leather. "I want to go down there,
close to the herd. To cover the action from ground
level."

Jake was not ready for another walk on the Mesozoic
wild side. It was late afternoon. In the cooling half-light
carnivores were bound to be more active and dangerous.

"Oh, *you* can stay up here. We'll combine ground
recordings with a wide-angle aerial sequence." She
panned her recorder. "Here come more carnivores. A
whole hunting pack."

Jake looked the newcomers over; they were taller than
A. megagracilis, chunkier, too. Full-sized tyrannosaurids. A half dozen black-and-tan boys (or gals) out to

raise hell among the herbivores. None were as big as
the one Peg had touched. The four largest were in the
lead, followed by two more gracile types. If Peg was
right, this was a hunting pride—four females and two
smaller (possibly younger) males. They did not stalk the
creekbeds, but ambled right toward the river, not caring
who saw them coming.

Jake had seen this dance of death before, on the
steppes of Central Asia, on the plains below Kiliman-
jaro. Carnivores approached casually from downwind.
The herd edged slowly upwind to keep from being ambushed, maintaining a healthy separation. Neither hunter
nor victim moved too quickly—neither wanted to ex-
haust their reserves. In the ultimate rush, a labored
breath might make all the difference.

And Peg itched to be in the middle of it. Jake began
to question the wisdom of picking an active young paleontologist who had never seen a battery of carnivore
teeth outside of a fossil formation. He set down on the
leeward periphery of the herd, giving her a comlink to
clip to her ear. "Take this *little fucker* with you."

"*Little fucker*?" English confused her again.

"Technical term. Just keep the link open."

Slipping the comlink into her ear, she swaggered off
toward the brush, showing long sweeps of thigh between
the slits in her shirt and the tops of her leggings. Jake
hoped this was not his last look at her.

Fighting a crosswind, he kept *Challenger* positioned
almost directly above Peg. *A. megagracilis* still worried
Jake the most—but he had lost the cheetahlike stalker
in the rough, and did not have time to hunt him up.

"How does it look? I have the herd in sight." Microamps made Peg sound like a flea in his ear.

"*A. megagracilis* is missing. Those big tyrannosaurs
are moving in line ahead, a couple of kilometers downwind." Jake judged that the big ones were getting ready
for a run-in. The triceratopses thought so too. They were

shifting their young into the herd center. Adults turned their horns toward the approaching carnivores, swiveling on their short front legs.

A game of bait and bluff began. Nature's ballet of death is never all-out battle. No carnosaur was going to charge into a hedge of horns. And no right-minded triceratops wanted to be separated from the retreating herd, singled out for slaughter. Heroism is not a herbivore survival trait. The most dim-witted triceratops must know that the carnosaurs were not out to annihilate the herd, just to make a meal out of one or two members. The trick was not to become the unlucky sacrifice.

"What's happening?" Stuck in the brush, Peg was missing everything. So much for being *on the scene.*

"Tyrannosaurs are fanning out, trying to turn a flank."

Defenseless duckbills scattered for the brush along the river.

"I'm heading over there."

"Don't get stepped on."

At that instant something spooked the herd—maybe the flanking tactics, maybe the bolting duckbills—for whatever reason, the triceratopses got their wind up and thundered downriver, tyrannosaurs sprinting at their heels. Jake stood frozen at the helm, awestruck by the living avalanche flattening the countryside. Thousands of elephant-sized dinosaurs stampeded at top speed, heads down and tails up, sides heaving. Even larger tyrannosaurs tried to dash in among them, slashing and snarling, attempting to cut down a victim while running flat out, meters ahead of the horns.

Death in the afternoon. Near-indescribable chaos. The only thing Jake could compare it with was a breakneck Lakota buffalo hunt. The dust-covered tyrannosaurs reminded him of Crazy Horse and Company, whooping in to make their kills.

Only this time they missed. Perhaps the horns came too close or the herd broke too soon, maybe it was all a feint—for whatever reason, the carnivores rolled out and regrouped.

Peg missed it all. "I can see the dust raised by the herd, but where are the tyrannosaurs?"

"They rolled right, half a klick short of you." A good thing, too.

"I'm going to work my way up this dry wash, staying to leeward of the herd." The wash was a flood channel connecting two loops of the river, a shortcut that let Peg keep abreast of the frightened herbivores.

Jake acknowledged, dipping down to scout the wash, looking for that sneaky culprit *A. megagracilis.* The fast little bastard might be anywhere by now.

A setting sun cast long, confusing shadows. Duckbills crouched like great frightened lizards in the greenery— huge overgrown iguanas trying to hide amid giant magnolias. The triceratops herd caught its collective breath. Rearmost adults turned, peering back into the dust, keeping a horned eye out for the pursuing tyrannosaur pack.

Challenger beeped him.

"Oh, I see them now," Peg hooted with triumph. "Here they come!"

"Who? Where?" Jake turned back to her. His jaw fell. Both he and the herd had been fooled. Under cover of dust and half-light, the tyrannosaurs had wheeled, shifting from line ahead to line abreast. Using Peg's shortcut, they were starting another run smack at the middle of the shaken herd, aiming to split it into two panicked segments.

Right in their path, Peg scrambled out of the wash, lying prone on the cutbank, her recorder running. Idiot luck had put her between the herd and the line of oncoming carnivores. Six frenzied tyrannosaurs rushed at her out of the twilight, teeth gleaming, tails straight, clawed feet chewing up the clay pan. For an awful instant, Jake saw her, insanely refusing to move.

Then the wave of claws, teeth, and muscle swept over her, and her comlink went dead.

Seeing the Sauropod

Jake's job made him a generalist, but he did imagine himself a specialist on Time—Newtonian Time, post-Einsteinian Time, non-Euclidean Time—he had even yawned through an endless lecture by Plato on the subject. His navmatrix gave him a hyperlight time sense that could carve days down to milliseconds or stretch them over millennia, never missing a click of the cosmic clock. The instant Peg disappeared beneath the charging carnivores Jake started counting nanoseconds—screaming for *Challenger* to land.

He knew that what was left of Peg needed immediate life support. A body, even one as classic as Peg's, could be regenerated. Bit by bit if need be. But nerve cells were slippery cases—as they died, they took away the memories that made Peg who she was. Brain-dead was dead.

He was out of the cabin before *Challenger* touched down, vaulting through a forward window, hitting the ground sprinting, medikit in hand.

Jake calculated he could have Peg on life support in seconds. Minutes would put her at the portal. But on the far end of the portal real medical care was still centuries off. There was no direct connection between the Uppermost Cretaceous and Home. At the other end of the Hell Creek anomaly medicine was still in the business of killing patients—cut-and-stitch butchery done by buffoons in disease-ridden hospitals. Surgeons *paid by the limb* spent their odd hours denouncing public health and germ theory.

As he ran, his mind searched calmly for ways to push time back, to retrieve minutes, even seconds—to recapture the instant before this all happened. In theory FTL made it possible to pull Peg out *before the tyrannosaurs hit her*. In well-traveled historical periods STOP teams routinely performed impossible rescues.

Not here though, not now. The Hell Creek anomaly was too new and on the edge, so poorly mapped Peg had feared they were in the Paleocene instead of the Mesozoic. A STOP team could not count on hitting the right millennium, much less the right moment. But if he could get her through the portal to a historic period—a STOP team could be waiting. That was Peg's ticket to an autodoc.

Simultaneously Jake cursed himself for letting Peg wander about, guided by nothing but a daft death wish. He was despicable, doing his job with a hard-on, so obsessed with bedding Peg that he gave in to her suicidal whims. Leaping over the crumpled lip of the wadi he steeled himself for his first look. So much depended on what shape she was in. What he had to work with.

Peg was sitting covered with dirt, elbows propped on her knees, recording the disappearing tyrannosaurs.

Jake landed next to her, hit wrong, bounced badly, and did a perfect pratfall.

Peg turned, startled by his impact. "Are you hurt?" she asked, setting down her recorder. "It's good you brought a medikit."

Taking the kit from his nerveless fingers, Peg was all over him, helping him sit up, checking for injuries, and brushing him off, making him feel twelve times worse. "Did you see the tyrannosaurids? That was a truly *essential* moment—they galloped right over me."

He sat there, stunned, saying nothing—flooded with relief and anger, all his guilt and fear turning to cold, hard fury.

"Feel better?" Her smile aimed at being helpful. "Could you look for my comlink? I think you landed on it. The *little fucker* flicked out in the fall."

Jake was wired to explode. He dug her comlink out of the dirt and slapped it into her palm, replying as diplomatically as he could, "I am responsible for your working safety. But since you are dead set on *hara-kiri*, have the decency to do it on your own *damn* time, so bystanders won't be blamed."

Peg looked coolly back. "Don't be anal," she advised. "Ever since passing the portal you have been in a testosterone frenzy—pawing me by the fire, bounding about saving me, making a farce out of a serious expedition."

He tried to argue, but she just turned huffy and academic. "Do you know what the stride length of a tyrannosaur is?"

"*Damned* large." Like the rest of it.

"Running flat out—four to five meters. All I needed to do was drop down, and they sailed right over me." Peg pointed to the first three-toed gouge, meters away in the middle of the streambed. One stride would have cleared a small ground car. "Stop thinking with your gonads. I was never in danger. No seven-ton carnosaur chasing a six-ton herbivore is going to care about a fifty-kilo mammal in its path. You are so edgy. It's a surprise FTL picked you."

Jake said nothing, knowing too well why he was here. FTL had not picked him—he had picked Peg, snapping up her and her Mesozoic project like a lovesick teen.

Cultural, academic, and entertainment institutions—as well as interested individuals—submitted field work proposals to FTL, which Faster-Than-Light filled at whim. Only STOP missions had priority. Cultural-scientific importance was meant to play some vague role in selection, but the real criterion was what veteran field agents thought they could accomplish. No one could be forced through a portal, and attrition was high, especially among first timers. Field agents succumbed to portal skips, excitable natives, and primitive medical beliefs. The stupid or gullible didn't last. Trips that looked too dangerous, or too trivial, had no chance of happening.

Senior agents could argue for promising assignments, and Jake had his own system for scouting fresh projects. Locking himself in his Syrtis Major studio, he ordered up a pot of coffee and a pipe of opium. Properly blasted, he had Biofile send him open cases one at a time.

Everybody was there—the good, the ugly, and the merely impossible. People wanted a word with long-dead relatives . . . Psychics needed predictions tested . . . A Ph.D. at Tehran U. wanted to shoot some Persian history in fourth century B.C. Mesopotamia . . . SAVE THE CHRISTIAN MARTYRS had a long list of worthies they wanted plucked from the flames. THE JEW-ISH COMMITTEE TO EXPOSE THE SAINTS had an even longer list of worthies they wanted blackened (and brought back to the future for trial.) An *el grosso* Feelie mogul needed background for a porno miniepic on the Marquis de Sade. Then came the cranks and crazies . . .

How to decide among so many admirable requests? Jake's opium-logged brain had not even tried. Peg and her Mesozoic proposal put everything else on hold. He must have replayed her proposal a dozen times, puffing on the opium pipe, getting every nuance of her voice, person, and presentation.

Her listings were incredible: Cuvier Fellow at the University of Paris at twenty-six . . . French, Latin, Classical Greek . . . swimming, yoga, *aikido* . . . Phi Beta Kappa, no criminal record . . . A neovegetarian and practicing nudist. Endorsements by everyone from the World Paleontological Congress to Teen Lesbians. A bright, well-balanced young professional, out to put her mark on the planet. Perfect. A field agent's prayer. Where could Jake go wrong?

The results had him doubting the wisdom of making crucial decisions in an opium stupor. But even his sober brain had failed to see the flaws. Uppermost Mesozoic was a brand-new period—farther back than ever, a high-risk, high-opportunity assignment Jake could not pass on, not if he wanted to stay at the cutting edge. Whoever came back from the Upper Cretaceous would *own* FTL.

Unless he fucked up. FTL was infamously unforgiving. Faster-Than-Light had an army of active agents and files full of wanna-bees; its ingratitude was boundless. One bad bounce, and you were out. FTL trips were too troublesome and expensive to allow failure—*for whatever reason*. Screw the pooch in some god-awful corner of the past, and your best bet was to marry that pooch and learn to farm—there was no point coming back.

FTL boasted off having a ninety-nine percent success rate—but that counted every time hop, no matter how safe or trivial. The actual failure rate on high-risk penetrations of new or chancy periods was one in five. Still not terribly ferocious, until you multiplied out the probabilities and saw that the chance of completing three such missions was only a shade over fifty percent—the chances of doing an even dozen were fewer than one in ten.

There were a million ways to fuck up. Portal failure. Chronic slips. Unattended details. Too little foresight. Too much imagination. Or just a run of bad luck. Jake was already considered far too *colorful* and accident-prone. Easily FTL's most raffish agent. Afflicted with more *joie de vivre* than *per regulation*. Only unbroken success made him able to pick among plum assignments—like steering Peg through the Mesozoic. But the bigger the assignment, the better the odds of going bust—*for whatever reason*.

Sitting in the dogwood-shaded wash, listening to Peg explain what a dolt he was, Jake thought how he had to succeed. Hell, he had to excel. Picking a crazed partner just because he wanted to fuck her did not justify failure, not to FTL. He tried to imagine what might work best with Peg, contrite apology or a vicious tongue-lashing.

Challenger beeped him.

With a bang and a crash the brush parted. *A. megagracilis* burst out of the magnolias. Jake recognized the rust brown spots and the cleaner, smaller, more gracile variation on the basic tyrannosaurid build.

Nerves shot, Jake suppressed a shriek, calling for his stunner. He thrust his hand into an empty armpit. No holster handed him a weapon. He had hopped out of *Challenger* carrying nothing more deadly than a medikit. If this long-legged tyrannosaurid had a toothache or a broken toe, Jake could handle it, otherwise he was caught short.

Fifty meters upwind a juvenile hadrosaur broke cover. Squawking in horror, the duckbill bolted from a four-legged crouch into dipedal flight. The two-ton dinosaur's green-and-black coloring, like old-fashioned camouflage, made it nearly invisible among the ferns and dogwoods. Megagracilis must have smelled out the baby duckbill, because the tyrannosaurid showed no surprise, springing right at its prey.

Seeing death coming, the terrified duckbill cut right. The tyrannosaurid cut even tighter, turning inside the bawling herbivore. They collided in a spray of dirt and gravel. Godzilla meets Baby Huey. Mercifully, it was quick.

Megagracilis got its jaws around the hadrosaur's neck, biting down. The duckbill's eyes bulged in terror. Slowly its thrashing subsided as *A. megagracilis* started to feed.

Jake sat rigid, so tense his muscles had set. Peg was right. To these terrible giants, two humans were a pair of bumps on the landscape. Insignificant bugs. While he and Peg argued, a game of eat and be eaten had gone on. Megagracilis had smelled out the hiding duckbill. The poor herbivore had watched death stalk closer, panicking at the last instant. Neither paid the least attention to the humans. Very deflating.

A glance at Peg was even more deflating. She was on her feet, shooting each slice of flesh as it came off the duckbill. The look on her face was otherworldly, completely relaxed—not smiling, not happy, merely transported.

By picking this young paleontologist, Jake had handed her the adventure of her life; an adventure at once astounding, romantic, professional, and damned near multiorgasmic—an epic in which Jake was only a poorly written stanza, necessary as the reactor, but certainly no more important.

Jake was cynical enough to consider using that truth. He could point out that if it were not for *him*, Peg would not be *here*. Jake was cynical enough to think it, but too proud to say it. He was not going to grovel.

He liked thinking of himself as witty, handsome, and as brave as he needed to be. Peg put a strain on that self-esteem. So it was time to give his libido a rest. Maybe they would not make love, but they would *damn* well work together. No more loose adventuring, waiting for lightning to strike. *Gung ho*, or no go. What he needed was a plan, something he could hold Peg to when she veered off on her next tangent.

Telling the navcomputer to illuminate the darkening wadi, he trotted back to the *Challenger*, slipped on his shoulder holster, and ordered an Irish coffee from the microstove. Mug in hand he walked back to the wash to watch *A. megagracilis* demolish dinner.

Coffee and whiskey had just the right bite for his mood, and he got back in time to witness a tail-lashing feeding frenzy. Two of the larger tyrannosaurids came strutting back from the bend in the river. Perhaps this pair missed their kills. Perhaps the pack had a falling out. In any event, the big tyrannosaurids decided baby duckbill would do nicely.

There was some snapping and snarling as *A. megagracilis* made a pretense of asserting property rights. The smaller carnivore was too quick to be hurt badly, but the outcome was never in doubt. The two tyrannosaurs settled down to a thieves' banquet. Megagracilis slunk off to hunt up another duckbill.

Jake saw a lesson in this. Megagracilis was a specialist, a speedy killer of small duckbills. Much as Jake admired the compact lines and well-honed technique, Jake was glad to be a generalist. The two tyrannosaurs were generalists—big enough to tackle a triceratops, but not too big to scavenge. Given enough time, generalists always won. Or so Jake hoped.

Peg, snub nose stuck in her viewfinder, was the specialist *par excellence*.

They walked back to *Challenger* together. Peg tossed her recorder on the chart table, propping moccasined feet beside it. "A totally essential day. I'm thrilled, famished, and exhausted—in that order."

She produced a huge shed tooth, pushing it toward Jake. "For your collection."

A peace offering. Dinosaurs shed their worn teeth, so tremendous canines weren't rare, but Peg seemed eager to make amends, to *be sociable*, despite a gritty weariness in the corners of her eyes.

Jake was touched. He served up mushroom moussaka and cabbage borscht, accompanied by a favorite Moselle. Outside, snapping bones added to the night noises—great crunching jaws broke up the last of the duckbill.

Peg nodded toward the noisy feast, "Giant carnivores are nice enough, but I still want to see sauropods."

Sauropods again. She had mentioned them the first

day. Jake knew these brontosaur-type, long-necked herbivores were the ultimate in dinosaurs—twenty to thirty
meters long, massing as much as a hundred tons.

Peg's sleepy eyes glowed. "Sauropods are essential
to this expedition, essential to the extinction question.
Essential to everything."

"We're unlikely to find them here in Hell Creek," he
pointed out.

She shrugged, "FTL picked Hell Creek. I wanted to
go straight to Morrison formation."

Her overspecialization showed. "Upper Cretaceous is
as far as the anomaly goes," Jake explained. Peg was
weak in Wormhole Theory. He had turned her original
proposal into something workable. Morrison formation
was Late Jurassic, maybe eighty million years farther
back. From where they sat a weekend in St. Tropez was
closer.

The Mesozoic was gigantic. He and Peg had only broken the surface. *T. rex* was nearer in time to human
civilization than to brontosaurus and the Great Age of
the Sauropods. Jake had brought them in as close as he
dared to the mysterious KT boundary that marked the
Cretaceous extinction, figuring the end is never a bad
place to start. Succeed here, then they could open other
anomalies, going farther back, seeing more.

But Peg wanted to see it all *now*. She had not come
sixty-odd million years to see a single slice of the past.
"What we have here in Hell Creek is an explosion of
new types: tyrannosaurids, triceratopses, and advanced
duckbills. Evolution in fast-forward. But it's essential to
know what is happening to older types as well, and sauropods are some of the oldest."

Jake was not a paleontologist, but he swore he could
feel the great extinction coming. Hell Creek dinosaurs
looked healthy enough—at petting range *T. rex* was ter-
rifying—but there was a frantic quality to dinosaur life
he did not see in the crocs and fisher-storks. At its upper

levels the net connecting life to life hummed with tension.

Peg cataloged the symptoms, "Carnosaurs forced to squabble over kills. Triceratops herds surging across the landscape, searching for water and sustenance. Poor harassed duckbills unable to protect their young."

Jake put in his pitch for generalism. "Aside from the ostrich types there are no hordes of small dinosaurs. No tiny generalists waiting to take over if the big boys falter."

Peg shook her head. "This whole show is propped atop the food chain." One day something would hit the props hard, and the crash would be tremendous. Even as they talked, world calamity hurtled through space-time toward Earth.

"We'll have plenty of time to go over Hell Creek in detail—we have to leave through here. Sauropods are an essential contrast to these new types. They are well-established herbivores, who have already survived numerous extinctions and cosmic collisions."

The notion of a sauropod hunt appealed to Jake. The long-necked herbivores were huge but harmless, unless they stepped on you. Seeing a sauropod was a sane ambition, compared to playing tag with tyrannosaurids. "So, where could we find large sauropods in the Uppermost Cretaceous?"

"Maybe in the highlands, certainly in South America."

Enjoying her enthusiasm, Jake had *Challenger* project maps of fossil finds onto the chart table. They reminded him of the charts that pretended to describe nineteenth century Africa. Fossils formed where sediments were being laid down, so the maps showed coastlines, river deltas, floodplains, and the like. Continental interiors were great blank areas.

Peg dismissed the Euramerican sauropods, "So-called *titanosaurs*, they hardly live up to their name. Not much bigger than duckbills.'' Euramerican predators were also small to medium—megalosaurs and dryptosaurs. *T. rex* would have roared through them like lion at a poodle show. Much of Europe was just plain underwater. Eastern North America, Greenland, and Scandinavia were united into Euramerica—but Southern Europe was a string of semiarid islands, some inhabited by dwarf dinosaurs a couple of meters long, quaint rather than impressive. Peg did not have time for evolutionary U-turns.

Jake suggested they ride the prevailing westerlies south and east, at least as far as North Africa. The Sahara was supposed to be a green tropical expanse, connected to Euramerica by the Spanish Isles.

Peg shook her head. ''West Africa will have more of those misnamed titanosaurs—bigger than the ones in Euramerica, but not by much. We can look in on them later, on our way to India.'' India was another huge blank spot, as mysterious as in the days before a Gama, thought to be terribly exotic—perhaps an island, perhaps attached to Africa.

She wanted to go straight to South America, even though it meant flying through the teeth of the megathermal, and the tropical storm belt. ''There we are sure to see *real* sauropods.''

Jake disliked the iffy weather, but he would cheerfully face a dozen tropical cyclones if he did not have to endure another tyrannosaur chase. And they'd see Hell Creek again on the way out—this was the only Mesozoic portal.

He agreed. Feeling that they had finally arrived, he took *Challenger* aloft for the night. In his evening systems check he noted Peg's recorder was drawing minimum power—on hold at the end of a file. She must have fallen asleep reviewing data. Curious, he interfaced with the recorder through its power intake, telling his compweb to break any encryption. The recorder code was a simple digital transformation, keyed to Peg's birthdate—

putting PEG with BIRTHDAY brought the date out of memory. The deciphered image went straight to Jake's optical lobe.

He was surprised by a familiar purple-blue sky. White vapor streaked the ruddy horizon. The recording had to come from Home; the image was not from the Mesozoic. It was not even from Earth.

Frozen in the 3V foreground was a group of teenage girls—young, gawky, big-eyed—leaning on each other, tired and triumphant. They wore respirators and altitude suits, but had doffed their masks for the recording. Thin lips were blue from cold and lack of oxygen. They were on Mars, the western summit of Olympus Mons; Jake recognized the red ocher Amazonis Planitia in the background. Phobos shone above them.

Olympus Summit was a typical tourist destination, but these weren't typical gate-hopping tourists. *They had climbed the sucker*. You could see the incredible hike in the girl's faces. And Peg was in the middle—very adult, very in charge.

Of course. Teen Lesbians. Peg was probably a Pack Mother or something. Her proud look, backed by the Plain of Amazons, explained part of his problem.

Next morning they scouted the proto-Rockies, finding dense impenetrable redwood forest. Peg thought the highlands might hold large sauropods. Jake did not disagree. "There might be ultrasaurs down there, or lost cities, or leprechauns, but the only way to know would be to tether *Challenger* to a sequoia and blunder about on foot—two people and no shock-rifle. The sauropods of the Rockies will have to wait."

Bayou country came next—lower, swampier, opened by waterways. Cajun tunes played in Jake's head, while Peg cataloged flora and fauna from the air. "Swamp cypress, cycads, tall stands of fir and pines . . ." They spotted a pack of small tyrannosaurids—*Nanotyrannus lancensis*, Peg thought, but she could not be sure without seeing their teeth. Nothing remotely resembled a sauropod.

Then came the sea. Green-white shorebreak. Blue water. Reefs and atolls. *Challenger* descended to top off the water ballast and fill the hydrogen cells. Peg took seawater samples and swam nude inside a reef. Small, toothed shore birds wheeled above.

Leaving balmy Montana, they sailed south and east along the Dakota shoreline. Most of Missouri and Mississippi were completely underwater. Peg sat on the transparent cabin deck shooting straight down to the sandy sea bottom, picking out marine reptiles, twelve to sixteen meter plesiosaurs, long-necked versions of the Loch Ness monster. She still worked in the nude aboard ship—but that had become mere entertainment. Jake admired her yoga positions over breakfast, then relaxed into his role of flying chauffeur.

He swung far enough east to sight the Euramerican shore, seeing duckbills in the Alabama swamps. "Alabama Song" played in his head as he set mental course for South America. He flew in bright sunshine alongside immense flocks of long-legged ducks, as big as flamingos.

This part of the trip was like coming home. Jake had learned airship technique in the twentieth century aboard the original *Graf Zeppelin*, working as a rigger for Lufthansa on the South America run—Frankfurt to Recife to Rio, then back to Germany by way of Seville. That was when Rio was Rio, not just another branch of Megapolis. He remembered fevered nights full of music, women and *Mardi Gras* with Nazi reichsmarks burning in his pockets. Not a bad time and place—between the world wars and before the AIDS pandemic—unless you were poor, or perhaps a Jew. He rummaged through his music files playing a samba, then "Bolero."

By now they were in the megathermal, the fevered blanket circling the waist of the planet. A perpetual steambath with temperatures in the wet one hundreds. Everything was sopping. Decks and bulkheads sweated. Pillows turned to warm sponges. Buckskin came apart in soggy clumps. Jake took to wearing only light cotton pants; anything more was intolerable.

Approaching the equatorial trough, the wind died to a whisper. Depressed by the heavy air of the doldrums, Jake dumped ballast and headed farther out to sea, hoping the higher marine air would be cooler. A mere ribbon of water separated South America from Asiameric and Africa, a seaway too small to be called the South Atlantic. The fishlike shadow of the airship swam over the waves.

Weather radar noted convective turbulence, an easterly wave of low pressure signaling a weak equatorial low.

Peg stood, recorder ready, anxious for her first glimpse of South America and its sauropods. As soon as they found a decent-size sauropod, Jake was going to give his charm another chance—catch Peg in a paleontological frenzy and anything was possible.

Tall anvilheads reared before them, a fluffy colonnade leading up to Olympus. High sea surface temperatures created warming unstable air masses. Typhoon weather, with storm pillars ten kilometers high.

Seeing a gap, Jake shot for blue sky and blue water, hoping to put the emerging storm cells behind him.

More white patches appeared ahead, boiling rags of mist that swelled rapidly into cottony thunderheads, roots gray with rain. Peg was disappointed to find the horizon clouding up. "I cannot get a clear view of the coast."

Not surprising. Weather was closing in from all sides, plunging the barometer into freefall. For the first time *Challenger* fought terrific headwinds. Rain spattered in the open window; fat searing drops hit Jake in the face.

Shielding her eyes with her viewfinder, Peg announced, "I see a black line to the south."

"That's the coast." He watched her go to maximum magnification. In this thickening storm she had as much chance of sighting Rio as she did of seeing a sauropod.

"It isn't getting any closer."

Jake nodded. "This headwind is a *bastard*. Maximum revolutions and ground speed is *falling*."

"Is that possible?"

"I would not have thought so an hour ago. But it's happening."

Challenger's twin propellers were churning at peak revolutions without gaining a meter. The headwind had topped 160 kilometers per hour. Strain on the ship was transmitted to Jake as a line of tension along his spine, humming from head to buttocks.

Peg complained that South America was slipping away. At last she let her recorder fall. "It's gone. Nothing but gray skies and gray wave caps." They were being blown backward by gale force winds.

Alamosaurus

The storm seized hold with astonishing speed. Inrushing winds reversed, then immobilized *Challenger*. Radar reported ominous rings of cumulonimbus spreading through dense stratiform clouds. The signature of a truly intense cyclonic storm—a hurricane being born around them.

Jake stole a glance at Peg, who hardly looked worried. Nothing new there. Much as he might admire her fine brain, Peg hadn't the sense to be scared. Mesozoic weather was advertised as mild. And at Home, cyclonic storms had long been tamed; satellites seeded them from orbit to remove energy as rain and limit crop damage. Aside from the unwary sailing buff, people simply avoided storms. No one except suicide cases went ballooning about in a typhoon.

But Jake had been through horrible blows before—rounding the Horn under hatches aboard a tea clipper, and clinging to the mast of a leaky Athenian coaster off Cape Matapan. He *knew* what it was like to have life hang at the whim of wind and sea. He did not need that replayed.

Lightning scrawled across the sky, connecting thunderheads. A thermal tugged at the airship. Jake applied maximum down elevator, to keep *Challenger* below her pressure height. He did not mean to vent hydrogen in a thunderstorm, where the column of valved gas could act as a conductor, drawing lightning straight to the ship. And every gram of lost buoyancy cut into *Challenger*'s chances of riding out the storm.

"There must be excess power in the reactor." Peg was still set on seeing the sauropods of South America.

"Sure, the props could rip the reactor right off the hull. Wouldn't help us much." They had to run before the storm. He reduced power on the port propeller, using starboard rudder to bring the airship about.

Challenger struggled to obey. Head winds beat at the control surfaces. Staggered by the buffeting, *Challenger* was blown sideways, then leaped ahead like a sprinting sauropod. Ground speed zoomed from less than zero to several hundred kilometers per hour.

Peg observed the transition with calm interest. "Where are we headed now?"

"North by northwest." So near the center of the swirling cloud mass, winds shifted too rapidly to give an exact heading.

Rain beat against the cabin, blotting out the sunlight. Windows closed. Interior lights winked on. Jake ordered a pot of *café au lait* from the microstove—it was never too soon to seek chemical stimulant. Who knows how long he'd be fighting this storm.

He started to pour, bracing himself against the heave of the deck.

Challenger shot upward, flinging hot coffee on Jake, Peg, and the surrounding bulkheads.

Yelling for more power and down elevator, Jake snagged a window frame with one hand and Peg with the other, keeping her from flying through the galley into the lounge. Despite his orders the ship continued to rise, sucked up at a sickening angle.

Jammed against Peg, with only wet coffee between them, Jake felt compelled to make conversation. "We're caught in a convection cell."

She nodded, eyes wide and staring.

Challenger started giving the altitude in hundred-meter steps as they neared pressure height, "Eight hundred meters, nine hundred meters, a thousand . . ."

"At twelve hundred meters we'll reach pressure height, and have to valve hydrogen, or the gas cells will rupture." This short exposition sounded absurdly calm even to Jake, who was leaving a lot unsaid. Hydrogen was what kept them aloft. They had no way to replace it. Lose too much, and they would be forced to land in an ugly sea.

"Pressure height," announced *Challenger*. "Butterfly valves opening." Feeling hydrogen gush from the ship, Jake ordered down elevator. The stall alarm rang in his head, but still they kept rising, borne aloft by a rushing bubble of air.

". . . fifteen hundred meters, sixteen hundred meters . . ."

More hydrogen spewed into the storm.

". . . twenty-three hundred meters, twenty-four hundred meters, twenty-five hundred meters . . ."

They could defy gravity only so long. "Brace yourself." He held harder to Peg.

At more than twice its pressure height the airship lurched to a stop. They teetered for several seconds. Then *Challenger* plunged into the boiling darkness.

"Dump ballast." Jake kept his lips tight, voicing the command in his head. Why show Peg how scared he was? Water ballast streamed from the ship. But now they were caught in a downdraft; deflating cells sucked air into the hull, offsetting the loss of water, threatening an oxyhydrogen explosion.

"Look, the ocean." Peg pointed. Rainswept waves appeared as they plummeted through the bottommost cloud layer.

Challenger righted herself so close to the whitecaps Jake could see spray flying from the chop. She began to climb again. Immediately Jake ordered added power and down elevator to counteract the climb. Each wild oscillation cost him both gas and ballast. The airship threatened to yo-yo until she lost all buoyancy and plunged into the sea.

Fresh water and hydrogen were all around him, but Jake had no notion of touching down to refill the tanks. Wind force was fearsome. Jake spotted waterspouts, a conga line of twisters sweeping over the waves. Lightning struck the ship with alarming regularity.

A year or so before Jake shipped on the *Graf*, an American helium airship, the *Akron*, stronger and heavier than *Challenger*, touched down in seas milder than these. Three survivors were plucked from the Atlantic. Admiral Moffett and seventy-some others went down with the ship; so did a smaller airship sent to find them. Not enviable odds. Nor did the Mesozoic have air-sea rescue. Jake didn't fancy their chances of flagging a ride on a passing plesiosaur.

Altitude figures started to tumble. Another wet downdraft had *Challenger* headed for the wave caps.

"Prepare for ditch procedure," the airship advised in a disinterested monotone. "Your lounge chairs double as life rafts."

Jake clutched the window frame, staring at Peg. "Maximum power. Up elevator." He could not see them riding out a typhoon in lounge chairs.

"Ditch procedure," repeated the ship. Emergency circuits had made their heartless calculations. "Warm water ditching. Remove excess clothing. Place your head between your knees."

Jake tuned *Challenger* out. He had played almost all his cards. Reactor power. Water ballast. Elevators. But the rainswept sea still rushed up at them. He had hoped to escape—now he had to settle for a stay of execution.

"Jettison reactor."

Propellers whirling, the reactor detached itself, plunging into the wave tops. An almighty surge lifted them up. Lightened by the loss of the reactor, *Challenger* shot skyward, reeling off new altitude numbers, ''six hundred, seven hundred, eight hundred meters . . .''

''What happened?'' Peg sounded like she'd fully expected to get wet.

''I dumped the reactor.''

''Won't we need it later?''

''It was that or touch down in berserk seas.'' Only the reactor massed enough to give the needed buoyancy.

Challenger tore through her old pressure height, ''. . . twelve hundred, thirteen hundred, fourteen hundred meters.''

At over two thousand meters they leveled off. Wind speed fell. The nonslip deck felt firmer now that they were free ballooning, no longer fighting the storm.

Jake let go of Peg and walked slowly over to the microstove, ordering a light lunch and considering options. The air was slick and sweaty at ninety-nine percent humidity. Water beaded on the cabin windows.

Peg followed him into the lounge. ''What now?''

''I suggest *soufflé aux blancs d'oeufs*. And the last of that Moselle. No sense saving good wine for after the crash.''

''Crash?''

He gave a sober nod. ''When the hurricane hits the coast of Asiamerica, we'll have to bring *Challenger* down.'' Unless they missed Asiamerica. He pictured them shooting the gap between the two continents, sailing out into the near-limitless Pacific. That would pretty much match his luck.

''How bad do you expect it to be?'' Peg asked casually, as though hardly involved.

''I've only been in one airship bang-up—aboard the *Graf Zeppelin*, returning to Pernambuco from Rio. We hit a heavy tropical squall a hundred meters above the field. Drove us smack down to the deck.'' Jake recalled the nauseating crunch. "We lost a rudder and came down hard on some poor Brazilian's shanty. Rammed the chimney right into the *Graf*'s hull. Breakfast was cooking, so smoke and sparks poured over tons of hydrogen and fuel gas."

He shook his head thoughtfully, "We'd have been blown back to Frankfurt, but an on-the-ball mechanic leaped out of his gondola and dashed in the front door of the shack. He grabbed a pot of coffee off the stove and put out the fire." Zeppelin crews were the best, one reason Jake had trained with them.

Peg smiled at the story. Jake did not add that it was the sort of luck you could not count on twice. Over *café au lait*, he considered making a final stab at seducing her—but only out of a sense of duty. The line he had been saving, "*look I got you here*," was now wildly inappropriate.

Night fell. They dozed in their respective armchairs, behind black, rain-streaked windows.

Near to dawn, Jake's compweb woke him. Light showed in the east. Thunderheads towered over a stratiform cloud plain—not a day for yoga and *Dawn Symphony*.

Peg lay curled in her armchair, studying the cloudscape. "Did you ever *see* anything so lovely?" The cloud plain was flat as polished ivory.

Jake nodded to starboard. "First sign of land."

A speck hung in the false dawn. Boosted vision brought it into focus—long leathery wings, a sharp-pointed head, and the compact body of a pterosaur.

Peg hopped out of her chair. "*Quetzalcoatlus*." Another nondinosaur—merely a huge flying reptile, but sufficiently incredible, a living creature with the wingspan of a hovership.

The pterosaur flew in formation with the crippled airship, narrow-pointed wings not even beating, staying aloft through sheer mastery of the sky. Jake's microamps played "Riders on the Storm." Listening to The Doors, looking into *Quetzalcoatlus*'s wrinkled face, Jake felt the full eeriness of this other Earth, where birds had teeth and huge reptiles had wings and beaks.

He also sensed the same evolutionary tension. The pterosaur was big, beautiful, and otherworldly, but fragile as well. Great size meant small numbers and over-specialization. If *Quetzalcoatlus* faltered, who would take its place? Not another pterosaur, because there *were* no others. Replacement would come from the flocks of tiny birds, growing ever more numerous.

"But it's not a marine animal." Peg recorded and cataloged furiously.

"Exactly. We must be headed inland." Assuming the pterosaur knew its way home. "Perhaps it was blown out to sea by the storm."

"Something to put in the report," she declared. Such certainty amused Jake. It was a better than even bet they would never get to file on this run.

Ghostly landforms appeared on the chart table. The Texas coast. This late in the Cretaceous, the Lone Star State was still taking shape. Much of what would be coastal plain remained underwater. The New Mexico highlands were steeper, not nearly so far inland.

In openmouthed astonishment, Jake watched the coastline shifting. *Storm surge.* Sea level was rising, submerging coastal islands, inundating lowlands. He marveled at the flood. "This storm won't let go. The flats are filling up. There may be no place to land short of the highlands."

Dawn turned to day. The tempest whirled inland, losing velocity. Jake watched the tail end of the proto-Rockies poke up through the cloud plain. Black islands in a foamy white sea.

"Gorgeous." Peg was in rapture.

Jake scanned the mountain spine—no sign of a landing site. Ground speed was still formidable. Without power or aerodynamic control, *Challenger* would batter herself against the passes.

"Strap in." A crash rushed toward them, shriveling hairs along his spine.

"But I can hardly see from that chair," Peg complained.

"We are going to hit badly." A wild understatement.

"Will being strapped down make a difference?"

"It might."

She shrugged, strapping the belt and harness across her body. It was plain that Peg did not plan to spend her last moments with her head between her knees. She meant to enjoy them. And record them. Her 3V was taking in everything.

Black pine tops broke through the clouds below; a high saddle lay dead ahead.

A disembodied voice announced, "Present course will terminate in three minutes." *Challenger* did not think they would make the saddle.

"Down five hundred meters." No sense in staying up here. Jake had to find a landing spot, or all his maneuvering would only succeed in smearing them on the oncoming saddle. Pine tops grew larger. Enhanced vision searched frantically for a clearing.

Challenger gave a two-minute warning.

"Down fifty meters." Conifer forest reached up to tear the guts out of the airship. Still no gap in the canopy.

"One minute."

No clearing. No opening. Not the slightest. Damn. No time either. He had to choose between rocks and treetops.

"Release remaining hydrogen." Jake braced himself, fingers digging into the inflatable seat.

Pine tops leaped at him. A giant sequoia slammed against the cabin, snapping and shuddering. Plastic shattered on impact; shards exploded through the lounge.

Thrown against his straps, Jake heard *Challenger* cracking like an aluminum eggshell. Metal shrieked. The cabin tore free from the hull. Another plunge. A jerk and fall, followed by a rain of debris.

Then stillness, eerie in its completeness.

Alive enough to hurt, Jake hung facedown in his straps, tasting blood and vomit in the back of his mouth. His head sang with pain.

Above the pain in his head he heard rain pelting the forest canopy high above—Cretaceous treetops getting a baptist downpour. It felt like the First Day of Creation.

Twisting about, he tried to get a look at Peg. It was blacker hanging in the treetops than it had been in the morning air above—the crushed and deflated hull formed a silver canopy, blocking the light. Rain dripped in. A stupendous hunk of pine was thrust through the lounge, disappearing into the chart room wall. Through the screen of boughs he saw the back of Peg's inflated chair.

"Peg," he called. "Are you there?"

"Where *would* I be? Was *that* it?"

"Was what it?"

"Are we going to fall some more?"

"*Hell*, I hope not." He reached out and tested the pine limb thrust between them. A meter more to port and it would have gotten him in the gut. It was thicker than his waist, hardly likely to break. "We've landed."

"Good." In a flurry of white limbs Peg unstrapped, dropping down to the rear bulkhead, which had become a deck. She pushed aside the foliage. "What about you? Alive or dead?"

"Alive, I think."

"Great." She helped undo his straps. "How do you feel?"

"Like *shit* hammered through a tiny hole." The Mesozoic was still tumbling. Would his legs work? Apparently.

They knelt together on the bulkhead, feeling for breaks. First his limbs, then Peg's. Soon they were just feeling, then stroking and caressing. They kissed. His tongue still worked. "Sorry about the blood."

"Oh, I don't mind." Peg had the Look. That same dreamy half smile he'd seen by the campfire in Hell Creek. Fumbling to get his pants down, Jake could barely believe they were *finally* going to fuck—in a shattered cabin, halfway up a tree.

She watched him strip, showing almost clinical interest. "You know, this is the wildest thing I have ever done."

"Not nearly." He kicked his pants off. "The wildest thing you ever did was to pat that tyrannosaur on the nose."

She laughed. "The second wildest, anyway."

"Wrong again. The second wildest was when you . . ." He pulled her to him. Seeing all those yoga positions had given him some great ideas.

"I mean I have never done anything like this before."

"Never made love atop a sequoia after ramming into a mountain? It won't be near so hard as it sounds." He slid his hand between her legs. Peg felt as good as he'd imagined.

"No, I mean I have never made love. Not to a *man*."

"*Shit and damnation*." His hand stopped. How could an attractive twenty-six-year-old not have had heterosex? "Why didn't you tell me?"

"I just did." She shrugged bare shoulders. "It makes this, you know, essential."

After sleeping half the night in a chair and caroming off a mountain, Jake was not sure how *essential* he could be. "Why didn't your sex therapist take care of this when you were a teenager?" Virginity had been cured ages ago.

"Sex therapy bored me. All those lectures on the joy of procreation."

"Right, I got the procreation lecture too." But it hadn't discouraged Jake from having heterosex—not completely at least. "So why are you starting now?"

"Because we made it. This is the *motherfucking* Mesozoic." She whacked her hand on his hip. "Besides, you saved my life. I owe you for that."

"Like *hell*. It's nothing but a plain everyday miracle we survived. You could just as well say I slammed you against a mountain, but didn't manage to kill you." Some conversation to be having with his hand in her crotch.

"Either way, you got me here." Peg wore an impish grin. Putting her hands on his cheeks, she kissed him again, taking her time.

Their lips parted. "Ever since I was a girl scraping for fossils, I dreamed of coming here. Someone was going to be the *first*. I worked and bled until I was the best young Ph.D. in the field. But none of that mattered, until you picked me. Jake Bento did that. No one else."

"You knew that I picked you?"

"Of course." She caressed his chest with short graceful strokes. "It's *essential* to know who will judge your proposals. If I can diagnose the personal life of a dead reptile from a shed tooth, I can certainly find out how FTL passes on its projects. To get here I had to interest the right person."

"Me?"

"You, or someone like you. It was not hard to figure out what you'd want."

"I'll be *fucked*."

"First, we have to see how much I remember from comparative biology." Her hand slid between his hips. "So this is what the adult male organ feels like. I haven't held a penis since playing sex therapist in kindergarten. But that one was not so big and active."

Flattered, Jake felt himself respond.

"Oh look, an erection," she murmured. "This is fun."

Her hips moved. Her breath came quicker. "You know, we could have done this that first night, after seeing the triceratops herd. But you crawled off to your cabin. I was too shy to go knocking on your door, making you think I was desperate."

Shy? Even at that point-instant, Jake knew it was never going to be easy with Peg. But there was no way he could stop—the woman was a prize, with more angles than a dodecahedron. He did his best to start slowly. It was her first time.

He'd barely got going, when her eyes went wide, "Oh my, the cabin's shaking."

"It only feels that way." He had hit his stride.

"No," she insisted, sitting bolt upright. Nearly giving Jake a hernia. "The whole tree is moving."

He felt it too. The cabin shook like it was getting set to fall again.

Seizing her recorder, she squirmed over to the window. "Come look, a sauropod." She lay there aiming the recorder. "An *Alamosaurus*. I can almost count the teeth."

Jake saw the beast's head from where he lay—framed by Peg and the window—its face tilted upward into the pouring wet, stripped greenery off a pine branch with short cylindrical teeth. One eye looked in at him.

Since Peg was not returning anytime soon, he crawled over to be with her. No denying it. Alamosaurus was tremendous, a titanosaur in more than name.

The head wasn't much larger than a horse's, but it attached to a great wrinkled neck arching down into the foliage. Half off its feet, the sauropod gripped the sequoia with huge forelimbs, eating vigorously. All the nutrition for its thirty-ton body had to be forced through a smallish mouth past simple peg teeth.

More than most dinosaurs, this one had that ancient,

lord-of-creation look. Sauropods were old, unbelievably ancient. They had seen continents separate and seas dry up, turning to shale and sandstone. The little proto-lemurs in the trees would come down, lose their tails, learn to walk upright and to build starships—but still would not be near as old as late Cretaceous sauropods.

Magnificent. Inspired by the sauropod, Jake ran his hands over Peg's hips, starting again where they had left off. Peg set the recorder down, rolling over to face him, eyes alight. "Do it. But quietly. Don't disturb the dinosaur."

Jake cocked his head toward the pine boughs and inflated furniture, "We can be more private and comfortable." He'd have happily made a nest for them.

"No." She shook her head violently. "I want to see the sauropod. It'll be absolutely essential. I've waited all my life for this."

Right. At least Jake did not have to worry about being *essential*. Alamosaurus had seen to that.

Three-Card Monte

The control deck was gone—sheared off in the crash, taking every bit of navigation and communications equipment, from long-wave radar to personal communicators.

Scouring the remains of the cabin, Jake salvaged what necessities they could realistically carry—medikits, microstove, sleeping bags, and some provisions—using a winch and cables to lower them to the ground. Peg studied titanosaurs, tropical birds, small mammals, and the refinements of heterosex. Given the need for caution, and frequent fucking, it took Jake five days to get them down out of the tree.

Then they headed north, through the foothills of the proto-Rockies. So long as Jake's navmatrix was sewn under his scalp he'd never get lost. Mashed and eaten maybe, but never lost.

It took half a year to walk back to Hell Creek, recording, collecting samples, sleeping in trees, living on whatever the medikits identified as edible. Jake could not imagine a finer honeymoon.

Then it was over. They stood beside the same billabong they had begun at six months before, taking last looks at the Uppermost Cretaceous—Peg could barely stand to let it go.

Systems check was a snap. He hardly had any equipment left. The missing shock-rifle no longer stood out, neatly swallowed by bigger calamities, showing it never pays to worry early. In a rare instance when Jake could *truly* see into the future, he foresaw a hellish feud brewing with FTL. He had crashed *Challenger*—losing the reactor, plus all their communications gear. They were coming back with their data recorders, a neural stunner, a couple of medikits, some clothes, and camping equipment. Everything else was gone. Abandoned, smashed to bits, or lost at sea.

Worse, he had hardly done half the assignment. Aside from the duckbills of Alabama, they had seen *nothing* outside Asiamerica. South America, Africa, India, and Australia-Antarctica were as mysterious as ever. The only fuck-ups he had not committed were calling in a STOP team, or losing his client.

And he was not home yet.

But after months of hiking north along the Rockies, their recorders could not hold a byte more of data. They were carrying an incalculable treasure. Highland species. Scores of new genera. Gene samples. Tissue cultures. DNA scans. Humanity's first look at the Mesozoic. If FTL did not treat them like returning heroes, they would start their own agency.

And he had added nicely to his artifact collection, finding another shed tooth, and a huge *Quetzalcoatlus* claw. Peg wanted to bring an egg. But she would have had to sit on it all the way Home. The incubator chamber had gone down with the reactor, and they were headed into winter.

Sweating, bundled up in spare clothing, Peg was finally overdressed. Jake cleared his head for the most dangerous part of the return. Riding a tropical hurricane was nothing compared to doing the blind drunkard's walk through a newly opened portal.

He engaged his navmatrix. The billabong, the flowering trees, the proto-birds all vanished.

Space-time blew about him, a near-infinite number of point-instants thrown together by the anomaly. This time he was not lugging the reactor. The compweb beneath his scalp produced just enough drag to act as an anchor as he searched for patterns in the vortex pointing to the far end of the anomaly. Luckily he had been through this portal once already, and spatiotemporal anomalies were roughly funnel-shaped, narrowing as they approached their points of origin. Each correct movement made the next one easier. Each mistake threatened to trigger a portal skip to an unintended point-instant, the vast majority of which were in intergalactic vacuum.

Jake did not know they had made it until he saw snow-covered badlands and felt the howling Montana wind. "Light My Fire" throbbed in his microamps.

Four Hunkpapa warriors sat waiting by a fire, wrapped in buffalo robes and wearing winter leggings made from Mackinaw trade blankets. Big fur caps half hid the flinty looks that passed for Lakota greetings. Their names were Swift Cloud, Bear Ribs, High Bear, and Sitting Bull, the Medicine Man and Strong Heart Chief. This was no longer the Mesozoic. Jake recognized the year Minniconjous called, The Winter When Ten Crows Were Killed.

As Jake and Peg flickered into the frigid air, Sitting Bull started to repack his redstone pipe—a sign that guests had arrived. "I see you, He-Who-Walks-Through-Winters."

"I see you, Sitting Bull." Jake knew sign language, and was fully programmed for Lakota. Peg had to make do with French.

Sitting Bull spoke for the group. He was only a year or so older than Peg, but already a big man among the Hunkpapa. "You have been gone long in the Spirit World, He-Who-Walks?"

Jake folded his legs and sat down across the fire from the Strong Heart Chief, settling naturally into a lotus pose Peg had taught him. "For me it has been six moons, maybe seven."

Sitting Bull's face split into a smile. "For us it has been only as long as it takes to light and smoke a pipe."

Jake made a sign that meant, "Marvelous are the ways of the Great Medicine." Lateral drift had deposited them a few minutes farther along the time stream. Which was normal. You never came back to the exact same point-instant.

"Your Walking-Wagon did not come back with you," Sitting Bull observed.

"My Walking-Wagon went south." Jake smashed his hands together to describe the wreck of the reactor.

"It is good we have new Hohe horses." Sitting Bull indicated a string of stolen ponies. He lit the pipe from the fire—offering a smoke to Grandmother Earth, Grandfather Sky, the Four Winds, and then to Jake.

Jake smoked, spreading out the gifts he had been gathering. Swift Cloud, Bear Ribs, and High Bear got shed tyrannosaurid teeth. He gave Sitting Bull the big *Quetzalcoatlus* claw. Everyone was pleased by the presents from the Spirit World, saying they were "*Sha-sha*," which meant, "Very red." Excellent.

Sitting Bull added, "Will He-Who-Walks and Red Woman come back with us to the camp circle?"

"*You betcha*," Jake accepted. The Hunkpapa laughed aloud. "You betcha" was Sitting Bull's favorite Americanism.

Jake helped Peg onto a stolen pony. The nearest nineteenth century portal was well to the south—off the coast of what was now Florida. But Sitting Bull's goodwill made them welcome in lodge circles as far as Paha Sapa, the Black Hills that sit at the Center of the World. Jake and Sitting Bull had always gotten on well, even more so since Peg accompanied him. Sitting Bull liked to have striking women in camp. He was the one who had given Peg the name Red Woman.

"We're in." Jake grinned, handing Peg her drag rope, thinking how remarkable Sitting Bull's taste in women was. Peg was *sha-sha*, very red, very excellent.

Back at camp, Sitting Bull threw Red Woman and He-Who-Walks-Through-Winters a wedding feast, more to impress Peg than to give Jake's union any religious sanction. Lakota marriages were catch-as-catch-can. Some couples stayed together all their lives. Others indulged in adultery, wife-giveaways, mate swapping, bride-buying, polygamy, kidnapping, and quick divorce. Lakota society was a happy mix of polite mayhem. Straitlaced on the surface, but seething underneath with the eternal question of who was sleeping with whom.

When the grass was up Sitting Bull's band was headed south. A big summer council was called for Bear Butte. Partly to be ready if "Mad Bull" Harney and his Long Knives returned. Harney was a brigadier general who had swept through Lakota territory, massacring Little Thunder's Burnt Thighs, taking hostages, and dictating treaty terms to the Lakota. General Harney appointed head chiefs for each tribe, outlawing robbery and loitering about the emigrant trails—then he left, without so much as a fare-ye-well.

The Northern Lakota were mystified. Glad Harney was gone, and hoping he was not coming back.

Jake told Sitting Bull he could go to Bear Butte with a light heart. The U.S. Senate would never ratify the hard-nosed treaty Harney had forced on the Lakota. Congress could be as fickle and inconsistent as Lakota marriage customs. The treaty was one more specious piece of paper that white society insisted the Lakotas sign, then was too busy to be bound by.

Sitting Bull was pleased, considering Jake clairvoyant when it came to events among the great chiefs in Washington. It was good to hear Mad Bull Harney would not be back anytime soon. One visit was plenty.

They rode south with Sitting Bull's band, parting near

Bear Butte, where the Medicine Chief made a final attempt to talk Jake into staying. "He-Who-Walks, end your wandering with us. We Lakotas live at the Center of the Earth, closest to the Great Medicine. The Teton Lakotas are the most numerous and prosperous of all the Lakotas. And the Hunkpapas are the foremost tribe among the Tetons. Where could you be happier than here?"

Where indeed. Throughout space-time, Jake had seen hundreds, maybe thousands of peoples utterly convinced they had the best of lives. Long ago he had learned not to argue.

Peg gave Sitting Bull a warm "*au revoir*," and they headed south, toward *Paha Sapa* and the Center of the World. The nearest FTL safe house was in New Orleans, a couple of thousand klicks to the south. Jake and Peg would have to hoof it down the Mississippi—watching their step all the way.

Past Paha Sapa—and Ash Hollow, where Mad Bull Harney had massacred Little Thunder's Burnt Thighs—they camped with some Cheyenne on the Solomon Fork of the Pawnee. Young Crazy Horse was there, along with Young Man Afraid, and other angry Oglalas, working up their Medicine, aiming to teach the Long Knives how to fight. A Cheyenne Medicine Man named Ice promised that the Long Knives' bullets would bounce off them. Jake did not wait to see how that worked out.

Instead he and Peg rode almost due east, until his navmatrix found the exact intersection of ninety-six degrees west longitude and thirty-nine degrees north latitude, a patch of prairie west of Topeka. There Jake dug down to retrieve a metal safe box left by a survey crew attached to the British North America project. He had helped bury it, and knew the box did not contain communicators—or any out-of-period gear. But the contents were bound to be useful. They were leaving The Winter When Ten Crows Were Killed, headed for 1857.

As he was filling in the hole, a cavalry column clattered up, led by a courtly young lieutenant with a Virginia accent. He immediately offered assistance. Didn't they know there were Indians about?

Jake wiped sweat and dust off his forehead, allowing that he had seen a few.

"Where may I ask were you headed?" The lieutenant naturally assumed they were lost.

"New Orleans."

Jake's destination provoked laughter all around. The young lieutenant vowed to take them as far as the "Abolitionist" ferry at Topeka. "In exchange for an introduction to yer lady." He doffed his plumed campaign hat. "Lieutenant Stuart, First U.S. Cavalry, at your service. James Ewell Brown Stuart. But you may call me Jeb."

When Jeb found out Peg could only speak French, he was delighted, inviting them to ride at the head of the column. The future *beau sabreur* of the Army of Northern Virginia escorted them all the way to Topeka.

There Jake traded their Hohe ponies for flatboat passage to Kanzas Landing. Three days later they were standing on the St. Louis docks, looking for a steamer to take them south. It was a simmering hot day on the River. A mile-long line of riverboats lay moored along the Saint Louis levee, angled upriver. The Big Muddy boiled past their prows—"Too thick to drink and too thin to plow." Layers of gleaming white gingerbread made them look like a flotilla of tall wedding cakes.

Jake turned up the magnification on his corneal lenses to read the names on the pilot houses. Hand painted lettering danced in the heat: *Altona, Polar Star, A. T. Lacey, Natchez, Northerner, Sunny South, Great Republic, Aleck Scott* . . .

Peg stood to one side, eyeing the throng pouring along plank sidewalks—flatboatmen, stevedores, sporting ladies, Mississippi desperadoes and the like. Everyone who made a living off the River. They were both doing their damnedest to look native—Jake had on fringed breeches and a buckskin jacket; Peg wore a Lakota doeskin dress trimmed with human hair. Her shoulder yoke and half-sleeves blazed with white quilling and bloodred crosses. A tall, red-haired white woman wearing tanned leather and scalp locks drew looks. Even in St. Louis. Also catcalls, obscene offers, and proposals of marriage.

All of which Peg acknowledged with an easy, open smile—not knowing any English, and having the dangerous habit of looking men straight in the eye.

"Found our connection." Jake took Peg by the elbow, steering her through the raucous babble.

Streetcars clanged, dropping off passengers. Horse drays and baggage vans jostled past leather-stockinged trappers, silk-hatted sharpies, and coffles of slaves. The microamps in Jake's middle ear played Stephen Foster, *"Ho! for Louisiana! I'm bound to leave this town . . ."*

Jake had found his steamer. And not just *any* steamer. He didn't need a set of bad boilers steered by a lightning pilot full of forty-rod whiskey—some drunken daredevil who'd tie down the safety valve, swearing to see his passengers in "Hell or Memphis." Cutthroat competition and superheated steam made riverboats prone to detonation. And in 1857, scientific metallurgy and federal safety inspectors were as far off as flying machines.

Normally Jake could have called up the names and dates of all major steamboat accidents, explosions, and misadventures. Only he never expected to be steamboating through antebellum North America. The files needed were thousands of years in the future. Not yet imagined, much less invented.

But the moment Jake saw the name *Aleck Scott*, a line popped up in his augmented memory (*"Who is I? Who is I? . . . I fires de middle door on de Aleck Scott."*) The *Scott* would get them to New Orleans safely, and in some style.

Pickpockets worked the wharf. Sporting ladies smiled at Jake. His microamps picked up French, Spanish, German, a pair of African tongues, and a dozen English dialects. Black boat workers, both slave and free, engaged in a lively crap shoot. Shrieks of, "YO-LEVEN," mixed with curses and appeals to Heaven in Yoruba and Mandingo. "The man's point is eight—eight's the point. Double-four. Half-dollar on de hard way . . ."

Farther down the dock two industrious sharpies were fleecing a drunken young "Awlins" planter at three-card monte—much to the disgust of a white-gloved mademoiselle, twirling her peach parasol and tugging at his arm. She rolled her almond eyes, muttering "*Merde*."

Jake planted Peg next to Mademoiselle Parasol and the monte game. Roustabouts rolled barrels up the *Scott*'s gangway, under the watchful eye of a mate with a marlinspike. A rope end dangled from the mate's hand, ready to speed the shiftless. Deck passengers lugged aboard bed ticking, blanket rolls, carpetbags, and barking dogs; somehow he and Peg had to join them.

Slung over Jake's shoulder was a beaded Lakota possible sack crammed with their Mesozoic data. A trove that was meant to go straight to a Home Period. They had to get to New Orleans—and then the Mid-Atlantic portal—as fast as antique transportation allowed. And at this point-instant Jake had precious little left to work with.

Opening the metal safebox he had retrieved west of Topeka, Jake dug past a hardbound copy of *Life on the Mississippi*, a pack of Steamboat #00 playing cards, two pairs of dice, and other such River essentials. The bottom of the box was lined with money, counterfeit copies good or better than the originals. Most of it was dated after 1860 and utterly useless at the moment. Jake shoved aside the Civil War greenbacks and Confederate currency, to get to the slim stock of antebellum banknotes.

The safebox was "clean," containing no out-of-period paraphernalia to alarm post–nineteenth century investigators. Someone here-and-now might find its contents damned odd, even spooky (a Mississippi senator named Jefferson Davis and a VMI professor of Natural Philosophy and Artillery Tactics—soon to be known as "Stonewall" Jackson—had their faces on the currency of a nonexistent country). But by the time people were equipped to properly date the box, it would merely be a bunch of old bills and curios.

Lying at the very bottom was a thin sheaf of fifties, claiming to be issued by the Kansas Valley Bank in Atchison. Tightfisted William Waddell, bank president and freight baron, frowned up at Jake. Perfect steamboat fare. He grabbed the bills, locked the box, and pocketed the key.

Straightening up, Jake realized Peg was talking to someone.

Damn. Peg was wonderful. The woman he loved, and a whiz with dinosaurs—or anything that had been dead for eons—but she had no experience in sliding easily through an inhabited era. Lack of English ought to have been enough—but Jake could hear her chattering away in French with Mademoiselle Parasol. It might as well have been Hindi. Jake had not programmed for French this trip, there being hardly any need for Romance languages in the Uppermost Cretaceous.

Peg took him by the arm, switching to agitated Universal. "Charlotte tells me her brother is being cheated."

In the short time it took Jake to find the banknotes, Mademoiselle Parasol had acquired a name and totally won Peg over. Peg nodded toward the young planter brother, propped against the monte table. "These men mean to rob him."

Jake did not doubt it. Charlotte's brother was an earnest young mark in a taffeta coat, baby-faced and tolerably drunk. About to fall prey to two river sharks who made their living off well-heeled innocents. Jake tried to indicate it was hardly their affair.

Peg insisted, her determined look framed by copper curls. It was pointless trying to pacify her. She could not see wrong being done without wanting it set right.

Mademoiselle pleaded too, first in a flood of French— then seeing Jake did not *parlez-vous*, she switched to soft Southern-accented English. "Won't you help us, suh? It's Daddy's money, from a land deal. A sum in trust—all the cash we have till the cotton comes in."

Mademoiselle Charlotte was the perfect damsel in distress. Hair like dark honey stuck to her wet forehead, pressed against skin as delicately colored as a fawn's. A high collar and rose cameo hid what had to be a graceful neck. One look told it all, the tragedy not just of Charlotte's half-foxed brother, but of the whole moonlight and honeysuckle South—"Ladies full of false pedigree, the pistol-hearted horsemen and the honeyed-mouth." It was not Jake's fight, not by half—he hardly relished risking everything to rescue some bumpkin in a silk suit. But Peg wouldn't back away, so neither could he.

Sighing, he set down the precious possible sack, prepared to act.

The monte game was pitched in the lee of a woodcutter's cart. The bearded cordwood peddler leaned on his load, sporting a black hat and shabby coat, eyeing the $2,000 in bills sitting on the table—looking like he could have put the money to use. So did half the hard cases in the crowd. That much money lying in open sight on the St. Louis levee invited violence.

The dealer and shill were well-dressed ruffians with full moustaches, wiry sideburns, and hard-edged Arkansas accents—a cold pair of card assassins who could have been scalp hunters in their spare time. The dealer accompanied his shuffle with a fast patter, full of *bon-*

homie and bullshit. "Keep yer eye on the Queen. The Queen of Love. She's yer card . . ."

Charlotte plucked at her brother's sleeve, begging to board the steamer. Half-turning, he shushed her in an overloud whisper—"Hush up. 'Tis ah sure thing." She shrugged off the alcoholic assurance, looking to Peg in despair.

Three-card monte was a knock on the old shell game. Three facedown cards, shuffled in plain sight. The mark bet he could keep track of one card, in this case the queen of hearts. "The Lucky Lady in Red . . ." Jake guessed the shill had already run off a tempting set of wins, taking the young planter into his "confidence," getting the boy to bet big.

By St. Louis standards this was all good, clever fun— a fool's game, crooked as a corkscrew. But if you couldn't hang on to your money, popular opinion held it to be safer in other hands.

And these two Arkansas bushwhackers aimed to back their scam with steel. Internal magnetic detectors told Jake they both carried suspicious amounts of ferrous metal. The dealer wore a holdout, and what looked to be a hideaway gun. The shill was good for a bowie knife.

Shuffling stopped. The young man in sweat-stained taffeta deliberated, swaying over the monte table. As he reached for a card, Jake stepped up, saying softly, "Your card is not there."

"What, suh?" Charlotte's brother cocked a bleary eye, seeing Jake for the first time.

Smiling, Jake reached down and rapped the table. "Your queen is not there."

"Well, where in damnation is she, suh?"

Jake gave a friendly nod toward the dealer. "That gent has the queen in his holdout." The confidence man gave Jake a go-to-hell look, signaling to the shill with his eyes and taking a hasty step back. He bumped into the wood cart, finding his escape blocked by the wood peddler, a stocky solid-looking brute who would not be easily moved. The crowd edged closer.

''What in blue heaven is a holdout?'' demanded Charlotte's drunken brother.

''This is a holdout.'' Still smiling, Jake reached inside his buckskin jacket, triggering his shoulder holster. The holster shoved his small flat neural stunner into his palm.

Lunging across the table, he grabbed the startled dealer's right elbow; spinning the struggling man about, Jake brought the stunner down with a chopping motion, pretended to hit him. The stunner hummed and the dealer collapsed. Jake slid back the man's sleeve. The queen of hearts peeped out from under the unconscious dealer's cuff, held in place by a metal spring.

Cursing, the young planter scooped up his cash, flipping over the cards on the table—three treys.

Jake expected the shill to fade into the throng. Instead the fellow proved alarmingly game, mouthing a blistering oath and shoving aside the drunken planter. A shining steel blade slid out of the shill's sleeve, and the monte shark aimed a ripping cut at Jake, screaming, ''Yew meddling buckskinned bastard.''

Charlotte's brother let out a startled yelp you could have heard in Texas. Jake swung the slumped dealer around as a shield, angling for a shot with his stunner.

Peg moved faster than any of them. As the shill roared past she calmly stepped into him, pivoting sideways, right hand falling naturally along his knife arm, locking it against her hip. Without applying undue pressure, she took a short half-step. The man's own momentum sent him sprawling face forward into a stagnant puddle.

She dropped to one knee, half-atop the startled shill, ready to break his arm if he persisted in struggling. *Ikkyo.* Jake recognized the *irimi* variation of Immobilization #1. Neat. Simple. Nearly unstoppable. He had seen her use it before on an overfriendly Lakota brave.

A third Arkansas ruffian had been sunning himself against the wood cart, looking mean but harmless. Suddenly he burst into action, jerking a belly gun from his waistband, a small cut-down cap and ball revolver.

Too late Jake realized there were three members to the monte team. This was the backup man—waving his sawed-off Navy Colt level with Peg's head.

Jake dropped the dealer, lifting his hands in surrender but holding tight to the stunner. Corneal lenses locked on the gunman's sweaty trigger finger. His compweb figured odds and angles, cutting time into slow mode. Peg still knelt atop the shill, directly in the line of fire, milliseconds away from having the back of her head blown off. Jake had maybe a quarter second to work in, not half enough time for a proper shot.

The bearded woodcutter had been resting lethargically against his cart—lynx eyes following the action, fingers curled around a short cordwood log. In a blur of motion he brought the thick chunk of cordwood cracking down across the backup man's wrist. The cut-down Colt went spinning. Howling, the gunman grabbed his wrist and hopped about.

Jake finished the job with his stunner. Two short, low hums and the hysteria subsided. The complaining gunman keeled over. A foot-long bowie knife slipped from the shill's nerveless fingers. Peg rolled the man upright to keep him from drowning in the mud.

The swift spasm of violence produced stunned silence along the wharf. For several seconds people stared at the three sleeping swindlers and the upturned treys. Then the dockside babble resumed. "Pay the line. Pay the line," shouted someone at the crap shoot. "Four bits—Man made his point." Previous losers slit the sleeping monte dealer's pockets, retrieving their loses, passing out his personal effects—a silver watch, silk hankies, and a small pepperbox pistol.

Hands shaking with relief, Jake bent over and picked

up the shill's Arkansas toothpick—"The Fifth Ace" was burned into the bowie's handle. Despite all the concealed steel, the monte game had been settled by an *aikido* hold, a piece of cordwood, and a plastic stunner. Three out, no shots, no deaths, and the Arkansas side retired.

Charlotte's brother had his own derringer out, a .45 caliber cap and ball original. He was waving the minicannon, wild to shoot someone now that the fight was over. Jake could see Peg preparing to disarm him, so he stepped over and offered his hand, trying to save the young ass further embarrassment.

Seeing the proffered hand, the drunken planter managed to pocket his pistol—still capped, cocked, and like to go off—while he pumped Jake's arm like a well handle. "*Mon Dieu*, that was wonderful. I've hardly seen the like."

Seminumb from seeing that Colt pointed at Peg's head, Jake fought manfully to disengage, insisting no thanks were needed.

"Nonsense, suh. Nonsense." The planter hauled out a flask of whiskey, offering it to Jake and the wood peddler, absolutely determined to be sociable.

The stocky peddler took the flask, staring thoughtfully at his hunk of cordwood, with the rapt concentration of a man who's decided to ram his head through a brick wall and is just about to do it. Now that the action was over, his movements were as slow and deliberate as Sitting Bull's. "Never seen a fellow fall so fast from a rap on the wrist," the woodcutter declared. "Must be something in the wood."

His level gaze shifted to Jake, "Unless you would like to explain, stranger?" The unblinking inspection would have done credit to a Pinkerton.

Jake shrugged. This round-shouldered fellow in a shabby coat was clearly no fool. He looked to be in his mid-thirties, and the quick way he reacted meant he must have seen action—maybe out West, or in the Mexican War. Without seeing the stunner hidden in Jake's hand, he knew something was amiss. Clearly the woodcutter was one of those alert, wide-awake gents who could organize an expedition or command an army—but happened to be carting wood and drinking whiskey. America was alive with backwoods geniuses fueled by moonshine. Rail-splitters who could run for president. They were what made the place so exciting—and so damned dangerous.

Taking a measured swig he thanked the young planter and handed back the flask, producing a bundle of Missouri stogies out of his battered coat. The peddler offered them around as though he had delivered a baby rather than broken a man's wrist, saying, ''That was some smooth sippin' whiskey. Straight scotch—Glenlivet I would guess?''

Charlotte's brother beamed, taking a cigar, ''Armand Marie d'Anton, at yer service.'' He managed a deep bow without tipping over. ''An' this is my sister, Charlotte Marie.''

Charlotte smiled and did a deft curtsy, ''The Maries are for our mother. An' just plain Danton was never good enough for Daddy.''

The woodcutter lifted his black slouch hat. ''Ulysses Simpson Grant at your service. You, Madame, may call me Sam.''

Of course. Jake chided his compweb for not seeing that coming—the shabby clothes, deep-set gaze, swift resolute action, and thorough knowledge of whiskey— the man was Sam Grant to a tee. He reminded Jake of Sitting Bull at a buffalo feed, passing out tobacco and playing the bluff, shy ladies' man.

''An' what is yer name, friend?'' Armand shoved the flask of scotch on to Jake—drunkenly insisting everyone share in the good feeling.

Jake groped for a name. It would do no good to have

"Jake Bento" attached to these events; he did not aim to get "known" on the River. Or to have these three cutthroats coming after him once they revived. "Rhett," he replied. "Rhett Butler. And this is Miss Scarlett O'Hara." He patted Peg's arm.

"But I heard my sister call her Peggy?"

Damn the French—he never knew what Peg was saying. "Scarlett's a nickname."

"Ah, I see, suh. With her red hair. A real fighter, too." Armand shook his head over the shill, still lying faceup in the mud puddle, mouth open, snoring like a shanghaied sailor. "Never seen an armed ruffian upended with such dispatch. What did she do to the fella?"

"*Aikido.*"

"Ya don't say? She made it look so easy. Are you planning to board the *Scott*?"

Jake admitted as much.

"Deck passage?"

He nodded. Doubtless that was all that could be had. This close to departure the boat would be bulging at the gunwales with paying passengers and slaves headed south.

"Then you must share our staterooms, suh. We have a pair, booked all the way through to Awlins."

Jake gave in. Short of taking another steamboat, there was no way of shedding this pair. Peg and Charlotte had their heads together, chatting each other up in French. They were alike as two peas, pretty and headstrong, happy to be going somewhere with someone new and interesting. He could have kicked Peg's doeskinned fanny. Instead he had to smile his thanks.

Grant nodded toward the three sleeping monte sharks, lying at odd angles in the mud with their pockets slit. "If you wish to call a constable, I would be pleased to stand witness."

Armand shrugged, "St. Louie can keep 'em, with my blessin', suh. I aim to board the *Scott*."

Sam Grant pushed his wood cart off through the crowd, happy to have some smart whiskey and a bit of action under his belt. In four years this ex-soldier in a moth-eaten coat would be the main field commander in the Department of Missouri. In twelve he would be president of the United States, the first full general since Washington, and the most famous living American. Jake had not expected to meet the savior of the Union pushing a wood cart along the St. Louis docks, but so far as people went the American West was still a very small place.

Armand marched up the *Aleck Scott*'s fantail gangway, lighting Grant's cigar and humming the "Marseillaise."

> Aux armes, citoyens!
> Formez vos battillons!
> Marchons, marchons . . .

Tipsy as a parson on holiday, and twice as happy. Jake had more misgivings.

Amid the mud and soot of St. Louis the big riverboat fairly shone. Jake saw roustabouts with swabs and holystones polishing decks long as a playing field. The *Aleck Scott* was a floating hotel-palace on a steam raft, sporting fluted pillars and ornate balustrades trimmed with white gingerbread. Propelled by two immense paddle wheels—one to port, the other to starboard—the steamer was a miracle of Yankee engineering married to Southern comfort, bigger than Nelson's flagship or Cleopatra's pleasure barge, but able to carry quality folk and common cargo over swamps shallower than the deep end of a swimming pool.

Uniformed servants met them at the rail, "Sir'n and Mam'n" like they were royalty coming aboard. Not so much as arching an eyebrow at Armand's drunken stagger or the scalp locks on Peg's dress. A glass of iced river water, topped with a sprig of mint, was thrust into Jake's hand. Letting the grit settle to the bottom, Jake took a sip. Service like this took some of the savageness out of the American wilderness.

After seeing their gear safely stowed in the state-rooms, he took a turn on the Texas deck. Whistles screeched. The "last bell" clanged, and pine resin smoke poured from gold-crowned stacks—"Dem dat ain't goin', please get ashore."

Deckhands massed on the forecastle gave a shout, and the band struck up a traveling tune:

> I wish I was in de land of cotton,
> Old times dar am not forgotten,
> Look away, look away . . .

Gangways went up, and the *Scott* got under way, forging through tiers of flatboats and lumber rafts, the pilot cutting in tight to show the riffraff who was queen on the River.

In minutes they were booming down the main channel, leaving the levee behind, each turn of the giant paddle wheels taking them closer to New Orleans and the Mid-Atlantic portal. St. Louis and its brown pall of woodsmoke disappeared round a green bend. Not a shade too swiftly for Jake, who was eager as hell to bid *bonne chance* to the American wilderness.

The *Aleck Scott*

Alone at the Texas rail, Jake watched "Ole Man River" rolling by three stories below. The immensity of the Mississippi always moved him, making his problems seem small. More than a mile wide for much of its length, the Father of the Waters drained a basin stretching from Maryland on the Atlantic to the Bitterroots along the Idaho border. This was the last vestige of the great Mesozoic seaway he had flown over (and Peg had swum in) sixty-five million years before.

Whatever future mischief Armand and Charlotte managed would have to be dealt with. First priority was to get Peg and the Cretaceous recordings downriver *pronto*. Losing *Challenger* was a big black mark. Jake did not need time travel to know that Faster-Than-Light would be unamused.

FTL had a poor sense of humor and precious little forgiveness. Any field agent who failed to deliver—*for whatever reason*—was an absolute liability. A round-trip to even the closest parts of the Mesozoic was the energy equivalent to traveling 130 million light-years at near-infinite acceleration—hideously energy expensive. Lose the Mesozoic data he was carrying, and Jake might as well jump ship in Memphis and learn to chop cotton, selling himself to the highest bidder.

FTL had the means to make a Memphis auction block

look appealing. Jake could end up on perpetual call in some god-awful corner of the past—like counting rats and corpses during the Black Death. (Froissart said "one third of the world died"—but what did Froissart know? Modern epidemiologists wanted *real* numbers, *exact* details—fatal symptoms, dead ticks, blood counts, and pus samples. Some poor sod had to supply them.) Jake had *seen* the fourteenth century. One visit was enough.

A steamer passed, billowing smoke, pulling a thirty-cord wood flat upriver. Whistles tooted. Sunlight sparkled off muddy water. Accordion music drifted up from roustabouts playing rollicking shanties in the bow:

> . . . one more river ta cross.
> Old Noah once he built an Ark,
> There's one more river ta cross.
> He patched it up with hickory bark,
> There's one more river ta cross . . .

At that moment the American wilderness did not seem exceedingly dangerous; stark and untamed maybe, but not actively hostile.

Jake could easily be too worried. Too prepared. They had seen a spot of trouble at the docks. (He was still recovering from the heavy adrenal rush.) But that was expected—St. Louis was a nasty place.

Putting all problems on hold, Jake sauntered down to the boiler deck for rum and recreation before joining Peg in their borrowed stateroom. Mid-deck on the *Scott* was one long plush salon, with Windsor armchairs, deep blue carpets, and shining spittoons—awash with enough liquor to float the boat. This flood of alcoholic refreshment seemed to be the main improvement in North America since the Mesozoic. Small wonder President Washington's first domestic crisis was a whiskey rebellion. The mahogany bar was lined with well-upholstered planters in evening suits—though it was not yet noon. Jake felt conspicuous in his leather breeches and Sitting Bull buckskins.

Talk at the bar was fairly raw. A brute named Forrest with a bad squint and a worse laugh was buying drinks, saying he had shot a runaway that morning. The man was pure Mississippi gothic, wearing a long black parson's wedding coat thrown open to show off a pair of holstered Colts, with butts reversed so either pistol could be drawn with either hand—the gunfighter's rig. Forrest assured the bar that a double load of buckshot was "the scientific cure fer a slave sufferin' from itchy feet."

A downriver gent dared to disagree, claiming he came from around Columbia, where there was "way too much nigger shootin'. Not two weeks ago a couple of boys kilt a slave on the road, jes for spite—a valuable nigger, *worth more than $1200.*"

Forrest gave him a narrow look saved for abolitionists and similar insects. "The Lord Almighty decreed slavery for the black man. If blood be spilt, sobeit. His will be done."

"Nonsense," insisted the soft-hearted fellow from Columbia, "you wouldn't shoot a mule that strayed. Shootin' a man's nigger is got ta be at least as bad as shootin' his mule."

Jake tried to edge away with his rum punch, before anyone asked his opinion—but two courtly gents in full funeral rig accosted him. The taller of the two was a glad-handing Missourian named Taylor, with a trim goatee and white cornsilk hair. He asked if Jake was indeed "fresh off the prairie."

Dressed in a Lakota dance costume and paying for his drink with a neatly faxed Atchison banknote, it would have been foolhardy for Jake to deny it. Taylor wanted to know if he had been through Nebraska—"We hear the Niobrara is prime cotton country."

Taylor's portly companion, a red-faced cotton monger named Benson, swore that Nebraska was big enough to make a dozen new slave states, "If it weren't for the rascally Republicans . . ."

Jake had been to the Niobrara and beyond, seeing nothing that resembled a cotton plantation, or a Republican—just several thousand rascally Lakotas; Oglalas, Burnt Thighs, Minniconjous and Northern Cheyenne. Each and every brave hopping mad over the Harney massacre and the army's murder of Old Conquering Bear. He tried to discourage the notion that Young Crazy Horse's people were eager to have Wasichu plow up the buffalo grass and plant cotton.

But these two Missourians were convinced slavery had a terrific future out West, already counting "Bleeding" Kansas as a slave state, talking like the whip and auction block would go on forever. Taylor had cashed in his plantation, being so long in cotton had killed the soil— "Couldn't grow a sweet potato in it no more. Now he was hauling his slaves downriver for sale. " 'Cept for my old mammy—an' one perky yellow handmaid. A pert piece—not yet sixteen an' nearly white."

Benson guffawed, slapping Taylor's back, calling him, "A sly coon."

Taylor gave a wink and nod, "Why in the dark, stab me if she ain't all white. I aim ta sell the rest in Louisiana, or Texas. Maybe Southern California—if I get so far."

"Slaves is sellin' well now?" ventured Benson.

"Shud say so." Taylor fingered his goatee, "What would you figure I got for a woman of thirty an' her year-old suckling?"

Benson considered. "It depends. How many children?"

"Four, since I bought her."

"I'd say six-fifty, seven hundred dollars."

"A Texan paid eight. Pickaninnies alone are good for two hundred the moment they're pupped."

Mildly sick, Jake excused himself, saying he had not

half realized times were so flush. He left them congratulating themselves on Buchanan's inauguration, blessing the Democrats and damning the Republicans, who meant to free the slaves—"Jes' for spite. Let them get in an' it's war for sure."

It was no news to Jake that this shaky union was about to bust its seams over slavery—he aimed to be long gone by then. Every period had a pulse as sharply defined as the lines in a spectrometer. Life on the River throbbed to the slap of paddle wheels, the click of dice, and the beat of minstrel tunes, accompanied by the snap of the whip. Jake did not make it that way, but FTL expected him to dance to the music.

Turning the porcelain knob on the stateroom, he noted the original oil painting on the door—a naval scene done in bold colors, the mighty *Constitution* pummeling a puny dismasted *Java*. Peg lounged in the cabin's wicker chair, barely contained in a gown borrowed from Charlotte—a cascade of creamy satin, stiffened with crinoline and several sizes too tight, making her look like a leggy red-haired trollop posing as a bride.

Jake shook his head, still feeling mulish over the unnecessary roughness at the monte table, "Enjoying yourself?"

"Why not?" Peg assumed a wicked smile. "Don't we deserve to?" Since the crash they had *walked* from New Mexico to Montana, then ridden to St. Louis—sleeping in trees, caves, creek beds, lean-tos, and Lakota tipis. Nothing so far put a notch on accommodations aboard the *Scott*—with its lace pillows, smart service, and china chamber pots.

Jake sat down on the neatly pressed and turned-back bunk—but could not get comfortable. "Look," he told her, "you don't realize how chancy it is, dealing with these people." The talk in the saloon was a too-vivid reminder of what life on the Mississippi was like.

"These people are as savage as Lakotas, they just go to more lengths to hide it."

"Charlotte is no savage," Peg replied, reaching over and lifting the rum punch out of Jake's hand. "And Armand would not be a nuisance if he cut his alcohol allowance." She took a sip.

"Damn it." Jake got up, trying to retrieve his rum, regretting he ever taught Peg to drink. "You did see those coffles of slaves being marched aboard?"

"I saw," she nodded soberly, setting the glass down on the deck, out of his reach, fending him off with her free hand—showing her usual complacency. Just like when she sashayed into that tyrannosaur-infested scrub at Hell Creek with nothing but her 3V recorder.

He scolded her. "Right now it is just fighting, flogging, and selling folks for fun and profit. Soon they are going to be killing themselves in droves, up and down this river. Is that savage enough?" He thought about Jeb Stuart, that courtly young cavalry officer who accosted them on the prairie. One of Custer's troopers was going to bring him down with a pistol ball at Yellow Tavern.

She grinned mischievously, brimming with sass and sin. "I'll show you savage. Take *it* out."

"Take what out?" Jake lunged for the glass.

She stopped him with her palm. A woman trained in unarmed combat was not always easy to handle. "You know. *This*." She pressed the flat of her hand against the front of his breeches. Gentle unbending pressure kept him from getting at his drink.

"Shit." Jake stopped struggling, giving up on the glass. The harder he pushed the deeper her hand sank into the leather patch at his crotch. Deft fingers were undoing the laces on his leggings. His was the first male organ Peg had been able to play with whenever she wanted.

"Look," he warned. "You won't win this argument by seducing me."

"Of course not." Acting very unconcerned Peg undid the last lace, pulling his leggings down, letting the leather drag over his hips. "Who's arguing?"

Using soft palm pressure she made room for her tongue between the top of his breeches and the base of his groin. "You worry too much," she told him, starting to lick.

Damn. Worrying was his job. Peg took her paleontology plenty seriously—back in the Mesozoic she had not let them rest or fuck until they had found a sauropod. A *big* sauropod.

He cast a panicky glance over his shoulder. Naturally he had not latched the stateroom door. At any moment Armand or Charlotte might burst in with a hearty *bonjour*. Or some overpolite butler would appear with a tray of tarts and ices, in time to catch Peg acting like a *houri* in a ball gown.

Leaning as far as he could with his breeches about his hips, he groped for the latch—all the time telling Peg not to stop, saying how much he *really* appreciated what she was doing. Fumbling with excitement, Jake finally got the cabin door locked, just as Peg was dragging him onto the bunk, whispering, "Tell me you care."

"I more than care," he told her, furiously undoing ribbons and lace, as he struggled to kick off the leggings. (A Lakota warrior merely whipped aside his breechcloth, but Jake had stupidly turned his leggings into regular pants.) "I'm absolutely crazy about you."

"Not about me, silly. I mean Armand and Charlotte. Do you care about them—as people?"

He sighed. "Probably too much." Any consideration for the "locals" went clean against FTL regulations, but Jake was not about to quote the appropriate regs. Peg was here, and FTL was in the far distant future.

"Good," she grinned.

Beneath the satin and crinoline was the same smooth strong body he had made love to in the Mesozoic. Flesh pressed against flesh, and he forgot about Armand and Charlotte, about the slaves in the hold and the good ole boys at the bar, about Forrest with his killing ways and gunfighter's rig, he even forgot about the Mesozoic recordings—forgot about everything but the moment.

When they were done he lay half atop her, kissing the long curve of her hip, savoring Peg's smell and feel, saving up memories in his compweb for those moments when she really petrified him. Peg might be wearying, but never unexciting. Pleased and drowsy, she rolled over, wrapping her legs about his middle, pulling him tight against her groin. She had just had one of those long operatic orgasms. "Charlotte hates slavery," Peg insisted. "She told me so."

Jake propped himself up on one elbow. He had *expected* to hear something like that. "Sure Charlotte hates slavery. Hates it every day. But she comes from a slave-holding *family*. Her wealth, her station, everything she has from Daddy's plantation to her frilly peach parasol, it all comes *from* slave labor."

Peg ran a wet finger down his bare chest. "She says at home slaves are like family. Their mother died—their father never remarried. She and Armand were nursed, rocked, and spanked by slaves. Totally raised by them, really."

It was plain Peg had totally fallen for Charlotte. Why not? Jake was drawn by the shy, soft drawl and smart, caring manner—Charlotte had courage and style by the bucket. But courage and style were not near enough. Jake thought about Taylor, relaxing at the bar, swearing he would never sell his old foster mother, or his pert young concubine. And Thomas Jefferson, writing passionately about man's equality, while he thumped his slave mistress—who was his daughter's playmate and his wife's half sister. "Buying and selling family only makes it worse."

* * *

By the time Jake left the stateroom, sunset had turned the Father of Waters into a river of fire. Black snags radiated blood red ripples. Leafy shorelines and long islands faded by stages into blue hills and purple shadow. Darkness crept out of the river, devouring the light.

The pilot on duty, a man named Bixby, rang three bells—the signal to land. Jake saw Captain Fitz-Roy stroll out of his drawing room at the forward end of the Texas deck.

"We will lay up here for the night," Bixby called down.

"Very well, suh," replied Fitz-Roy, stiff and proper in his kid gloves and plug-tile hat, a diamond stickpin showing on his shirtfront. Captains on river steamers were pure ornament—like the gilt deer horns above the ship's bell—it was the pilot who carried the ship in his hands.

And Horace Bixby was one of the best, the man who would one day steer Sam Grant's gunboats downriver. (A prime factor in Jake's picking the *Aleck Scott*.) Twelve hundred uncharted miles of twisting channel lay between St. Louis and the Gulf, without a single bell buoy or lighthouse—if Bixby did not care to run downstream in the dark on a low river, then the whole blazing palace must tie up till morning at some plantation dock.

Normally Jake would not have minded. The *Scott* had been a delight—a splendid stateroom, rum punch from a plush bar, making love with Peg—it hardly felt like work. But complications had piled up at a feverish rate. Three angry Arkansas monte players were apt to be coming downriver, aiming to wreak vengeance on Rhett Butler. And the compweb Jake relied on to foretell disaster kept yammering that Armand and Charlotte were like as not to land in more trouble.

Dinner was a full dress business, rich hearty Southern fare and huge portions—beefsteak, pork chops, hoe cakes, sweet yams, Indian corn, stewed chicken, fried potatoes, with all manner of pies for desert—whatever the passengers did not finish went onto the "grub pile" for the roustabouts to pick over. Service was spotless, white napkins, white tablecloths, white livery: only the faces on the waiters were black.

Peg and Charlotte sat on either side of Jake speaking French across his plate, making him realize how unfair he had been, expecting Peg not to latch on to the one person she could *talk* to. And Charlotte *was* god-awful gay and attractive. He felt himself being totally taken in by her "Awlins belle" pose, despite the depths of anger and ambition he sensed beneath it.

As they left the table she seized his arm, saying in a sweet Southern lilt they should all go for a stroll. Wine had come with dinner. The smell of her perfume, the raw feel of flesh under silk were frankly overpowering. Just hearing her whisper "Mistah But-lah" in his ear was enough to make him want to walk the length of the Mississippi for her. Under the charm and flirtation, Jake sensed stoic courage calling out to him, saying, "You claim to be a man. You claim to have courage and compassion—Well, I need you to be strong."

All she actually whispered was, "Help me keep Armand away from the gambling."

Jake agreed. Once the tables were cleared, the brandy and cards would be out. Gamblers infested the big riverboats. Forrest was already waving a speckled-backed deck, inviting Taylor to take another beating at poker. Benson allowed that he, too, might have some money left to lose.

It did not surprise Jake that Forrest was a poker shark. The romantic "Gaylord Ravenal" image of the Mississippi gambler, all silk suit and smooth manners, was an invention of later, more innocent times. Most men who made their living by fleecing the traveling public were crude thugs, posing as upcountry hicks or traveling preachers. The chivalrous, dashing gentleman was apt to be the pigeon—a young well-to-do plunger like Armand, who would bet wildly, play badly, and end up busted.

Gents pulled up chairs, chuckling over Taylor's losses, and the way he bet one of his slaves—''Havin' a good-lookin' young houseboy stand up ta back a silly little inside straight that he had not a prayer of fillin'.''

Taking Armand's arm, Jake suggested a walk down the gangway and along the levee. The night was warm, lit by the four-story steamer ablaze with lamps and candles. Swamp frogs kept up their eternal obscene chorus, ''Let's fuck. Let's fuck . . .''

Peg and Charlotte walked arm in arm, chatting in French. Jake and Armand shared a clay jug, full of raw bourbon. Under the influence of the crude corn liquor, Armand confessed his losses. While Jake and Peg had been playing spoon in their stateroom, Armand had been busily losing at poker. The two thousand Jake had saved from the monte table was gone—''Along with a mite more.''

''How much more?''

''Seven thousand.''

Nine thousand in one afternoon. Jake pondered how deep the man's pockets might be.

''But I aim ta win it back . . .''

Such breezy confidence raised shivers. Jake's compweb predicted Armand was headed for a terrible fall. Sam Grant drank out of boredom, but Armand needed no excuse, and while Grant could be counted on to sober up for a crisis—like the coming civil war—Armand would barely notice the commotion. The man was not a mean drunk, but he was a serene and irresponsible one, able to make the most hideous mistakes and be miserably sorry afterward. What the next century would call an ''addictive personality.'' Only, antebellum Missouri did not offer twelve-step counseling or an outback addicts anonymous. Therapy was still in the "pluck 'em an' plant 'em" stage.

"... these are decent chaps, who've gladly taken my note in hand."

Christ. Armand's pockets were already emptied; which meant no free ride downriver—in fact Jake could see himself having to cover Armand's losses. Setting his compweb to furiously estimating how he might raise the capital, Jake remembered Jenghiz Khan's heartfelt warning—"Save a man's life and he's yours forever." The jovial old Mongol had assured Jake that for the chronically unlucky the best cure was massacre.

A big brightly lit steamer went blazing by, churning upriver. Sparks flew from her funnels, throwing light over dark rippling water. She gave the tied-up *Scott* a whistle blast, while a band played "Swanee River." Steamers ran day and night upriver, even in low water, since the current supplied steerageway. The contrariness of the Mississippi let river steamers make better time running against the current than with it.

"How does it work?" Armand asked. "You speaking English, and Peggy speaking French?" Jake had wondered when Armand would tumble to that. The problem with this imposture was that he and Peg never knew what the other was saying. Thank God they were almost to Cairo, maybe three days from New Orleans.

"And this other language, the one you speak between the two of you. May I ask what it is?"

There was no use trying to explain Universal. Jake looked about and lowered his voice—"It's Rumanian."

"Really, suh?"

"Yes," Jake confessed. "Our names are not really Rhett Butler and Scarlett O'Hara."

"I thought as much," Armand whispered back.

"No one is to know," Jake warned. "But we are Rumanian royalty traveling in disguise, seeing the West incognito."

Armand admitted suspecting something of the sort, "I mean with your strange outfits. And Miss Peg bein' absolutely new to America. What are your real names, if I may be bold?"

"Swear not to tell a soul." Jake kept up the conspiratorial tone, as if frogs on the levee might report the conversation. "Not a word. Not even to Charlotte."

"On my hon-ah, suh."

"I am the Count Dracula. Peg is my countess."

"I'll be damned." Armand whistled, taking a swig and staring at Peg's back. Ample skin showed above her borrowed dress—a Transylvanian countess in castoffs.

"If you ask, Peg is bound to deny it," Jake warned.

"Of course." Armand understood. He tipped back the corn liquor jug, took a long pull, then cast it aside with a clean hollow clunk.

A cry came from down beneath the levee on the river side, followed by a sharp smack and a whimper.

Jake saw Peg turn in the direction of the sound, pause momentarily, then disappear over the lip of the levee, into the darkness along the low bank. He dashed after her, setting his corneal lenses for night vision, turning up his microamps.

Shadows leaped into stark contrast. Footfalls sounded like thunder—accompanied by the crack of blows. Someone down by the riverbank was screaming, "Oh, don't suh." (Smack.) "Please, dear God—dat's enuff." (Whack.)

At the edge of the levee, he caught sight of Peg sliding down the embankment. Below them, between the bank and the levee, a girl of thirteen or fourteen was lying full length on the ground—groaning, sobbing, choking. A burly fellow in a rumpled suit and slouch hat, sporting a big handlebar moustache, stood astride her hips. He was laying into her with what looked like a leather crop or dog whip. Jake could not see the girl's face—her arms were flung forward protecting her head—but the man's expression showed neither anger or excitement. He swung his whip with cool determination, giving no sign of letting up.

Jake called down, "Stop."

The man looked up, "Suh?"

"What are you doing?" It was all Jake could think to say.

"Whut does it look lak I'm doin'. I'm beatin' the shit out of this li'bitch."

"But why?"

"I got my reasons. An' I'd take it kindly if you did not interrupt." It was clear the cowering girl was black, most probably a slave—the man beating her was likely to be well within his legal rights, indeed he might be enforcing the law.

Out the corner of his eye, Jake saw Peg reach the bottom of the embankment and scramble to her feet. Charlotte cursed at the fellow with the dog whip, calling him "bastard" and "demon." The man did not seem to care, raising his arm and turning back to his work.

Armand stood at his sister's side, keeping her from following Peg down the bank. The scariest aspect of slavery was the way brutality, rape, even murder could be such casual matters in a country busy boasting at being free and democratic. No wonder Missouri bordered on Bleeding Kansas. In Jake's estimation, anyone unmoved by such beatings was just as likely to horsewhip a loved one. Or shoot a stranger over cards. A whole nation, or at least half of one, was gripped in violent schizophrenia, careening toward civil war—making Armand's eerie calm as awful as the blows themselves. The courtly Awlins gentleman showed no sympathy for the child under the lash, merely attempting to restrain his sister.

There was no restraining Peg. Once upright, she walked straight over to the man with the whip. Peg was tall for a woman, but the big backwoodsman towered over her, his hand half-raised to strike. Seeing her coming, he relaxed a bit, saying, ''Ma'am, I'll oblige you . . .''

Jake never did hear how the poor brute expected Peg to oblige him. She seized the back of his whip hand, at the same time catching his forearm above the wrist, pressing into the nerves as she stepped forward.

Only Jake's corneal lenses and compweb playback allowed him to follow her movement. It was *yonkyo*. Immobilization #4. One of the most painful holds in *aikido*. The man gasped and went tumbling tail end up, dropping his whip with an undignified howl, his arm bent at a terrible angle.

Peg leaned casually into the fall, putting her body behind her knee, snapping the man's forearm. Then she stepped back into defensive stance, warily watching him writhe in agony on the ground.

Jake bounded down the slope to be at her side in case the fellow came up with a gun. The beaten girl scampered up, vanishing into the dark along the bank—as if she did not aim to stop this side of Minnesota. Massa groaned, rolled over, tried to rise, then slumped back—utterly astonished at what had happened to his arm.

Peg was not even breathing hard, but Jake read cool fury in her eyes. It was the first time he had seen her intentionally hurt anyone—or anything. ''I could have done that more discreetly with the stunner,'' he reminded her.

She eyed him evenly. ''It wouldn't have given me half the satisfaction.''

Jake managed to hustle her back to the top of the bank. By then the man was sitting up, cursing, cradling his broken arm, promising to set the law on them, swearing that, ''Filthy riverboat trash an' cheap whores got no right assaultin' honest folk. No right at'all.'' Blood dripped down his moustache from landing facefirst in gravelly mud.

Charlotte cussed back, calling him a "vile, ignorant coward—lower than the dumb-as-dirt hands in Daddy's fields."

Armand tried to hush his sister, saying it was nothing.

Jake was not so sure, nodding toward the *Scott*— "The boat will be tied until dawn. What if this fellow comes back with his buddies, or even the law?"

The young planter laughed. "Really, suh? An' what will he say? That a young lady off the *Aleck Scott* took away his whip, freed his nigger, an' broke his arm? No driver with a gram of self-respect would admit that. Depend on it, by the time he tells his story he will have been set upon by at least a dozen armed abolitionists, led by old John Brown in the flesh."

Maybe. Hopefully. Jake despaired of ever getting downriver without a stir. Complications kept multiplying at an absolutely furious pace. Peg had cheerfully added criminal assault—and probably slave stealing—to passing bad banknotes and creating a commotion at dockside. All within a half day of St. Louis.

They left the man sitting on the mudbank screaming threats and spitting teeth.

Hat Island

First light filtered through the stateroom shutters. Jake realized that the thudding he felt was not *T. rex* thundering over the mudflats—it was the *Scott*'s paddle wheels slapping the river. They were under way again.

Peg lay next to him, a red-haired sleeping angel. Kissing her lightly, he slid off the bunk and slipped into his buckskins, ambling out to see dawn from the middle deck rail. Lamps and lanterns burned dim. Banks rolled by in steel gray silhouette and heavy shadow. It was just light enough to make out snags on the river and the faint riffle of sandbars. Birdsong rose up to surround the *Scott*.

In the dew of morning things did not look so bad. No backwoods bloodhound gestapo had stormed aboard to arrest them for assault, slave theft, impersonating fictional characters, and interfering with child abuse. With a megaram memory reaching back into the Mesozoic, Jake had no trouble recalling the night before. Charlotte's anger. Armand's indifference. Peg's fury. Heaven knew what would happen if they did not get to New Orleans in a hurry. They could not just amble downriver, thrashing every ruffian careless enough to cross their path. Custom, law, and culture were dead against it.

"So, you could not sleep either."

He spun about.

Half a step behind him stood Charlotte, cool and composed in a frothy ball gown, wearing white gloves and parasol—an hour ahead of the sun. Her tawny disobedient hair tamed by a tortoiseshell comb. Hollows beneath her eyes said she had missed sleep, or been crying.

Jake admitted last night's nastiness was worse than dodging dinosaurs.

"Dinosaurs?" She pressed her lip in puzzlement.

"Big prehistoric lizards," he explained.

Charlotte laughed, showing white even teeth, "Like in Hyde Park, *n'est-ce pas*? Daddy took us ta London for the Great Exhibition." Fake iguanodons decorated the Crystal Palace gardens. She was sharp and knowledgeable, not embarrassed to own a mind ahead of her time.

Charlotte turned serious, "Ah never saw anything so brutal as last night."

He lifted an eyebrow. "Surely you have seen field hands beaten." Driving with a whip was fairly common.

"Field hands, yes"—she eyed him primly from beneath the parasol—"to keep 'em at it. But with women a crack in the air, or a light stroke across the shoulders is *totally* adequate. *We* know work when we see it— *men* are more likely ta be found lazin' about. There is no need ta beat helpless girls inta the ground. Daddy never, never treats *his people* that way."

His people? Charlotte was awfully choice with her English, never using the word nigger, or even slave— reminding Jake of Robert E. Lee. (Jake had ridden with Marse Robert at Antietam as part of the British North America project.) General Lee hated to say "Yanks" or "the enemy"—calling the bluecoats potting shots at him "those people." As if they were unruly neighbors. Terribly courtly. But Jake doubted that Charlotte and Bobby Lee had all that much in common, aside from a distaste for slavery and vulgar idioms.

The greens and gold of morning reflected off the mirror-smooth river. Jake asked if Charlotte knew about Armand's losses. Charlotte grimaced, "Daddy's money's gone—an' we are seven thousan' in debt ta the vultures."

Jake ventured that their sole hope was getting to New Orleans as fast as manageable.

Tipping back her parasol, Charlotte gave the water an intent look. "If we get out ahn the River before nightfall. An' get free of this low water. Then the pilots can quit lollygaggin' an run the boat night an' day." By "out ahn the River" she meant the lower River, below Cairo, where the Ohio flowed in and the water was higher.

Leaning forward, she laid her hand on Jake's arm, to get his full attention. And succeed in setting off a tingle that threatened to crash his compweb. "See how close the pilots are cuttin' their crossin's."

The *Scott* had been thrashing comfortably along in midstream, making full advantage of the current—now as they rounded a point, the long slanting line of a sandbar lay on the water a cable's length ahead. But the pilot kept doggedly on, cutting the shortest course past the sandy scrub pine peninsula.

"Look!" Charlotte leaned closer. "He's gonna just trim the bar."

The pilot cut the crossing razor-fine, aiming for the low oily spot at the head of the reef—a stagnant sheen on the surface marked by an ugly tangle of cottonwood snags. As they plowed onto the bar Jake felt the *Scott* hesitate, refusing to answer the helm, as if she feared shallow water.

Gripping the rail, he jacked up his microamps to catch the leadsman's calls. "Half twain . . . Quarter twain . . . Quarter-less-twain . . . Eight even."

Suddenly the suction broke and the *Scott* surged forward, throwing a great wave off the bow, mounting the reef with less than two feet of water beneath her bottom. Jake sensed Bixby's hand at the wheel.

"Pretty tight piloting," Charlotte concluded, releasing his arm. "We are not the only ones eagar ta make Cairo. If we make Hat Island by dusk, I imagine the pilots would risk runnin' the rest." Hat Island was the last hard crossing above Cairo.

Jake was surprised by how well she knew the River and riverboating. He listened to her tell about seeing England as a young teen—riding double-decker buses, reading *Punch*, and watching the America's Cup race around the Isle of Wight. Charlotte was far sharper than Armand: alert and curious, with a mind more like Sam Grant's. Jake liked that, though it made him wary—he could not fool her with fairy tales about Transylvanian royalty.

She gave him an immediate jolt by asking, "How long have you known Peg?"

What could he say? Eons. A month's training on Mars. Six months in the Mesozoic. Sixty-five million years since then. "Less than a year—but it seems like much longer."

Charlotte gave a knowing nod—"I can well imagine. Every moment wi' her is amazin'. An incredible woman."

That was Peg. Perfectly incredible. A Reformed Vegetarian who hated meat, but happily broke a man's arm. Jake had seen this chemistry before—two lively young women, accustomed to compliments and advances, tended to discount male attention. They knew what men wanted. Female approval had a whole other depth and dimension.

Peg herself appeared, and they traded *bonjours*, bursting into a flood of French. Every so often Charlotte would translate, so Jake would not be left out. He and Peg were lovers, expedition partners from a horribly advanced society with a universal language—but sweet, savage, honey-haired Charlotte had to tell him what Peg was saying.

Between translations he furiously considered how he might make some fast capital. Jake dearly needed a decent faxcopier and the proper sort of paper.

By breakfast it was plain the pilots were cutting *every* crossing tight, trying to make time despite low water and a corkscrew channel. Whenever the boat passed a point or island, passengers leaped up from their grits and hoecakes, craning to see just how close the pilot meant to cut the next crossing. A race mentality developed, though last night's docking had killed any chance of a record run. Riverwise gents in evening coats lined the rail, puffing cigars and betting on when they would make Cairo. With side bets on close crossings. Would the pilot mount the reef, or run aground? Westerners wagered on anything.

Odds ran near even until late in the forenoon, when one of the pilots—not Bixby—put the boat aground.

The grounding brought everyone to the rail, watching mud boil up from the bottom as the engines labored. By fine-tuning his microamps, Jake could hear commands echoing down the pilot's speaking tube. "Port, port . . . Now full astern . . . Snatch her! Snatch her!"

The boat stayed stuck. Odds on reaching Cairo that night took a plunge. Each hour on the mudbank brought them down another notch, until sharps offered two, even three to one against getting "out on the River." And found few takers.

Then Bixby took the helm. The *Scott* shuddered and scraped, groaning as if she meant to give birth. Polite stewards herded the passengers onto the fantail. "Hard a 'port, hard a 'port . . . Starboard! Starboard! Full astern," rattled down the speaking tube. The *Scott* raised her bow and slid off the shoal.

"Six-and-inches," sang the leadsman. "Seven feet! Eight . . ." They were booming down the channel again.

Pressed into the crowd on the fantail, Jake found himself alongside Taylor and the Missourian's teenage mistress—a sad-eyed girl the color of cream in coffee. As pretty as Taylor pictured her, but her fixed smile faded whenever Massa looked away.

The tall planter took out his watch, a massive Jurgensen with a diamond stem—as cold and expensive as the girl on his arm. He squinted at the timepiece, then snapped the gold cover shut. "That tears it. Another night on the bank. We'll never make Cairo now."

Reaching into his jacket, Jake hauled out one of his fake Atchison notes. "Here's fifty bucks that says we will make Hat Island, and are out on the river tonight."

Taylor blinked, "By Gawd, friend—what odds do yew want?"

Jake shrugged. "Whatever you think fair."

"This morning I would have asked two-ta-three. Now I'd put two hundred against that fifty—an' still call it theft."

"Done," Jake declared.

Word spread among the sporting types that the backwoods gent named Butler was as good as giving away fifties, betting they would clear Hat Island despite the delay. Sharps swooped down to make an easy plucking.

Charlotte tugged at Jake's arm, aghast, asking if he had gone mad—"You're another lunatic gambler. Bad as Armand."

No one could be that bad. "We need the money," he reminded her, rumpling a fifty to make it more like prairie currency—someone had to make good on Armand's debts. "And this isn't gambling."

She snorted, "What would yew call it?"

"A sure thing."

Peg dismissed Charlotte's alarm. Coming from a society without money, Peg would not have known a fifty-dollar bill from a French postcard. She habitually left all such decisions to Jake. It was his *job* to get her back to civilization; if that required betting on riverboats, or running buffalo with Sitting Bull, it was fine with her. Jake was *supposed* to know what he was doing.

The grounding and commotion even brought Armand out of bed and onto the middle deck, whiskey in hand, complaining of a vicious hangover. He took immediate interest in Jake's wagering—but with flat pockets all he could do was hold the stakes. Odds shifted throughout the afternoon, falling near to even as the pilots made better time, leaping back to three and four to one at every delay and bad crossing. His betting partners entertained Jake by extolling the horrors of the Hat Island crossing, with its maze of snags and sunken reefs—"not ta mention the wrecks of previous boats"—the only *safe* way to run the reef was to shave the island so close the stewards could "pick plums from the Texas rail."

Jake continued to pull in bets, becoming the subject of keen attention—which couldn't be helped. Deckhands gave him appraising looks. Servants made extra sure his glass was full, with a fresh sprig of mint in his julep. The wild gent in buckskins with the bowie knife— "Mistah But-lah"—was backing their boat with cash money against half the sharps on board—"an' your confidence in da ol' gal *Scott* is sore appreciated. Yew bet."

Bixby's cub, an apprenticed pilot named Sam with dark curly hair and a well-tended moustache, came down the companionway from the hurricane deck to get "a lungful of air." The young Missourian claimed things were too tense in the pilothouse for anyone as lowly as a cub pilot to dare draw breath. No one was standing regular watches—each man ran whatever bit of river he knew best. Sam swore that if they just cleared Hat Island he would give up cigars and spirituous liquors, "for at least the balance of the week."

By sunset Bixby was back at the wheel. Pocket watches were out as daylight ticked away. With the sun touching the horizon, Hat Island hove into sight; a chorus of "too bad" and "too late" went around the middeck—there was no chance of making the island before dark. Tucking their watches in their waistcoats, gamblers turned to see how Jake took his beating. Armand slapped him on the back, ''Losin's not terribly hard. Once ya get the hang of it.''

Forrest, the bad-mannered shark in a parson's coat, demanded to know when Jake planned to pay up.

Quietly Jake asked Armand for the stake money. Counting out ten fifties, he held them up for Forrest and the others to see. ''Here's five hundred that says Bixby runs Hat Island *in the dark*.''

''Damn,'' Armand shook his head, ''yer worse than I am. That money is already lost.''

Taylor agreed.

''A side bet,'' Jake insisted, waving the money under Forrest's long nose. ''Four to one. Or eat your words.''

''Wait,'' demanded Benson, ''what ya gonna pay us with when yew lose?''

''Take it out of his hide,'' roared Forrest, grabbing the five hundred. Benson and Taylor backed down, not looking eager to challenge the big mean-spirited parson and his brace of pistols. Jake's detectors also registered a knife in the man's boot and a blackjack up his sleeve. Reverend Forrest taught a tough Sunday school.

Attention turned to the pilothouse, listening for the three bells that signaled the boat would land.

The sun set. No bells rang. The boat bore on, thrashing into the gloom above Hat Island. Sporting gents on the middle deck exchanged amazed looks. A call echoed off the hurricane roof, ''Starboard lead, larboard lead!''

Out of the darkness in the bow came the sonorous chant of the leadsman. ''By the mark three . . . Quarterless-three . . . Half twain . . .'' The river was shoaling beneath the hull.

''By God he aims to run it,'' breathed Benson. The crowd around him gave an amen. And then silence. With Bixby at the wheel, the whole huge boat with its load of paying passengers, penned slaves, plush carpets, crystal chandeliers, and quarter million in cargo was bearing down on the Hat Island bar—running the reef and sunken wrecks, low water or no.

Bixby rang two bells. Jake's microamps picked up the jingling reply from the engine room. Steam whistled through the cocks. Engines stopped beating, and the great boat slowed, drifting downstream, torches and lanterns blazing, without enough steerageway to answer the rudder.

By now the night was bone black, the only mark of progress being the eerie cry of the invisible leadsman— "Quarter-less-twain . . . Eight-an'-a-half . . . Eight even!" The bar was rising up beneath the drifting boat, ready to tear the bottom out.

"Look!" cried a voice in the night. "The Island."

Adjusting his lenses for night vision, Jake saw the head of Hat Island looming over the boat. Bixby's voice descended the speaking tube, ordering the engine room to stand ready. Forrest stood frozen half a pace away, the five hundred clutched in his hand, sweat beading on his bearded face. Taylor's mouth hung open. His slave-mistress was wide-eyed.

"Seven-an'-a-half . . . Seven . . ." The leadsman's calls came quicker.

With only inches of black water under the bow, Jake heard branches bang against the overhead rails. Hat Island was reaching out to snag the *Scott*. There came a sudden lurch, then the dreaded grate of wood on sand.

Benson blinked and swallowed, "Heaven help us, we've touched bottom." In a moment it would be all-hands-to-the-pumps.

Bixby's voice banged down the speaking tube—"Full ahead! Hard down, Ben—Give 'er all she's got. Snatch her! Snatch her hard!"

Steam slammed into the cylinders, timbers groaned as the huge boat hung on the reef, dragging in the sand.

With a convulsive shudder, she mounted the bar and slid down the other side.

The leadsman in the bow sang out, "Nine feet . . . Nine-an'-a-half . . . Ten . . ." And then, "By-the-MARK-TWAIN."

They were back booming full bore down the channel, headed south in grand style. Jake plucked the five hundred from Forrest's startled grasp, saying, "Thankee, gents. Drinks on me when we get to Cairo."

Pandemonium erupted. Cheers rang and bells clanged. Sports at the rail raised a yahoo, lighting up cheroots and slapping backs. From pilothouse to engine room the boat rocked with good feeling and relief—except perhaps for the slaves chained in steerage, though if the *Scott* had ripped out her bottom out on the Hat Island reef, they'd have been the first to know.

Benson pumped Jake's hand, vowing he'd be damned if he had ever seen the like of it. Gents who could not wait for Cairo brought out bottles, toasting Jake and Bixby. Gamblers began to pay up.

Jake braced Forrest for the $2,000, wary of the pair of pistols in the man's belt. The tall, bearded gambler was totally taken aback by Bixby's success, his face twisted in puzzled consternation. (Jake found the flabbergasted frown heartwarming.) Forrest pulled a bundle of bills from inside his parson's coat, counted out his losses, spit a quid of tobacco onto the money, then handed it to Jake. Good feeling went only so far.

Charlotte giggled in Jake's ear, "That's Daddy's two thousand dollars—He's the man who fleeced Armand." Jake saw a measure of justice. Forrest merely glared hard at Charlotte, like he meant to hurt her too, if he could.

The party lasted out the midwatch, and into the morning, seeing the *Scott* well "onto the River."

Jake awoke next afternoon in high fettle, just in time for Peg and Charlotte to hurry him through a late breakfast. They had an invitation to ascend to the pilot-house—Bixby wanted to meet the man who bet on Hat Island.

Armand stayed comatose in his cabin, snoring impressively through the partition.

Jake took his coffee on the Texas deck, surveying an utterly splendid day. The River spread in all directions, looking like a broad shining arm of the sea, dotted with barges and flatboats. Dense woodland lined the banks, broken by farms, woodyards, and plantation docks. The Illinois shore was long gone—now there were slave states on either side Missouri to starboard, Tennessee to port. His compweb kept thankful track of each passing klick. They were plowing along, well below Belmont in the big loop between Island No. 10 and New Madrid. Ahead of them lay the drowned lands of southern Missouri, to the south rose the precipices shielding the Tennessee interior. The River was so twisted that they were steaming nearly due north to get south—half the trip could have been saved by walking to Memphis.

The pilothouse was a roomy glass cupola, with red-gold curtains, a big woodstove, brass spittoons, and a high-backed bench for the "river inspectors"—visiting pilots who traveled at company expense, to check the level of water "out on the River." (They favored the grandest boats with the best service, making the *Scott* a natural choice.) But today the splendid glassed-in cabin was deserted, except for Bixby, his cub Sam, and a white-aproned Texas tender named Hosea, who served iced tea and fresh coffee.

The great Bixby proved to be a slender, alert gent just over thirty, with curly hair and a captain's bearing. He did very little in the way of piloting. The water level was ample. The banks clearly marked. His cub clung nervously to the wheel, following the crooked channel.

Every so often Bixby would call for a sounding, remark on some passing point, or take a moment to reprimand Sam's steering; otherwise, he was content to relax on a leather sofa, basking in the glory of having run Hat Island in the dark.

He asked Jake, "How could you know I would run the reef? I did not decide myself until near to dusk."

Jake dodged the truth—that he had read it in a book which would not see print for decades. Instead he fell back on "gambler's instinct," hinting he had tremendous faith in Bixby's piloting—which he did.

He took care not to lay it on too thick; Bixby was not the sort to fall for flattery. Like most people who were extremely good at what they did, Bixby was his own best critic, with a level estimate of his abilities. It was safer and simpler for Jake to play the spendthrift sport with more nerve than sense. The river brimmed with them.

Peg and Charlotte surprised them by demanding that the white-haired steward introduce himself, and join in the conversation. Charlotte had a natural way with servants and slaves, never showing a hint of color prejudice. And Peg barely knew such a thing existed.

It turned out that the steward's name was not Hosea, but Cundazo-soo-zaduka. He spoke Cajun French, English, and several African tongues, having been born in Guinea to a good family—before being kidnapped and brought to America half a century ago.

Charlotte claimed she could tell breeding—even in a riverboat butler—and did not doubt that Hosea had been born to a princely house in Africa.

The old ex-slave was plainly touched. "If the young miss means to make me an African prince—then ah guess that's what ah was." He told stories about boyhood in Africa and about first seeing the Blue Ridge—"lyin' on the horizon like a dark slice of heaven."

Since Hosea had his freedom, Bixby asked if he ever considered going back to Africa—"You being a prince there an' all."

Hosea laughed, "White folks is always tryin' ta get us ta go back ta Africa. An awful waste, specially after all the bother of bringin' us here. No, suh. When ah get too old for the River, ah'll live all the time in Awlins. There's where the variety is, the music an' gay society. Rather be eatin' red beans in Awlins than lordin' over all the heathen in Africa.''

Conversation lapsed, and everyone enjoyed Sam's antics at the helm. The cub was brand-new to downriver piloting, careening all over the channel, climbing the wheel with eyes wide when he thought he saw a shoal coming up.

The approach of Memphis ended Sam's ordeal. Bixby rang the landing bells and took the wheel. By the time they left the Memphis bluffs behind, it was dusk, and Bixby's replacement came up. The great man went below, with Charlotte on one arm, Peg on the other, and Prince Hosea carrying the tea tray.

Sam collapsed on the high-backed bench. Digging into his pocket, he brought out a slim memorandum book and stared hopelessly at the pages.

"Problems?" Jake inquired.

"None whatever," Sam replied in a lazy drawl, continuing to give the book a puzzled, sorrowful look. "I just wish I had stuck to my original ambition."

"Which was?"

"Takin' boat up the Amazon. Bringin' the Good News to the cannibals—or at worst givin'em a change of diet. I was so busy banging both sides of the channel I couldn't mark the points as we passed."

Seeing the blank pages confronting the cub, Jake could not resist tripping in his compweb and rattling off every point, island, bend, reef, and sounding that Bixby had called out for the whole four-hour watch.

"Slow down, slow down," Sam wrote furiously. It took time, but he got it all down, every last sandbar and cottonwood snag. Then he closed the book, looking cau-

tiously up at Jake—"Slap me twice and call me stupid,
but how did yew do that?"

"Gambler's memory," Jake answered airily.

Sam gave Jake a curious look as he pocketed the
book. "That was a mean job of memorizing. You've got
a passable future in river piloting."

Jake thanked him for the thought, but assured Sam
that drinking, gambling, and loafing with the ladies took
up all the time he could spare.

Sam said he saw the sense in that. "I believe we've
missed supper, but may I buy you a scotch?"

"Certainly," Jake smiled, recalling to Sam his vow
to give up spirituous liquor if they made Hat Island.

The cub assumed a superior air. "That promise was
made in the sovereign state of Missouri. I only mean ta
wet the half of me that's in Tennessee."

As they descended the stairs Hosea came hurrying to
meet them, grave and gray-faced. "Mistah Butler, your
woman—the redheaded one—is in an uproar. She's
breakin' down a stateroom door."

Damning his complacency, Jake took the steps two at
a time with Sam at his heels.

When they got to the middle deck a crowd had already
gathered. Weaving his way through the press of servants
and curious types, he saw that the door to Armand's
stateroom was off its hinges, its oil painting torn and
trampled.

Peg had Armand down on the floor, practicing hold
#2 on him, twisting the little .45 caliber derringer out of
his grasp. A grim-faced Charlotte stood watching. Armand was sobbing.

Jake stopped at the broken door, his compweb warning him that worse was coming. Peg looked up, explain-
ing in perplexed Universal, "There was nothing else to
do. He was going to harm himself."

"Why in Heaven's name?" Jake asked in English;
hoping Charlotte would answer, so he and Peg could

preserve some of their cover. But she merely picked up the cocked and loaded derringer, shoving it into her purse.

Forrest answered for her, pushing to the front of the crowd. "Mama's boy could not stand his losses." With a mean dry laugh he explained there had been another round of poker, and Armand had again been the loser.

"What did he bet with?" Jake did not trust Forrest's fustest-with-the-mostest manner.

"Can't say it matters"—Forrest shrugged—" 'cause the little flat lost it all. I'm here ta claim the last of it."

Charlotte straightened up, turning her back to her brother, whispering, "Ah am ready," so softly Jake almost needed his microamps to hear her.

"Then come smartly." Forrest stepped forward.

"Wait." Jake moved to stop them. Peg was still holding Armand face down, his sobs soaking the carpet.

"You'd do well not ta stick in an oar," warned Forrest, opening his coat to free his gunfighter's rig. His grin shone like a guillotine, goading Jake to make a move.

Charlotte touched Jake's arm, the way she had that morning, begging, "Please, let it be. From the day I was old enough to know, I expected this would happen. The moment has come. There is nothin' ta be done."

"What in hell?" Too much was happening for Jake's compweb to keep pace.

"Fooled ya, did she?" Forrest's smile became a cold sneer, alive with malice. "Yawl were takin' in by a little nigger girl, playin' at being free. Takes more than white gloves and a parasol ta hide a mustee from me. She's yellow an' frenchified, but a nigger nonetheless." He tapped his breast pocket. "An' I got her bill of ownership."

Peg rocked back, relaxing her hold, ready to spring. She could not follow the words, but she could read faces and intent. Armand moaned and rolled over, holding his head.

Gripping Jake's sleeve, Charlotte looked straight into his face. "This man's right. If I don't go now, there is gonna be blood. An' the law will back him."

They both knew that Peg would not hesitate to go up against a tall villain sporting a knife, blackjack, and brace of pistols. But Forrest had the terrible weight of slave society behind him. Peg could not take on the entire boat.

Giving a sharp shudder, Charlotte let go of Jake and followed Forrest out.

"How could he take her?" Peg demanded in alarmed Universal. She was on her feet, undecided and uncomprehending, but ready to dive through the broken door if necessary and drag Charlotte back despite the arsenal Forrest toted about.

Jake could feel her gaze on him, urging him to set things right. Angry and helpless, he jerked Armand upright, determined to shake sense out of the sodden oaf. "So Charlotte's not your sister?"

"Half sister," Armand admitted, still busy being sorry for himself. Between sobs he spilled the whole story. "Mother died when I was born. Daddy had a quadroon mistress—already with child, meant ta be my wet nurse." Daddy had simply renamed his mistress Marie, just as you would give a new name to a dog or a horse. She mothered both children.

"The only mother I knew," Armand whimpered. "I was at her breast before Charlotte Marie was even born."

Charlotte was an octaroon, the daughter of a white and a quadroon. It explained so much—her brown eyes and darker hair—also the gloves and parasol at every hour of the day. She must have been terrified of darkening up, of showing her mother's color. Poor, poor Charlotte. She should have stayed in London. The second she set foot on British soil she was free. Only her home held her in bondage.

Jake seized Armand's flask. Bracing himself with a fast dollop of scotch, he tried to explain to Peg—no easy task.

"But she is more white than black," Peg objected. Charlotte was two shades lighter than Jake's Mesozoic-Mississippi tan.

"Doesn't matter," Jake told her. Not for nothing was slavery known as "the peculiar institution"—a charming combination of racism and rapacious profit making. The product of master and slave was legally a slave—perfectly salable. Large parts of the free white population had no hope of correctly naming their fathers, but the fact that one of Charlotte's eight great-grandparents had been black made her as salable as moonshine or molasses (more so, since moonshining was technically illegal—unlike the sale of young women).

Peg was shocked. "That's absurd."

"No, it's the law." Jake did not try to argue the justice of it. Turning back to Armand, he demanded, "Why the hell didn't her father free her?" Daddy could have done it anytime.

Armand shook his head. "Father always plays his cards close ta the vest. He would have freed her—when she got ta be twenty-one, or if he found the right husband. Till then, I was supposed to look out for her."

Jake swore softly—half in Universal, half in Lakota. "But instead you lost her to that snake Forrest. How in blazes did you get back in the game?"

The elegant idiot mopped his nose, looking miserable. "I bet yer money."

"And lost it." Jake got madder by the microsecond, saddled with this self-indulgent clown. That money had been Jake's backup, his safety margin in a merciless period when everything was for sale. Life. Love. Liberty. Even people. It was lucky Charlotte had taken the der-

ringer, because Jake would have cheerfully returned it
to Armand, helping him to steady his aim and work the
trigger.

"Ah lost it all," Armand sniffled, "ta the last *sou*."

Jake looked around the cabin. It was clean as a whistle. "No baggage, no belongings?"

"Yours also." The hopeless ass hid his head in his
hands.

Jake's jaw dropped. Alarms clanged in his compweb.
"What about my lockbox and possible sack?" Spinning
about, Jake lunged toward the door, to check their stateroom for the precious Mesozoic data. Armand seized at
the fringe on Jake's leggings, crying, "Wait, it ain't yer
cabin no more. Forrest won that too."

Peg stood poised and mystified, bursting to take action—mercifully the last exchange had not been translated.

Shaking off Armand's alcoholic grip, Jake shoved a
path down the hall to his former stateroom. Forrest
would not be able to open the lockbox, but he was bound
to be mystified by what he found in the beaded possible
sack. Given the man's slim wits and short temper, he
might leave off trying to puzzle out the contents and just
heave the priceless recordings into the river.

Jake grabbed the porcelain knob. The door was
latched. He pulled and pounded.

A gruff voice advised, "Go away."

He pounded louder.

"Damn yew," yelled the man inside. "I'm busy—
an' in no need o' company."

Peg was at Jake's shoulder, demanding an explanation. Instead he told her, "Break down the door."

She stepped back, aiming a karate kick. "Be careful,"
he warned, drawing his stunner, "the fellow is armed."

A yell echoed within, followed by the hollow boom
of a black powder .45. Jake flinched, but no bullet burst

from the door. Microamps estimated something soft had stopped the ball.

Peg completed her kick. The door crashed open in a shower of splinters. Gunsmoke spilled into the hall.

Jake stepped inside, stunner ready. Forrest staggered backwards into his arms, looking absolutely astonished and bleeding furiously. A fist-sized spot of blood on the man's shirtfront became an expanding blotch, staining the white shirt, wetting his pants, streaming down his coat sleeves.

Charlotte sat on the lower bunk, wedged against the wall, small and defiant, tears furrowing her cheeks, the derringer clutched in her gloved hand—smoke curled up from the pistol's round black muzzle.

Down-the-River

Gawkers crowded about the busted stateroom door, staring at Jake as he tore open the gambler's shirtfront, doing what he could with CPR and a medikit. Servants worked around him, righting furniture and mopping up. Derringers were notoriously useless at more than a dozen feet—at hailing distance, a man with a derringer might bang away at you all day without your finding it out. But at arm's length Charlotte didn't need to be Daniel Boone to put a ball the size of a hickory nut through Forrest's pump.

Not getting a flicker of a pulse, Jake gave up playing Florence Nightingale—nothing shy of cardiac surgery could have saved his patient, and Jake was not up to doing open-heart work with bare hands and a bowie knife.

Hell, he had not much liked the bastard to begin with. The homicidal card shark had been totally detestable even on a two-day acquaintance. Straightening up, Jake passed the flask of scotch to Sam, telling him to bar the doorway and keep the crowd at bay. He needed time and space to think in.

"Sure 'nuff." Sam propped himself in the doorway, taking a sip and eyeing the splintered door. "Only teach your woman the proper way to enter a room. By the time we make Bayou Sara we won't have a serviceable door aboard the steamer.''

Jake splashed his hands in the stateroom basin, asking Charlotte what had happened—for form's sake. The evidence was almighty plain.

Pushing honey-dark hair out of her eyes, she stared hard at the far wall, as though she could read her future in the filigree, eyes avoiding the body sprawled on the floor. ''He tole me he was gonna teach me ta behave. Claimed frenchified ways had given me airs—but fortunately he knew the cure. I told him not ta touch me. He grabbed me anyway, swearin' he was a hands-on trainer. Sayin' a nigger must learn never ta say no. I warned him, but he would not let go.''

Enough said. Jake pocketed the derringer and nodded to Peg. With the help of Taylor's young mistress, Peg hustled Charlotte into the adjoining stateroom, where she would not have Forrest lying eyes-up in front of her. The crowd at the door parted hastily, closing behind them.

Hosea, prince of Africa, was directing the cleanup, working with a tear in his eye that wasn't for the deceased. Jake asked Sam what jurisdiction they might be in.

Sam shrugged, owning that River justice was horribly chancy. ''Depends on where we land. Helena is the next port of call. I guess Arkansas will hold the trial.''

''Hain't gonna be no trial.'' Hosea's white-haired head wagged dolefully. ''Befo' I had my freedom, I was a groom in West Texas. I saw a Mexican girl stab a white man ta death—defending her husband. Weren't no trial. They took her to a bridge over a creek an' hung her. She were pretty an' full of ginger, jes like Miss Charlotte. Took off her hat, tossed it ta the crowd, an' put the noose around her own neck. Texans gave a cheer an' pushed her off. Arkansas will do the same ta Miss Charlotte—hain't no call for a trial.'' Prophecy complete, Hosea departed, carrying bloody laundry.

Sam stepped smartly aside. Captain Fitz-Roy pushed through the crowd, grim-faced—with Bixby in his wake—demanding to know what in hell was happening.

From the damage to the door and the gory mess Jake had made attempting CPR, it looked like Forrest was done in with a howitzer. Jake outlined events. Witnesses abounded, and any attempt to embroider would only annoy Fitz-Roy.

Muttering a genteel curse, the Captain dropped to his knee, telling Bixby, "I aim ta get the possessions—be my witness."

Going through Forrest's coat and trousers, Fitz-Roy came up with a card pack, the knife, and blackjack, Charlotte's bill of ownership, and a bundle of cash. Forrest's Colts hung by the door—he must have figured fists, knife, and lead sap were sufficient for what he wanted. Fitz-Roy passed each object to Bixby, who handed them on to Sam.

Jake made an apologetic noise, pointing out that some of the man's so-called possessions belonged to him— "Most particularly a Lakota possible sack. Also some money. But mainly the sack."

Fitz-Roy stood up, shaking his head, "My dear Count Dracula, that is not how I heard it. Ah fear you have even lost your claim to this cabin."

Dear Count Dracula? Armand was as hopeless at keeping a "secret" as he was at holding on to money.

Jake did his damnedest to act the outraged Rumanian aristocrat. Antebellum society had a charming respect for eccentricity, and Jake could get sympathy by playing the buckskinned count. Bobby Lee's staff would be a wild menagerie, with young Mr. Stuart riding off in the middle of night maneuvers to dance with the ladies behind enemy lines. And Stonewall Jackson falling to his knees in battle, getting tactical advice from the Almighty. Jackson's second, General Ewell, had fits of imagining he was a bird, chirping at dinner.

Jake pointed out that Forrest would hardly be needing the stateroom. They could roll the gambler up in the bloodstained carpet and plant him in the River. Anything more elaborate was a waste of good bottomland.

Fitz-Roy grimaced. "No, no, my dear Count, Mr. Forrest will be gettin' other accommodations. But there are previous claims on his cabin an' property." He turned slightly—Taylor and his hee-hawing partner had worked their way through the crowd—"These two had a compact with the deceased."

Benson gaped down at the corpse, but Taylor smoothly produced a notarized piece of paper. As cool as an estate executor, he declared the paper was a contract between himself, Benson, and Forrest, stipulating that in event of a death the two survivors would divide the dead man's effects—"This cabin, its contents, *any* slaves he owned, it all comes ta us."

It was a typical river gamblers' tontine—and the Missourian evidently thought Charlotte was not a total loss, or that some use might be squeezed from her before handing her over to Arkansas law.

The best defense is counterattack. Jake ignored the proffered compact. Taking Forrest's cards from Sam, he flipped through the deck. His compweb compared faces to the speckled pattern on the backs. Just noticeable differences leaped out in the upper-left corners—seemingly random speckles shifted from card to card, dots appeared and disappeared. Forrest's winning streak was explained.

He passed the pack to Fitz-Roy. "These are marked."

"Really." The captain elevated an eyebrow.

"Hold up a card."

Fitz-Roy slipped a card out of the middle of the pack and held it up, the speckled back toward Jake.

"Big Casino. Ten of diamonds."

"By damn, they are," swore Fitz-Roy. "How could you tell?"

His compweb had easily broken the code—but that was minor. "How else could the prime loser at the poker table turn out to be this crook's heir?" Jake motioned toward Taylor, while giving the corpse a healthy kick.

Forrest did not complain, but Taylor reared back, sputtering indignation, saying he never knew the cards were "readers."

Expressing mild disbelief, Jake put his case to Fitz-Roy. "You've got a gambling ring on your boat. Go through Forrest's money—you'll find a batch of newly issued Atchison banknotes. Everyone knows I bet those notes on the Hat Island crossing—and won. A dozen gents saw me snatch them out of Forrest's hand last night. How did they get back in his pocket? Bixby and Sam can swear I spent the whole afternoon in the pilot-house, and never so much as passed the poker tables."

Jake was setting Armand up for fraud and theft—but frankly he did not give a damn, the drunken oaf deserved it. A stint in jail might do him good. Maybe sober him out. Or at least give him a new look at life.

"Forrest fleeced your passengers with marked cards, while these two happy losers pulled in victims." The pair of planters had acted as high-class shills, Benson posing as an amiable Bacchus, while Taylor played the well-heeled brahmin with his coffle of slaves and pretty yellow mistress. The contract they had hoped to collect on became damning evidence.

Fitz-Roy looked stricken. River captains tolerated gambling as part of the entertainment—run your boat like a Sunday school, and you could count on traveling half-empty. High-flying planters, stupid with cotton money, were the lifeblood of the luxury trade. But for a big expensive boat like the *Scott* to harbor cheats would cost even more customers.

Fitz-Roy glanced to his pilot. Bixby looked taken aback—the man who would soon be running Grant's gunboats had small sympathy for Taylor's commerce in women.

The *Aleck Scott* was a curious microcosm of slave society. Headed south, her hold stuffed with human cargo, and her saloon crammed with boozy gents cheating each other with cheerful abandon—she still had a Yankee pilot and a black crew. Cotton money might pay their wages, but from the minstrel band on the boiler deck to the stokers in the hold, it was free labor that kept the *Scott* fed, happy, and afloat.

None of the crew cared to have a hand in hanging Charlotte. In the eyes of Bixby, Sam, Hosea, and the rest, Forrest had tried to compound robbery with rape. And Charlotte had paid him off with an ounce of lead— a fit occasion for drinks all around. Cads like Forrest got everyone to knuckle under by blustering about threatening violence; but fewer and fewer folks liked it. In four years Grant and Lincoln would call their bluff.

But it would not be up to the crew. Unless Jake acted fast, Charlotte's fate would rest with a Phillips County judge and jury, who were bound to take a sterner view of young women ventilating their owners.

Taylor temporized, telling Jake, "My partner and I would be pleased ta return anythin' yew can prove is yours."

The Missourian had made an astonishingly better offer than he realized. The Mesozoic data was all FTL would care about—easily worth a million Charlottes. Taylor was offering to let Jake skate Home with the secrets of the Uppermost Cretaceous. Just what regulations *required* Jake to do—FTL's prime directive being *don't fuck with the locals*. The future didn't give a hoot about what happened to Charlotte Marie d'Anton.

Fitz-Roy turned to Jake. "My dear Count Dracula, would that satisfy?" The captain plainly hoped it would.

"No. Not near enough." Remembering Charlotte's musical laugh, Jake could not stomach the thought of her life being jerked out by a noose just to please FTL and the state of Arkansas. Inability to follow regulations was a grievous character flaw, but one Jake had cheerfully learned to live with. He would not let Charlotte go, even if it cost him the scientific prize of the ages. Besides, Peg would no doubt break both his legs.

But if he pushed too much, Fitz-Roy would turn the whole mess over to a judge.

Jake swore on his honor as a Transylvanian count that he had no intent to evade the law. He merely aimed to settle the matter of ownership. (Then head off into the blue with Peg and Charlotte, the moment Fitz-Roy showed them his back.) "Give me a fair chance at one of your stud tables," he demanded. "A single game of Down-the-River with a square deal and an honest deck. Winner take everything."

Fitz-Roy brightened. Jake was proposing something irresistible to the River temperament—an *affaire d'honneur*, with poker cards in place of pistols.

"More than square," declared the captain, seeing a way to satisfy both honor and the crew. Win or lose no blame could be laid on him.

Taylor tried to wriggle loose, protesting innocence, citing his notorious run of bad luck.

Fitz-Roy tut-tutted, "Nonsense, friend. You saw the good count read Forrest's cards—like they were a dime novel. Luck had never to do with it. Either meet the count at the table, or throw in yer claim."

The crowd clamored agreement. Taylor's newfound aversion to poker got nothing but a good guffaw. First a murder, now a sudden death round of cards—this promised to be one memorable night on the River.

Taylor had to go along, or lose what little credit he had left; besides with Benson to back him, he had a better than even chance. Jake had to beat both of them to win.

All that remained was to put it to Peg in the neighboring cabin. She was there, was standing watch over Charlotte like a lioness with a wounded cub. It was fully night now, and the stateroom smelled of stale sweat and lampblack. Armand lay on a bunk looking mournful. Jake couldn't muster a milligram of sympathy. Things would have gone far smoother if Armand *had* blown his brains out. But he'd bungled that, too.

As quick as he could translate events into Universal, Jake told Peg what was happening. She was incredulous. "A card game? Over such a serious matter."

"Serious matters are better left to poker," Jake assured her. The alternative was trial by jury, a quaint anachronism discarded centuries before Peg was born. At best trials were a tedious subterfuge for shifting responsibility—and in Helena they were likely to see the law at its worst. "The question would be put before a semirandom panel of twelve citizens—from which females and nonwhites are specifically excluded."

Peg was appalled. "Excluded? For what possible purpose?"

Jake shrugged—"I suppose to secure a conviction in cases like this."

Slave law made a vicious mockery out of "trial by your peers." Charlotte would see no pretty young mustees sitting in the jury box. In fact no women of any sort—young, old, pretty or plain, slave or free. She'd be a black woman with white man's blood on her lace gloves, facing a panel of slaveholders and property owners. Jake did not need Hosea to tell him there would be a hanging in Helena.

"Then let's play cards." Peg took Charlotte's arm and made for the companionway leading to the main salon. She had absolute faith in Jake when it came to pasteboards and paper currency.

Ambling behind, Jake paused at the port rail to sip Armand's Glenlivet and breathe the evening air. Slipping the derringer out of his pocket, he let the tiny pistol drop into the dark river. Exit the murder weapon—its splash lost in the slap of the huge port paddle wheel. If only he could have done the same to Forrest. The less evidence to bother a court the better.

The long maindeck saloon was mirrored like Versailles. Blue cigar smoke hung about the gaudy chandeliers and silver filigree. The air beneath reeked of cheap peach brandy—made by pouring raw bourbon over burnt peach pits soaked in fish oil and nitric acid. Baton Rouge planters and Creole dandies crowded three deep around the green baize tables, sharing brandy smashes with decorative bare-shouldered *cocottes*, their bosoms half out of their ball gowns. All chatting gaily at top volume, as a backwoods bishop thumped his Bible, quoting Jeremiah at the sinning throng.

Stewards bustled about the poker table, putting out quail *pâté* and a clean spittoon.

Jake took a leather-backed seat, telling his compweb and microamps to get baseline readings on his opponents, to pick out stress, inflection, subvocals and pulse rate fluctuations. Benson looked to be a plunger, gorging on *pâté* and bantering with his buddies. But Taylor played it cool-as-be-damned, and would probably favor a neat, scientific game.

Flanked by Bixby and Sam, Fitz-Roy counted out $15,000 in flat rectangular mother-of-pearl markers. This represented Armand's losses, with Charlotte chivalrously valued at $2000—the priceless Mesozoic recordings were hardly valued at all, merely thrown in to round out the prize. The saloon bartender produced a pack of club-cards with plain white backs, passing them to Jake for inspection.

After a fast flip through the deck, Jake slid the cards to Sam, saying, "You deal."

The cub pilot started to protest. Jake cut him short, insisting they needed a neutral dealer, adding significantly—"Just don't shuffle the spots off 'em."

Sam rolled his eyes and sat down, asking if there was any more of that good Glenlivet. Then he started to shuffle nervously, using a big overhand riverboat shuffle that is really no shuffle at all.

Jake passed Sam Armand's flask and settled back, giving Peg and Charlotte a thin, reassuring smile. Peg returned a grin. Charlotte's numb expression did not change.

During the short flip through the deck his compweb had marked the location of every card. He watched Sam give the pack to Benson to cut—that fast shuffle and cut could not hope to mix the cards completely. The memorized sequence was merely broken into strings of varying lengths; and Jake could count on his compweb to reconstruct the deck in his head. As each string appeared in play he would hopefully know what Benson and Taylor's hole cards were, and what might be coming up. He had picked "Down-the-River," seven-card stud, an exact brand of poker that maximized his advantages. Each player got seven cards, three down, four up—with betting rounds after the third, fourth, fifth, sixth, and seventh cards. The player who made the best five-card poker hand won the pot.

Sam took the pack back from Benson, looking up at Fitz-Roy.

The captain ceremoniously placed $5000 in pearl plaques before each player, saying, "*Messieurs*, you may start—*les jeux sont faits*." Benson gave a grunt. Taylor shot his cuffs and flexed his fingers, telling Sam to deal.

The cub pilot fumbled out the first cards, three to each player, two down, the final one faceup. As the cards flicked out, silence fell over the table. The bishop's lamentations grew louder.

Jake surveyed his hand and the faceup cards. Taylor showed a five, Benson a deuce. Jake had a jack and seven down, another seven up. His compweb got to see the first and last cards dealt, and every third card in between, making it easy to fill in the blanks. Benson had an ace and deuce down. Taylor's hole cards were a pair of queens. It was as if the compweb could look right through the white backs of the club-cards and *see* Taylor's queens kissing the green baize table.

But knowledge did not make Jake's pair any higher—two sevens is a losing hand in Down-the-River. Jake passed.

Taylor eagerly bet $500, sliding five white plaques into the center of the table—confirming he did have two hidden queens, which beat anything showing. Benson with a pair and an ace matched his partner's $500.

Normally Jake would have tossed in his sevens. (The odds ran thirteen to one against a low pair.) But his compweb buzzed to tell him that *if the current string held* the top card in Sam's hand was another seven, the card he needed to beat Taylor's queens. Calling the next card in the deck was always problematic—the card could easily be the start of a new sequence—so the compweb kicked the problem to Jake.

Trusting to Sam's slovenly shuffle, he shoved $500 into the pot.

Sam dealt. Spectators leaned closer, applauding or chuckling at each card as it appeared. First came Jake's seven, followed by a king for Taylor and the nine of clubs for Benson.

Everyone bet. Jake buoyed by his three sevens. Taylor counting on his queens. Benson fishing for another ace.

Three more cards came sliding faceup across the table. Nothing for Jake. Nothing for Taylor—whose two queens looked horribly lonely. (The compweb predicted Taylor would fold.) But Benson got his ace, the ace of diamonds. (Jake's microamps registered the jump in pulse and sharp inhale, as surely as if Benson had shouted—"Hot damn. Matched my ace.") He had aces up, with two cards coming, two chances to make aces full.

Jake quizzed his compweb. The string containing the ace of diamonds went four, jack, seven and then another ace. If that sequence held, Benson was heading for a neat fall. He could not get his aces full without Jake getting a fourth seven.

Carefully Jake counted out five white plaques to bait the trap. Taylor hesitated, then called. Jake wished he had gone for a full thousand—now was the time to raise Taylor out. But Benson snapped at the bait—doubling Jake's bet.

Jake called Benson's raise. Taylor looked wistfully at the plaques in the pot, then folded his two lonely queens. It was just Jake and Benson now.

The next round went as predicted, four and jack—no improvement. Jake checked. Benson pounced, piling ten white plaques into the pot. Jake called. Peg watched each play, showing keen interest in the mysteries of poker. Charlotte hung on her arm, looking lovely and woebegone.

Benson was staring hard at the deck, sweat beading on his neck, willing that ace to be there. Sam announced gravely, "Last cards, gents. Down and dirty."

Two white rectangles skittered across the green table. Jake tipped the corner of his final card. A fourth seven peeked back.

Benson shoved the last of his $5000 into the pot. No need to read his pulse to know he had gotten that third ace. Jake called.

Flipping over his aces full, Benson gave a guffaw and wiped *pâté* off his fingers, reaching out to rake in the oversize pot. He had a full house, aces over deuces. Out of more than two million possible poker hands, only a few score could beat it.

Jake shook his head, turning up his down cards.

Benson's outstretched arms sagged against the table.

Flabbergasted, he stared at the four sevens, and his useless aces. He was busted flat on the first deal, holding a pat hand that should have been a winner. The crowd around him crowed—"Damned shame when a full house don't answer."

Peg was pleased. Charlotte showed hardly a speck of emotion, having troubles that went far beyond a hand of poker. "*La partie continue*," Sam intoned dryly. Now Jake had $12,000 to match against Taylor's $3000.

But Taylor took the next hand with kings up, getting back $1500 of what he had lost. The fastest most sophisticated computing did Jake not a damn bit of good if he did not have the cards.

Peg still smiled. Jake's losses looked small compared to what he had won from Benson. But it left him with only one hand in the deck, and the odds nearly even.

By the third draw of the final hand there was $4000 in the pot. Jake had a straight to the queen, but only the eight, nine, and ten showing. Taylor had a four flush showing—six, nine, ten and ace, all spades. According to Jake's compweb Taylor's down cards were two red treys.

Ace high, Taylor bet a thousand. With the deck out of treys, the Missourian must be trying for the flush. He needed one more spade to beat down Jake's straight. Seven spades had seen play. Taylor had four more in his hand, leaving two at large, the jack and the deuce. With only seven cards left in the deck, Taylor should have had almost a one in four chance of filling his flush—sufficient to justify his bet.

But Jake's jack in the hole was the jack of spades. The only remaining spade was the deuce. Little Casino. Taylor's chances were a slim one in seven. Jake queried his compweb. Little Casino lay nestled between the ten of hearts and the five of clubs. No help there. Neither card had been played.

Jake decided to go with the odds, matching Taylor's

bet and raising him $1500. It would take all Taylor had left to call.

The Missourian eyed the plaques in the pot and the four flush he had showing, estimating chances. He could throw in his hand, leaving the table with $1,500; not enough to lay a claim to Charlotte, but a handsome two days' earnings in a dollar-a-day economy. Or he could stake it all on finding that last spade.

Jake waited. His compweb replayed a sound bite from the day before, about how Taylor bet one of his house-boys on a hand "he had not a prayer of fillin'." But that was with Forrest's "readers." Would he do the same in a real game?

Touts and sharps begged Taylor to call. They were taking side bets on each card. At best Jake showed a possible straight. A spade flush would be a sure winner. Sam sat sweating over the last seven cards, waiting.

Taylor pushed his plaques into the pot. Sam fumbled nervously, managing to get out the last two facedown cards.

Jake tipped his card up.

Shit. The ten of hearts stared back at him—a spattering of blood red splotches. Taylor had to have the deuce, filling out his flush. The compweb's calculations guaranteed it. Little casino was going to sink Jake, costing him a $9000 pot, leaving Taylor with a healthy claim on Charlotte.

Stunned, Jake sat facing sure defeat. His luck had seemed unbeatable. And he had so needed a win to clear the deck for his getaway. Feeling how Benson must have felt, he groped for the flask of scotch, unscrewing the cap from the nipple.

"Damn," Taylor flipped over his final card in blank disgust. It was the five of clubs. He had missed his flush by a single spade.

Jake set down the Glenlivet untouched. His compweb screamed foul. The card should have been the deuce of

spades. Sam's clumsy overhand shuffle could not have
lifted Little Casino out from between the ten and five.
But instead of an ace high flush, Taylor was holding a
simpering pair of threes. Eager faces looked to Jake.

He turned over his straight to thunderous applause.

Men pounded him on the back, calling him lucky as
all get out. One hell of a fine fellow. Jake could only
stare at Taylor's five of clubs, sensing something uncanny. Something his compweb could not explain.
Maybe miracles did happen.

He sat back, basking in praise he did not deserve,
while Fitz-Roy counted out his money. Strangers vied
to buy him drinks. Taylor leaned across the table offering congratulations, "Damnedest game of Down-the-
River I ever saw. Proud ta be at the table—though I had
ta pay for the honor."

Shaking the Missourian's hand, Jake stood up, ac-
cepting his unexpected triumph, taking the bill of ownership, lining his pockets with cash.

Maybe his luck *was* unbeatable. There remained the
trifling matter of getting off the boat—but the tide had
clearly turned—he figured Fitz-Roy to keep a light
watch, a bribable steward or two. Jake had taken infinite
pains to appear trustworthy, playing the clean-as-the-
prairie gentleman in a den of thieves and gamblers. He
was a Rumanian count for Christ's sake. Royalty did not
cross the Atlantic to abscond with fugitive slaves . . .

"Stop." A barn-sized gent barred his way, standing
foursquare between the tables. Glenlivet froze in Jake's
gut. The fellow's Arkansas accent was as raw as a rusty
saw, and he fixed Jake with a peculiar slantendicular
look, as though he were trying to be sure of his man.

Jake had no such problem. Thanks to his compweb,
he never forgot a face. Or a voice. The last time he heard
that downriver drawl, it had been slurred with hate. This
bristling ruffian was the man whose bowie knife Jake
carried in his belt. It was the shill from the monte game

at the Saint Louis docks—his coat still torn and muddy, his disposition unimproved. Behind him crowded the squinting dealer and the angry backup man, waving his bandaged wrist, swearing, "This fellow is wanted fer assault in St. Louiee. An' we're here ta see the law upheld."

South to Freedom

Dragged down to earth, Jake listened to Captain Fitz-Roy's surprised stammer, "Wanted, yew say? On what grounds, suh? Count Dracula's a guest here, came all the way from Russia . . ."

". . . Rumania," called out a scholar in the crowd.

"Dracula, be damned." The shill spit tobacco juice. "If he's a count, I'm the black-assed Queen of Sheba. His name's Butler. Rhett Butler. An' he's wanted fer assault, him an' that red-haired whore he runs with."

Of course Jake denied it. But whom could he call as a witness? Sam Grant was inconveniently far upriver. Armand was worthless, exposed as a lying, thieving, drunkard. Charlotte was a slave facing a murder charge. And Peg was his codefendant. Still he damned their eyes, demanding to see a warrant—which he knew they could hardly have.

Fitz-Roy backed him. "Yes, stranger, where's your warrant? Do you claim to be a constable?"

The shill quieted down, aiming a foxy smile at Fitz-Roy, "There was no time. We missed this boat at Cairo, an' came down rail from Columbus, just managing to get aboard at Memphis." His gaze shifted to Jake, eyes bright as a bowie. "But, ah wired ahead. There *will* be a warrant waitin' in Helena."

Blast the telegraph. It was absolutely unfair that a time

period dependent on slave labor and outhouse plumbing should have speed-of-light communications.

Fitz-Roy asked what good the shill supposed a Missouri warrant would do in Arkansas.

"Oh, it'll be all legal-like," the shill assured everyone at the top of his lungs. "My brother is a sheriff down in Columbia—an' he's comin' upriver ta meet us."

Columbia, of course. Jake recalled the gent at the bar telling Forrest there was "entirely too much nigger shootin' down around Columbia." Law enforcement in that neck of lower River had to be rare and artful.

The shill cracked a vicious smile, grinning at Jake. "Yew ken bet that when we get ta Helena, Count Gawdalmighty Butlah is gonna be damned sorry he took ta assaultin' honest folk." The flint-faced bastard seemed supremely confident that what law there was in Helena would happily back him. More *mal hombres* shoved their way forward, a mean nervous posse, toting long guns and double-barreled pistols; made up of kinfolk, jailmates, and bushwhackers-for-hire, collected as the monte crew came south. The crowd parted sharply for these two-legged wolves.

One look, and Fitz-Roy tossed in his cards, "My dear Count, I fear these charges an' countercharges won't be answered in a night. An' now that yew are the owner o' Miss d'Anton—you'll be aimin' ta get off in Helena anyway. If only to know what'll happen to yer two thousand-dollar property."

Getting off in Helena was the last thing Jake intended. He would far rather have done the breaststroke through a bayou full of gators, but in no time he was sitting in a stateroom—one that had a door—his pockets stuffed with useless cash. On the far side of the door, interested parties and passenger-volunteers took turns standing watch, with the balance of the vigilantes within call.

Charlotte sat beside him on the bunk, her head on his shoulder, having hardly spoken since shooting Forrest.

Peg sat on her other side, comforting her in French.

The hideous irony was that for once Jake was absolutely innocent. After committing crimes and misdemeanors up and down the Mississippi, passing bad money, freeing slaves, assaulting overseers, destroying evidence, and abetting murder, he and Peg were going to be given over to the law for their one more or less legal act—breaking up that rigged monte game. But no amount of truth or bluster could move Fitz-Roy. No one who worked the River could afford to be overweighted with scruples; the captain must have guessed that if Jake was not guilty of this, he was certainly guilty of something.

Charlotte looked up at him. "Forrest was right," she whispered. "I was only playin' at being free. Like when we were kids, an' used ta pretend ta have tea parties in the kitchen, spinnin' tales about what we would do if we were grown."

Jake told her he was pretty much a playactor himself.

"Because you're not really a Rumanian count?"

He admitted the fraud.

"Well, suh, whatever happens, you are a prince ta me." Warm lips brushed his. Her kiss was chaste and tongueless, with a mere hint of provocation—but awfully like a good-bye.

"What now?" asked Peg, clearly game for anything, even taking on the posse bare-handed.

"We wait," Jake declared. If it weren't for the monte team, they could have counted on a lax warden and a score of chances to escape. Now they had one slim chance—"In the wee hours the watch outside will be down to a few sleepy souls. Quick use of the stunner should take care of them."

"And then?" Peg was warming to the scheme.

"We improvise."

With luck they could steal a skiff and strike out for the Mississippi shore. The *Scott* must have a sounding yawl, or even a captain's gig. But the absolute worst of it was they were separated from their luggage. Jake no longer had the possible sack. Nor could he imagine himself banging about the boat in search of it. Which meant he faced complete ruin even if they somehow escaped. The Faster-Than-Light agency would have a cosmic fit when he tried to explain losing the data to a trio of crooked monte players. FTL had a ferocious disregard for extenuating circumstances or innovative excuses. Keeping that cheerful thought foremost, he set his compweb for a couple of hours before dawn and put himself to sleep.

He was still dozing, waiting for the compweb to wake him, when microamps reported a soft rap at the door. The stunner was in his hand before his feet hit the floor.

Peg came instantly alert, braced to take action.

Belly tensing, Jake tiptoed over, slipping the latch.

Through the door crack, he saw Armand looking in, sheepish but sober. Holding a finger to his lips, Armand whispered, "Wake Charlotte Marie."

Peg was already doing that. Opening the door wider, Jake saw the monte dealer and an ugly pair of vigilantes sprawled on the deck, snoring over a clay jug.

"Mustah been the booze," chuckled Armand. "Never trust backwoods forty-rod—not fer standin' watch. This'll do yew better." He handed Jake a cup of coffee.

Jake opened the door wide. Behind the young planter was a ring of black faces. Jake recognized Hosea, also a huge roustabout with a Mandingo accent and rows of ceremonial scars ribbing his cheeks. Wooden bosun's clubs and lengths of pipe gleamed in the lamplight.

Hosea nodded sagely, saying, "Come along, day-clean hain't far off."

Jake stammered thanks all around as they slid into the center of the crowd. Tall deckhands and big fellows from the blackgang closed about them. Stepping over the sleeping guards, they marched down the carpeted hall, a moving wall of bodies, passing closed stateroom doors, making for the companionway leading down to the maindeck.

A late-night tippler staggered down the companionway, took one look at the determined phalanx, and darted up toward the Texas.

Jake heard landing bells ring as they emerged into the hot, black night. Sam was waiting by the port gangway, holding a hooded lamp. Piled at his feet were their possessions, including the lockbox and the beaded Lakota possible sack. The cub tipped his cap, "We have ta make a landin' at the Davis plantation"—he nodded toward the invisible Mississippi shore. "Thought you might want ta know:"

Swiftly checking the contents of the possible sack, Jake assured Sam he was god-awful relieved to learn about the unscheduled landing. And to have a hand with the luggage. Eternally grateful in fact. Philips County might easily call what Sam was doing, "aiding and abetting"—itself a hanging offense.

Sam shook his head. "Miss Charlotte deserves a brass band welcome for what she did, with the keys ta Helena thrown in—though a court would not see it that way." He cracked a Huck Finn grin. "But I guess I've been studyin' middling hard for the gallows myself."

Jake took a sip of the coffee growing cold in his hand. The night was black as the Devil's basement; he did not doubt the ability of a Mississippi pilot to find the right plantation dock, guided by nothing but the twists in the River.

Orders echoed down the speaking tubes. The boat slowed. Jake felt the deck shudder as the great port wheel stopped, then turned backwards, churning up the black water. The boat glided to a stop. The gangway thumped down.

Sam lifted up his lantern, illuminating the circle of crewmen, and the nervous sparkle in his own eyes. "All ashore that's goin' ashore—Count Dracula O'Hara Butler, or whatever yer name turns out ta be . . .''

Jake bent down, opened the lockbox, and found his copy of *Life on the Mississippi*—fishing out a writing stylus, he turned to the title page. ''Make it out to 'Jake'.''

Sam stared at the book, taken clean aback. ''What? You want me to sign this 'Sam Clemens'—I never wrote it.''

''Just make it, 'Mark Twain,' '' Jake told him.

Sam shook his head, worried a bit over the stylus, then scrawled ''Mark Twain'' across the title page. Slipping in something to mark the place, he handed book and stylus back, begging, ''Get gone, friend. Or we're all be standin' before a judge, tellin' stretchers.''

Jake glanced at the title page. The bookmark was a white-backed club-card—a black deuce. Little Casino. The two of spades Taylor had needed, but never got. Sam's smile twinkled in the lamplight.

Hosea called out in a heavy plantation twang, ''Marse Davis—may ah takes yer bag.'' Jake, Peg, Charlotte, and Armand hustled down the dock onto the Mississippi shore. The gangway lifted and the *Scott* slid away into the night, churning toward the Arkansas side, showering sparks in her wake.

The lower river was up. This was Yazoo country, and the Davis plantation dock was a little wooden island, surrounded by marsh and canebrake. Jake hated the risk of waiting on daylight, yet they could hardly blunder off into neck-deep water. After an hour or so of sitting in darkness, slapping at no-see-ums, Peg announced, ''There's a light approaching.''

Jake saw it too, a yellow glow, growing larger, bobbing between the tree boles. ''Swamp gas,'' he suggested.

''A will-o'-the-wisp,'' whispered Charlotte.

It was neither. The light turned out to be a lantern in

the bow of a skiff, poled by a girl of nine or eleven. Gliding her pirogue expertly up to the dock, she asked in all innocence, ''Are yawl the mail boat, come early?''

Knowing a godsend when he saw it, Jake knelt down into the circle of light cast by the lantern, thumbing through his wad of bills—watching the girl's eyes widen. He explained that they were not the mail boat, but he would pay cash money for quiet passage to some point of solid ground. The urchin eagerly agreed.

Solid ground proved to be a way off. At first light they were still poling over flooded bottoms and frog swamp, past cabins on stilts decked with hanging moss. Cows eyed their progress, standing placidly in breast-high water. Finally the child gondolier brought them to rising ground and a dry road. Jake paid her off, asking in some detail how they might catch a train to Memphis. It was plain she had never seen a locomotive in her life, but Jake left her with the absolute impression that they were headed north, to Tennessee and the free states.

At a ferry over the Coldwater Jake hired a horse and wagon to take them up the bluffs and into Holly Springs, bypassing the railroad to Memphis. Instead they caught the Central Line from Grand Junction, headed south.

Having done his level best to point pursuers north-ward—the natural direction of flight—Jake meant to make for Awlins again. Rolling down the center of the state, his microamps played ''City of New Orleans'' in time to the beat of the rails, past Oxford and Grenada, along the banks of the Big Black. They changed trains in Jackson, for a Jackson and Great Northern coach car that took them around Lake Pontchartrain into New Orleans, half a day behind the *Scott*.

The FTL way station in New Orleans was a two-story house built on ''made ground'' below river level. It faced a cemetery—row on row of graying marble vaults—a city of the dead, inhabited by little lizards that crept over the marble tombs snapping up huge mosquitoes.

The house itself was similar to the homes across Canal Street in the Vieux Carré, the old French Quarter, with wrought-iron balconies and rose-tinted plaster, reminding Jake of the color of light in wine. The ground floor masqueraded as a dim little voodoo parlor decorated with tasseled hangings, plush cushions, black candles, and parts of small dead animals. The odor of orange peels and burnt chicken feathers clung to gray lace curtains.

Seated behind a crystal ball was Mama Pleasant, the shop's proprietress. She greeted them with a bit of spirit talk, mumbling, "Yew done be expected."

That much was true—FTL informed her whenever a mislaid expedition "done be expected." The rest was mumbo jumbo. Mama Pleasant was actually a professor emeritus of Afro-American Religions from Tulane, semiretired. She ran the way station and turned a small profit for FTL, predicting local elections, cotton futures, and the like—but never with one hundred percent accuracy, to keep her from being overrun by customers.

She turned to Charlotte with a crinkled smile, "Young lady, I see yew takin' a long trip." More or less inevitable—wherever Charlotte was going had to be a long way from here.

It fell upon Jake to bid Armand good-bye, giving the astonished young planter all that remained of the money. Jake had no use for it—the Atchison banknotes were his contribution to a chronically underinflated economy.

"But what about Charlotte Marie?" Armand eyed the money nervously. "You're takin' her with yew? I mean, is Rumania a free country?"

"Most days. She'll be well beyond reach of the fugitive slave laws and the Dred Scott decision."

On the long reach of plank walk bordering the River, Jake, Peg, and Charlotte boarded a tiny seagoing towboat, with a low tapered hull and a high walking beam. No one paid them the least attention. The roadstead was packed with shipping, everything from coasters and fishing smacks to steam packets, tall clippers, and a great line of riverboats. New Orleans was the Paris of the Indies. Half the world seemed to be passing through the port, headed upriver into the North American interior, or out through the passes of the Mississippi, to Europe and South America.

Mama Pleasant steered the towboat downriver, past Chalmette and Point a la Hache, to the passes of the Mississippi, that weird end of the River where the channel runs between thin fingers of land forty miles into the Gulf of Mexico, finally meeting the sea. Off Grand Pass Jake, Peg, and Charlotte transferred to a gray schooner-rigged Baltimore Clipper—about the best all-around sailer built before the twentieth century, with speed crafted into every line.

Charlotte was stunned to discover the *Flying Dutchman* had no crew. Holograms worked the rigging and answered hails from the quarterdeck. She swore she had never seen the like.

"All done with machinery and mirrors," Jake assured her, suggesting she get used to such wonders.

Lines creaked, sails unfurled by themselves, and the anchor came thundering up. Aside from the ghostly 3V crew, the clipper looked and sounded like any other sailing ship, groaning with each pitch and roll like a huge untuned choir organ. In less than a fortnight the *Flying Dutchman* beat her way around Key West, through the Straits of Florida and the Providence Channel into the Atlantic, showing a clean pair of heels to inquisitive revenue cutters and a navy brig. A fusion reactor and propellerless drive buried in the hull made sure the *Dutchman* was never boarded for inspection—she would show up only as a log report of a hellishly fast schooner, name and origin unknown, last seen headed hull down into the Bermuda Triangle.

THE PLEISTOCENE HORIZON

Our ancestors were forever young, in a world without want, and still they were not happy . . .

—Acoma Creation story

Home

Jake got everyone out of their fusion-heated cabins for
Transition. Pale stars shone overhead. First light backlit
the eastern horizon, brightening the water; a low breeze
blew out of the cloudless steel blue sky. The Bermuda
Triangle was a mystic stretch of ocean, renowned since
Shakespeare's time for wrecks and disappearances. A
perfect location for the Mid-Atlantic portal.

His compweb counted down.

They entered the portal. Wind and sea vanished. The
Dutchman hung suspended in a blank void, outside
space and time. Charlotte gasped, grabbing at Peg for
support.

Jake's navmatrix marked off timeless nanoseconds.
Right on schedule the sea reappeared. The *Dutchman*
lurched onto a new tack, masts and cordage groaning,
one gunwale slapping the wave crests. A new tack, on
a latter-day Atlantic. The sea was no longer green-white,
but dirty gray, rolling under almost-solid cloudbank.
Wind whipped out of nowhere, driving a single slanting
line of afternoon sun across the waves.

Jake's corneal lenses picked out a spark of light, dropping through the hole in the overcast, then skimming
low over the waves, growing larger—a STOP hovership.
He braced himself against the heave of the deck, and

141

picked up the beaded possible sack, preparing to board. His microamps rolled out:

Swing low, sweet chariot,
Comin' for to carry me home.
I looked over Jordan an' what did I see . . .

The thump of rotors grew from a distant hum into a mechanical hurricane, hammering at the plank deck, drowning the words in his head. The hovership was a boat-helicopter hermaphrodite, thirty meters across and almost as long, a shining lifting body hull married to a set of stubby wings. Jet powered tilt-rotors cut circles of flame in the overcast—twin halos for a plasti-metal Kali Mata, a many-handed All Mother, stocked with sick-bays, comlinks, hypnotic gases, and heavy weapons, an omnitalented saver-killer, healer-destroyer, cybersmart and laser-sighted, Chandi fierce and user-friendly. The Godmother of all UFOs. STOP was stenciled on her fuselage in tall red letters.

Hovering over the *Flying Dutchman*'s foremast, the STOP ship lowered a clear bubble cabin to within a half meter of the tar-stained deck. Rope ends danced in the propwash.

Jake undogged the bubble, bowed to Charlotte, and shouted, "Your carriage, Madame." The *Awlins belle* looked dubious. Peg called out reassurance in French. Together they coaxed her in.

Jake swore the pressure cabin was copacetic—airtight and all right. Better than all right. Settling into the cabin's cushioned interior, he gave a huge heartfelt sigh. The hatch sealed and they were hoisted aloft. He had done it. For the first time since *Challenger* went down, Jake savored the flat bland taste of recycled air. Sitting with the possible sack in his lap, he took comfort in the complete unnaturalness of his surroundings—every edge seamless, crisply joined and computer correct.

Wind and spray beat against the plastic, but nothing could touch him. He was Home—in the disciplined hands of FTL—any further mishaps, disasters, or misadventures were someone else's show.

The cable hummed, reeling them up. Peg and Charlotte pressed their faces to the clear bubble, exclaiming in French—neither had ever ridden in a STOP hovership before. Jake had ridden in them more times than a veteran field agent would want to admit.

Through the transparent deck he could see the *Flying Dutchman* coming onto the opposite tack, already tiny against gray foaming sea. She was beginning another of her endless runs through the Mid-Atlantic portal. This gateway in the sea was opened to shuttle ships and equipment into the historic periods. The *Dutchman* could enter any time period in which sea level was not radically different—say anytime between the ice ages and the Greenhouse Meltdown. The tall ship got plenty of use.

Abruptly, the shining hull of the hovership engulfed them, replacing sea and sky with gleaming interior. The ready room was jammed with grinning STOP team members, wearing blanked video jackets bulging over half armor, with comlinks clipped to their ears. The sickbay autodocs stood empty—thankfully unneeded.

Eager hands undogged the hatch. A special-weapons tech with a linebacker's body and a hardcracker smile, yelled out, "Well hell, Jake. Welcome Home, boy. Glad ta see ya back."

Someone gave a sarcastic cheer.

"Where ya been keepin' it?"

"Haven't seen you since the Fall of Rome."

He stepped out to ironic applause, still wearing his Sitting Bull buckskins.

A com-tech thumbed the audio switch on her communicator, backfeeding the signal into a shrill wolf whistle. "Look at the leather."

Jake did a swift pirouette, showing off the Lakota dance costume, enjoying the mildly suppressed tension between field agents and STOP teams.

STOP stood for Special Temporal Operations. "Special Ops" almost always meant retrieving field agents. Missions could be as easy as this simple mid-ocean pickup, or as hellish as finding and extracting a scattered team and tons of artifacts from the sack of Rome. (At night, with the city in flames, arrows flying, and Alaric's Visigoths howling at the team's heels.) STOP teams owed their existence to field agents, and many field agents owed their lives to STOP teams, so relations should have been cordial—but humans aren't built that way.

The big weapons tech rolled his eyes in mock surprise. "Hey Jake, where's yer blimp?"

He thrust his keg-sized head into the pressure bubble and glanced about, as if expecting to see *Challenger* stowed between Peg and Charlotte. "What happened to her?"

"Don't tell us you lost it." The team leader gave her head a doleful shake. She had frizzy black hair and dark Judeo-Arab-Afro features, with a crescent moon and a Mogen David tattooed on her cheek. Team members snickered, knowing Jake's airship must be long gone. Why else would they be there?

Dealing with the dirty underside of time travel gave STOP teams a cynical view of field agents. Agents were considered the glory hogs, screwing around in the past, seeing the sights, hobnobbing with the great and not-so-great, and teaching the locals fancy ways to fornicate— then squealing STOP when the going got tough. STOP teams hardly so much as *saw* a field agent unless said agent had fucked up in some awkward part of the past.

Likewise, for a field agent, calling in a STOP team was a no-win deal, an admission that things had gone seriously sour for the agent in place—provoking head shakes, and triggering a full-blown inquiry, with the chance of reprimand, demotion, or worse. Agents were firmly convinced that *they* had the worst of it, sweating alongside the locals, putting lives on the line for recordings and data, always expecting the unexpected—while STOP teams minutely planned each operation, training in air-conditioned comfort, spoiled by special gadgets and gourmet rations. Faster-than-light travel allowed STOP to take weeks, even months, preparing for an operation that lasted only minutes in real time. Teams arrived hyped and ready, with pre-positioned backup, chemically protected against fear and fatigue, enjoying every conceivable edge.

Jake had done enough liaison work to see things from both sides. STOP teams took terrible risks, too. No amount of preparation and planning could hope to cope with full-blown temporal disaster. In one ghastly operation that still gave him nightmares, Jake had seen three STOP teams fed through a Bronze Age portal, trying to retrieve first the agents, then the original team, then the backup. Only to have nothing come back—no clue as to who or what had swallowed them. It was like shoving people and equipment into a black hole. To Jake's immense relief, FTL punched erase on the operation, sealing the portal, and tagging the anomaly with a warning beacon. Jake had been on standby—set to guide a fourth team in.

"Come on, share it, bro," the weapons tech demanded. "Did you *even* get to the Mesozoic?"

A bated silence followed. This *was* the bottom line.

Jake grinned broadly, patting the possible sack. That ended the banter. Frontline operatives hardly ever argued with success. FTL might grouse about losing *Challenger* and missing mountains of data, but any operation you could hobble away from was five-by-five with these folks.

Peg and Charlotte emerged. The jocular contempt for

field agents did not extend to them. Peg was a paleontologist. And Charlotte was obviously a displaced local—a problem STOP teams were intensively drilled to deal with. Women went into action, making a space where Charlotte could feel secure and comfortable, watching her for signs of temporal shock—treating her just the way an *Awlins belle* might expect to be treated in "civilized" company. Peg served tea and translated.

The hovership did a quick eyeballs-out turn and headed for the Bahamas. Mission accomplished.

Jake was free to decompress, feeling that vast weariness that meant a trip was truly over. Slumping into a window seat, he ordered refreshments. The facilities aboard STOP hoverships were legendary—full galleys, outrageous autobars, autodocs stocked with more than just the usual alkaloids. Synthetic opiates. Medicinal hallucinogens. Jake felt a tremendous temptation to overindulge. He deserved it—Hell, he *needed* it. At some point a mind-altering binge was absolutely essential, if only to maintain a symmetrical strain on his system.

But the Bahamas lay just below the horizon. Civilization hurtled toward him. First Quarantine. Then debriefing. He could not afford to arrive totally deranged, so he kept his requests within limits. With his personal clock still set at dawn—summer of 1857—Jake settled for an Irish coffee, while the galley whipped up *huevos rancheros*.

Moments like this were easily the most outlandish part of his profession. He might be doing the most risky edgework in some vile corner of the past—but everything you could ask for was only a portal away. Safe, comfortable transport. Spiked coffee. Breakfasts cooked to order.

Not that antebellum America was all that vile. Already the shocks and alarms Jake had suffered were fading. Scalping, slavery, lynch law, life-or-death gambles had all left no permanent scars—not on Jake anyway.

And he had seen worse, far worse. In the wake of that aforementioned Roman holiday, Jake had scrambled aboard a STOP ship, shoving a pile of priceless scrolls ahead of him. Instead of Charlotte getting tea and sympathy, the STOP crew had been holding down a screaming girl, gang-raped by Huns and trying to throw herself from the hovercraft. Autodocs were treating everything from smoke inhalation to a javelin in the spleen. A hectic, heart-stopping operation. But as Dark Age Europe whipped beneath the tight formation of hoverships (a fiery portent worthy of the Fall of Rome) Jake sat down to a stiff sherry and *quiche au roquefort* with *petits pois au beurre*. Not even the Fall of Rome took away the need to eat—and eat well.

In the seconds it took his eggs to cook, Jake sipped his whiskeyed coffee and watched the waves skim beneath him. Right then it amazed him that he could ever leave such comfort. But he would go back. Back to burning Rome if need be. Or even worse. Jenghiz Khan made Alaric the Goth look like a gentleman. No matter how outlandishly comfortable things were at Home, Jake would feel the absolute need to hang himself out again, taking indefensible risks. Why? To better savor civilization? Because Home Period was *too* outlandishly comfortable? He could not say. And this was not the point-instant to dissect hazy motives. This was the place-moment to recoup, reprogram, and get ready to reap some benefits.

Peg settled in beside him, still holding on to Charlotte's hand. Charlotte stood staring wide-eyed out the window. The blue waters of the Bermuda Triangle had given way to aqua-white shoals, so clear Jake could see the sandy bottom. A pair of big white sharks circled in the lee of a sunken reef.

The Bahamas hove into sight, green-and-white jigsaw shapes lying on the sea. Charlotte whispered, "Where are we headed?"

"Quarantine."

"Where is that?"

Jake pointed out the window. "The second island to port." He explained how FTL favored the box within a box system, to protect Home Period from unwanted intrusions. Space-time was too big and untamed to be trusted. Going back could not "change" history—but nothing kept history from playing hell with the present.

"We have to pass through several portals, layers of gates, each more carefully controlled than the last." The system resembled nothing so much as Dante's Inferno, an inverted pyramid of ever-tightening security. The Hell Creek portal had been totally unguarded, with the Mesozoic at one end and the American West at the other. The Mid-Atlantic portal was carefully watched by nuclear subs and orbital surveillance. And Quarantine was the most secure portal this side of Luna.

All gates went back into the past—the laws of physics prevented gates from being pushed forward into the future. It was impossible to pioneer an anomaly to a point-instant that had not yet occurred—probing the past was chancy enough. Until Jake and Peg got there, the Mesozoic had been largely *terra incognita*. To protect Home Period from possible contamination, the portal was opened in a backward, semisavage period—1850s Montana—where teams could have easy access, without much local interference. Any havoc emerging from Hell Creek would spill into preatomic North America— where history assured them the effects would be minimal. Or at least unnoticed.

Jake told Charlotte that Quarantine was not nearly as ferocious as the name implied. "Simple medichecks is all." Charlotte seemed sturdy and durable, and nineteenth century bacteria did not terrify anyone here-and-now.

Seeing the island grow beneath them, Charlotte shook her head. "And then where?"

"Paris," Jake replied. "You'll love it." Probably she would—but the Paris that Peg meant to take her to would not be the city of Louis Napoleon, Victor Hugo, and George Sand, of Delacroix frescoes and Meyerbee operas. It was no longer even the capital of France (a country nearly as long gone as antebellum America). Peg's Paris was merely a pleasant, touristy branch of Megapolis.

Peg laid her free hand on Jake's shoulder, saying in Universal, "She's going to have to be walked through this. I want to get her in and out of Quarantine, and to my place in Paris as fast as possible. Before I have to tackle that World Paleontology Convention."

Jake nodded. Charlotte was plainly suffering from time shock. Not a bad case, but enough to call for TLC. "Sure, I'll handle getting on line. After that, they will be so wrapped up with the recordings you'll have half a day to yourselves."

Peg smiled and pecked him on the cheek.

The hovership landed on a sunny atoll newly won back from the sea. During the Greenhouse Meltdown the entire Bahama chain had been submerged. Collapse of the hydrocarbon economy and the current mini–ice age had reduced sea levels worldwide. The FTL undersea substation on Quarantine was now above water. But the blue-green lagoon was empty. No pleasure craft, no sun-bathers, no beach bums. In this period the Atlantic atoll had no speed-of-light gates, just a faster-than-light portal, keeping traffic to a minimum.

Quarantine substation retained some of its old formidable nature from its underwater days. Heavy metal pressure domes hunkered next to the hoverpad. The humped backs of docked submarines poked out of the waves at the tip of a jetty on the seaward side of the island.

The medicheck was a mere formality—a last going-over before being released into Home Period. Peg and

Charlotte went through decontamination together. Jake followed at a gentlemanly distance, stripping down and submitting to microscopic inspection, letting sensors draw blood and search under his toenails. No unpleasant surprises were discovered. The Hell Creek portal had been opened in nineteenth century Montana to ensure that anything unpleasant from the Mesozoic would have been discovered and dealt with ages ago. "Let the past pay," was the FTL motto.

Quarantine was mainly a barrier against more exotic threats. Like time bandits. Or other hyperlight species. Literally anything was possible.

This final faster-than-light gate was the least impressive. A sterile windowless containment hemisphere, painted a soothing green with a yellow circle on the floor to mark the gate. Step through the circle and you disappeared—to reemerge in the same room centuries later. Hyperlight computers kept traffic flowing, making minor timing adjustments to prevent travelers from running into each other.

Jake stepped through the circle. Suddenly the hemisphere was no longer empty. A cheering crowd of substation techs and smiling well-wishers blinked into existence, packing the metal bubble. Word had flashed ahead of them—the *First* Mesozoic Expedition was back! The applause that had greeted Peg and Charlotte still echoed off curving concrete. A sign of what Jake could expect from here on.

Aside from cheers and handclapping, no one said a thing. No "I have returned." No "one small step." There was no need. In minutes the solar system—or as much of it as cared—would hear what had happened. These FTL stay-at-homes just wanted to *be here*. A moment to bore the grandkids with.

The women were politely acknowledging the applause. Peg grinned. Charlotte did a demure curtsy. After what she had been through, Rumania—or wherever this was—certainly owed her a welcome.

Ahead was an open hatch. Warm breezes blew through it. Blue Bahama sky blazed beyond.

Jake caught up, and helped usher Charlotte outside, into the differences centuries had wrought. Now there were boats in the bay, tall spritsailed yachts and home-built balsa catamarans. The lagoon thronged with people, swimming, splashing, boating. None bothered to applaud—they were too busy soaking in the sun to notice history being made, or remade.

Quarantine did not *belong* to FTL. The whole of the Bahamas chain belonged to everyone, and no one. Here-and-now, land ownership hardly existed. People had use-rights to almost every accessible point in the solar system and beyond (*accessible* being the key qualification), but private property was a rare commodity above the level of a prefab cubicle or a family plot. Beyond the substation the Bahama atoll was open to anyone who could manage to get there.

A dozen meters away on the sand stood a speed-of-light kiosk.

Halfway there Charlotte balked to catch her breath, brought up sharp by the nude scene on the beach. Ghost schooners and hoverships had been mere wonders, but here lay acres of exposed human flesh—brown, pink, and tan bodies. Ordinary folks had stripped to the buff in droves, lying hip to buttocks trying to see how dark they could get. It was something to write home to Louisiana about.

Tourists hovered around the kiosk hoping for handouts. A pair of painfully thin girls—their ribs poking out over hard curves of pelvic bone—accosted Jake with wan smiles, asking if he had food in his pack. "You won't need it where you're going."

A similarly destitute, but well-endowed young gent

accosted Peg and Charlotte—offering his services for a handful of rice, or a sandwich.

Jake shrugged, saying all he had was Mesozoic tissue samples—frozen dinosaur chromosomes and the like. The thin, winsome pair was not impressed, though moments before the same news had cheered a room packed with people. His fifteen minutes of fame were already up.

Peg punched a Paris code on the kiosk, giving Jake a good-bye kiss. Charlotte offered her hand, ostentatiously ignoring the well-hung young moocher still making his pitch. The two women vanished together.

The portal cycled. Jake caught a brief glimpse of a Paris street and the tall green column marking the Place de la Bastille. Then Peg and Charlotte were replaced by a grinning young tourist wearing an ultralight pack bulging with freeze-dried meals. Nylon straps pulled her shoulders back, perking up her breasts. Giving Jake a breezy greeting, she dodged the nude panhandlers and dashed for the beach, not wanting to waste a nanosecond of her stay. She clearly did not care that he had just gotten back from the Cretaceous.

Like any decent island paradise, the Bahamas were populated way beyond carrying capacity. To compensate, local speed-of-light gates operated on a two-for-one basis. Two people had to exit before one could enter. Tourists toted their own food. The ones hanging around the gate had overstayed their meal supply, and were on a forced diets, obliged to scrounge off of new arrivals and boat owners—otherwise it was back through the portal to make room for someone new. STOP teams and the substation crew had their own rations and transport—one of FTL's many perks—making duty in the Bahamas pretty blissful. Home Period's moneyless economy leaned heavily on job satisfaction.

Since he was leaving, the gate welcomed Jake. He did not need to punch a destination, his compweb and navmatrix merged effortlessly with the gate controls, sending him where he wanted to go. The gate ahead was being held open for him.

He stepped out of the blinding Bahama sun into an enormous reception room, with high ceilings, twin fireplaces, and a tall harpsichord in one corner. It had been morning in the Bahamas, but it was afternoon in Ile-de-France—a six-hour time difference. A golden glow filtered through wraparound windows.

Beyond the windows Jake could see Paris. Gray kilometer-high cubes dominated the suburbs, four to the north of the Seine, two to the south. Lines of parkland and geodomes stretched toward the Old City. His corneal lenses could just make out the curving ribbon of the Seine, with Ile de la Cité, Notre Dame, and the Eiffel Tower, looking like historic miniatures at the hub of the overgrown metropolis.

The room was at full capacity. Aside from the gate on hold for him and Peg, every entrance was maxed-out. No one could enter until someone left. As he stepped in everyone turned to look. Women smiled. Men started clapping. Jake was getting used to being greeted by immediate applause; already this handclapping was less thrilling than the cheers at the substation.

Besides, most of what he saw was 3V illusion. The people were real—FTL heavyweights, Sorbonne academics, Feelie moguls, media luminaries, anyone whose *persona* required them to be *on the scene*. But his nav-matrix told him the windows were solid walls backed by layers of circuitry. The reception room was at the center of a seventh kilometer-high cube, sited south of the Seine. Wraparound projection gave any room in the monolith an exterior view, not just of Paris, but of any part of the known universe, any world that could be pictured or imagined.

Aside from the spontaneous applause there was a minimum of ceremony. No one introduced him. No speeches were needed. Everyone *knew* why they were there. This was a prearranged "historic moment"—planned long before he left for the Mesozoic.

In fact Jake and Peg had left from this very room, this *very* party—a mere forty minutes or so ago, "real time." While they had spent months in the Mesozoic and nineteenth century North America, going up and down the Mississippi Valley and through the Bermuda Triangle twice, these people had been lounging about. Talking. Enjoying the *déjeuner* spread out on massive ornamental sideboards and struggling not to look bored. Forty minutes of small talk could easily be more trying than a year in the past.

Now came the payback. Applause was merely polite acknowledgment. Jake was about to amaze everyone with the world's first *real* look at dinosaurs. Anything less was going to be an absolute disappointment.

A Louis XIV salon table occupied one corner of the room, opposite the harpsichord. Lying atop the table was a gleaming metal slab, slotted to take recordings. Mirror-shaded blinders and a 3V headband dangled from superconducting wires. In a single smooth motion, Jake set down the possible sack and took up the blinders and headband, positioning himself on a velvet-cushioned stool.

A tiny record chip was already in his hand.

Eventually all the recordings would be downloaded into public memory, immediately accessible at any terminal in the solar system. But this was the *once only*, real-time, *first look*. Inserting the chip, he slipped the blinders over his eyes, plugged terminals into his ears, and tightened the headband.

The roomful of smiling people was replaced by matte gray nothingness. Dermatrodes hidden in the headband made contact with his sensory centers—disorienting numbness settled over him. He could no longer feel the table in front of him, or the stool beneath his butt.

Consciousness shrank down to a tiny spark in near-infinite grayness. A blank sensorium hungry for data. Newton called gravity the Sensorium of God. Jake was not so grandiose, but the sensorium he was hooked into went about as far as gravity could reach. His images, his sensations, would sweep around the planet in less than a second, radiating speed-of-light ripples throughout the solar system.

A couple of seconds to Luna. Minutes to Venus and Mars. The Sorbonne reception they would see it in 3V sense-surround, but the people plugged into public Feel-ie channels would see, hear, and feel it, more or less as it happened to Jake.

FTL estimated that only one-half of one percent of the home system population gave a hoot about time travel—with a whole spiral arm to explore and settle, plus the mindless excitement of 3V, the present offered more wonders than most people had time for. But the system's population topped forty billion. "One-half of one percent" meant two hundred million people were tuning in. Not an audience to disappoint.

Knowing that a healthy chunk of history was show biz, Jake had stayed up nights aboard the *Dutchman*, splicing together Home Period's first glimpse of the Mesozoic. His first day's campfire encounter with the triceratops herd had been delightful in its own way—but folks could laugh at that later. He started with their 101st day.

Baby Duckbills

Gray sensorium gave way to hard light hitting a dry winding wash, edged by ferns, vines, and flowering trees. Fat blue flies whined about. Jake felt hot thick Mesozoic air against his skin. He was back.

In the middle of the arroyo stood his old buddy *Albertosaurus megagracilis*. The angular three-ton carnosaur looked gaunt and deadly with its rusty leopard-spotted back, long toothy snout, and great graceful hind legs. Its light underbelly was spattered with red mud.

Jake could not hear the gasp that must have gone around the room in the Sorbonne, but he could *feel* the way his own heart raced. So could his systemwide audience. Sense-surround did not let you be very much of a hero.

The big theropod was nine meters long and stood three meters at the hip. Jake would have come up to about mid-thigh, if he had been incautious enough to saunter over. The forelimbs were tiny even by tyrannosaurid standards. It probably used them to pick its pointed teeth.

Peg was beside him, placidly recording, wearing her Crow gift shirt and a satisfied expression.

By now Jake's shock-rifle was ancient history, and his neural stunner would not have made this monster sleepy. Nor was the big speedster anywhere near as safe as the dozing tyrannosaur Peg had touched on their second day at Hell Creek. *A. megagracilis* was awake, alert, and macabrely hungry. Dangling from its jaws was a mauled and dying juvenile duckbill.

A. megagracilis stood staring at Jake, as if he and Peg were some sort of exotic antipasto suddenly appearing on the takeout menu. It would have been a simple matter for the swift theropod to drop the struggling duckbill and dash over for a quick taste—just to see if Jake was edible. If it did, they had no hope of outrunning those huge jaws. The best he and Peg could do was to break in opposite directions. One might get away while the other was being sampled.

But *A. megagracilis* stuck to the old albertosaur dictum—a duckbill in the mouth is better than a pair of bipeds in the bush.

And his horribleness had more pressing problems. Something even more terrible was stirring the dogwoods. Warned by his microamps, Jake reached out and drew Peg back—slowly, so as not to alarm the wary carnivore. They crouched behind a pillarlike cycad stump, shielded by low bracken.

The albertosaur was off in a shot, pounding over the hardpan with the little duckbill locked in its jaws, raising clouds of fine white dust.

Striding along in *A. megagracilis*'s tracks, acting like it owned the landscape (which it did) was *T. rex*. Jake hiked up the gain on his lenses. This was a medium specimen, no more than twelve meters long, but heavy-boned and thick-limbed, outbulking *A. megagracilis* by two to one. The top of the carnosaur pecking order. The tyrannosaur's powerful body and huge battery of teeth made it plain why *A. megagracilis* was rare, and getting rarer. Both the albertosaur and the duckbills it fed on were losing out in the Late Cretaceous arms race. Only triceratops could stand up to tyrannosaurus. Big unarmored herbivores and medium-sized carnivores were being squeezed out.

T. rex pulled up short, stopping right where the albertosaur had stood. Turning to look sideways, it stared right at Jake, giving him the same suspicious slantendicular look he had gotten from that big Arkansas ruffian aboard the *Aleck Scott*.

Jake went rigid behind the screen of slick, green fronds, hyperventilating to slow his heart rate, trying to *become* the cycad. The beast was hungry and frustrated enough to devour anything that moved.

And it was obviously wondering what the albertosaur had been looking at. Behind the beast's intent look lurked a brain bigger than Jake's. Which might not be good enough to get the carnosaur into the Sorbonne— but it was not an intelligence to be trifled with. Especially when it had missed a meal.

For once Peg froze, too, coolly continuing to record, but giving the brute nothing to go for. Showing off her practical grasp of carnosaur behavior. Nanoseconds tumbled in Jake's compweb. Nothing moved except the fronds in front of them, rustling in the blast furnace breeze. Then *T. rex* lumbered off after the albertosaur.

Jake breathed softly.

Peg bounced up. "Let's not lose them. That tyrannosaur must be famished."

"Right." To Jake that sounded like an excellent reason not to disturb the six-ton killer. But he knew better than to debate orders. They set off following in the ogre's three-toed tracks.

Running down a hungry tyrannosaur proved harder than Peg imagined. A couple of klicks down the streambed, the tracks veered sharply to starboard, and went crashing off into the greenery. "Stride lengths increasing," Peg shouted. "It's spotted something." Jake bounded reluctantly behind her.

Fortunately, it was fruitless. From the stride length *T.*

rex was doing 20–30 kph. They had no hope of keeping up. The trail burst into open country, plowing through thorny berry bushes, then hitting a stretch of bedrock and vanishing altogether.

They stood alone under the grueling sun, sweaty, dirty, and scratched by berry bushes. Jake's lungs heaved like bellows, burnt raw by the kiln-hot air. The Uppermost Mesozoic seemed very vast and empty. Kilometers of scraggly berry bushes ended in a broad expanse of bedrock and lava flow, containing a pair of silly mammals millions of years from home. A line of blue volcanoes smoked in the hazy distance.

"Let's backtrack," Peg decided. "We can see where that duckbill came from."

They hiked back to the creek bed, aiming to find the albertosaur's trail and follow it in the other direction. Until he got to the Mesozoic, Jake had merely thought of dinosaurs as big. He never imagined the brutes would be so tough to find, or keep up with.

Morning turned to noontime and the temperature soared from hot to intolerable. (Here Jake did a judicious edit, deciding not to treat his audience to the long backtrack, followed by a lunch break, sex, and a short *siesta*. When he started again all they would know was that he was rested, fed, and happy—folks could draw their own conclusions.) By afternoon the landscape had gotten more lively. Peg spotted a pair of *Troodon*, jackal-sized, predatory proto-birds, with sickle-clawed feet, binocular vision, and short, clawed forelimbs in place of wings. They seemed to be stalking something, but she could not tell what. "Maybe a small mammal," she ventured.

Jake silently rooted for the mammal. He was primed to sympathize with something cute and furry.

One of the old, old, beliefs about dinosaurs was that they were crowded out by "superior" mammalian intelligence and physiology. But he and Peg had seen small sign of that in the Latest Cretaceous. By now mammals had been around for better than 150 million years—about as long as dinosaurs—and had not progressed much beyond the small-furry-bug-eater stage. If they aimed to take over, they were taking their sweet time. More likely they were just trying not to become lunch.

Peg signaled silently, and they followed the two *Troodon* into the brush, trying to see what they were up to—without treading on their tails. They seemed to be following an established trail, a narrow game path overgrown with vines and creepers. Patches of red earth showed between pockets of leafy shade.

Wiping sweat from his eyes, Jake wished that lunch had included a cold beer. The main thing the Mesozoic lacked was a string of decent microbreweries. Just as he concluded that they had lost the *Troodon*, Jake was brought up short by a loud, abrupt hoot. Peg froze, holding up a dusty hand, stopping him in mid-step. The sound had come from a few meters ahead—and no *Troodon* had ever made it.

They waited, but the hoot was not repeated. Jake jacked up his microamps. A low snapping and crunching grew in volume until it sounded like a forest being felled. He had his compweb fix the location—a few meters ahead and to the right.

Squeezing Peg's hand, he pointed. She set off again, sliding noiselessly between branches, as cool as Daniel Boone. Jake did his best to imitate.

The crunch and grind grew louder. Then ceased. A knife-sharp cry came from the thicket. Peg took a step, then stiffened. Birds exploded out of the brush ahead.

Jake jacked up the gain on his lenses, trying to bore through the tangle with sheer optical overkill. Greenery grew and expanded. Twigs turned into giant limbs. Veins on leaves stood out like river deltas. It was no good. With lenses on full and his microamps on high gain, all he could tell was that they were meters away from something really big.

Suddenly the dogwood in front of them leaned alarmingly, then snapped back, showering them with leaves and petals. Whatever was there was close enough to touch, but completely hidden. Peg danced from foot to foot, trying to peer through the vegetation.

Jake took her arm, tugging silently. If they worked their way around the thicket, they might actually *see* what they were blundering into.

Peg nodded in agreement. Jake unsheathed his heavy bush knife, hacking a path through the brush—and finding it tough going. Someone had already given the grove a thorough working over. A head-high pile of dogwood trunks blocked his path, stripped of their leaves and smaller branches. Something big had clearly been feeding.

In negotiating the dogwood abatis, Jake managed to lose the dinosaur completely. The beast must have moved off. Jake knew his navmatrix would not get that turned around, even in a maze of fallen trunks and tall slick ferns.

A series of red clay mounds broke through the bracken, each about two meters across, and a meter or so high. They were hard as concrete—like truncated termite hills. Jake scrambled atop the nearest one, hoping for a better view, and gasped at what he saw.

"What is it?" Peg pulled herself up behind him, eager to see. He made room for her atop the mound. "Hadrosaurs," she breathed happily. "A whole herd."

Beyond the screen of dogwoods was a wide mudflat crisscrossed by alkaline channels, shining with silica. Hundreds, maybe thousands of hadrosaurs filled up the flat, some moving, some sitting, some honking and hooting at each other. They were big duckbills, ten to twelve meters long, but their movements were fluid, graceful, and birdlike. Crested heads bobbed back and forth as they walked, balancing two or three tons of body mass slung between huge hips. Their shorter forelimbs were used to get up and down, to tear off branches, or to move the mud around.

The duckbills had been busy landscaping. Between the braided streams, the ground was covered with humped mounds—some thatched over with cut vegetation, others bare. They were much too regularly spaced to be natural. The hadrosaurs had clearly heaped them up for reasons of their own.

"They're nesting," Peg answered Jake's unvoiced question.

She was right as usual. Adjusting the gain on his lenses, Jake spotted juveniles in among the adults— some only half a meter long and gaping to be fed. This was the nursery where *A. megagracilis* had gotten his baby duckbill. His compweb replayed the sticky reddish mud splashed on the carnosaur's belly.

"The mounds are nests," Peg declared. "Some are still incubating under heaps of vegetation—others are old and empty—like the one we're standing on."

Jake looked down. The red-orange mound beneath their feet had a bowl-shaped depression on top, half-filled by erosion. Flecks of white eggshell were mixed in with the mud.

"Look at their teeth," Peg told him, still enamored with dinosaur dental work. Sauropods like *Alamosaurus* might be ten times as hefty, but they were amateurs in the dental department; their small peglike teeth could not compare to the duckbill's huge battery of self-sharpening grinders. Fresh teeth replaced the older ones, continually renewing the chewing surface.

Duckbills chewed with a peculiar sideways motion that allowed them to use both sides of the mouth at once. And the hadrosaur's body was mostly digestive tract balanced by a long stiff tail, making them near-perfect mowing machines. Any plant unlucky enough to get in their way was likely to be mashed, shredded, and sent down the gullet. Small wonder fast-spreading, flowering plants were replacing ferns and horsetails.

Jake had never thought much of duckbills, who seemed to be a dying breed—more and more marginalized by the big carnivores and heavily armed ceratopsians. But up close they impressed him. Not just with their eating ability, but also with their organization. Their rookery was well hidden—nearly invisible until you were virtually on top of it. Each nest was carefully spaced about a hadrosaur length apart, and the babies were being fed and cared for until they were able to move with the herd.

"Look how cute the little ones are." Peg pointed to a clutch of nearby juveniles, newly emerged from their nest and clinging together for company. They bobbed about, active and curious, scratching the ground and snapping at bugs. Aside from what their parents brought them, there was not much to eat around the nests, the nearby vegetation having been pruned and trampled by the adults.

Jake began to see duckbills as something other than food for the carnosaurs. They were cooperative, intelligent, even charming. Some had bright green-black camouflage, while the others were more dully colored, slate gray and mud green. Males and females? Most likely. They all seemed to be one species.

So what if duckbills did not have much of a future? No dinosaur did.

"It's *essential* to look at a nest." Peg obviously did not mean the empty one they were standing on. She slid down and started worming her way forward. Jake squirmed after her. The closer he got, the more it reminded him of a giant bird rookery—hot, noisy, spattered with duckbill droppings and smelling of rotting vegetation. Heat of fermentation must help incubate the eggs.

Swarms of flies rose from the rotting leaves, snapped at by a small shrewlike mammal. Birds pecked at snails and brine shrimp among the braided streams. A large pterosaur circled overhead—then dropped like a leather-winged dragon, scattering the flocks.

Peg reached the nearest nest, lifted the vegetation, and peered inside. "I see nine eggs, hard-shelled, with surface ridges, arranged in an open spiral with . . ."

She never got to finish.

All hell broke loose. The nearest adult duckbill reared up, honking at top volume. Others imitated this action, hooting and bellowing like mad. A duckbill stampede headed their way.

Jake sprang to his feet, telling his shoulder holster to produce his stunner. He grabbed Peg by the scruff of her Crow gift shirt. "Get up," he shouted. "Get moving."

She was up in an instant, hastily shoving the rotting vegetation back atop the nest.

Jake cursed her for being so neat, hauling her backwards into the dogwoods. A dozen huge duckbills were charging at them, honking angrily, like giant green-skinned turkeys gone berserk. And this tail-lashing band of duckbills was after him and Peg—no error there.

Jake was comfortably used to being ignored by dinosaurs. That morning's intense hungry look from *T. rex* was the best he could boast of. Terror-stricken, he dragged Peg into cover, pushing her along the trail he had cut through the dogwoods. With several angry hadrosaurs bellowing at their heels.

Tuning his microamps to wide angle, he picked up more hadrosaurs, crashing through the tangle on either hand. They were hooting to each other, signaling their positions, letting the herd know they had their prey trapped.

He hoisted Peg over the pile of dead dogwoods, near where they had heard that first hadrosaur. Then he dodged left, trusting his navmatrix to find the *Troodon* trail they had followed into the thicket.

Those *Troodon* should have been a warning. They were small carnosaurs, low-down egg-stealers and baby duckbill eaters, hanging about the nursery. But he had seen none near to the rookery. Now he knew why.

The hadrosaurs had excellent defenses against small bipedal predators. Jake was appalled at the horrid mistake he had committed. Carnosaurs ignored them because they were not much of a meal, but with these rampaging duckbills it was a different matter. They weren't hungry, this was a communal response—a herd of homicidal herbivores protecting its nests.

He found the *Troodon* trail, shouting to Peg, "Here, this is the way."

Before he had gone a dozen meters down the narrow trail, he ran right into a hadrosaur coming the other way. Jake nearly screamed in frustration. Cooperative intelligence had lost its charm now that the herd was bent on tracking them down and stomping them into the red mud.

He tried his stunner on full power. The enraged hadrosaur did not even stumble.

Jake holstered the useless stunner. Exhausted, panic-stricken, spattered with mud, he hauled Peg back into the tangle of dogwoods. They crouched back to back, armed only with their recorders. Jake did not need microamps to hear the duckbills closing in, hooting and roaring in the undergrowth.

Beneath the tangle of fallen dogwoods, he could see their leathery three-toed feet, churning the muck. Then massive sides and tails appeared, splintering the dogwoods overhead. Twigs and bark rained down. His compweb issued a stern warning—in seconds he would be mashed flat.

Day One

Always leave them wanting more.

Jake put down his headband. The rampaging duckbills disappeared, replaced by an audience frozen in anticipation, staring wide-eyed at the windows.

It was no longer afternoon in the Cretaceous—it was now night in Ile-de-France. Paris, City of Light, glittered within her necklace of suburbs, like a diamond tiara laid on black felt. Tall cones of light illuminated Montmartre and the Eiffel Tower. Hours had passed, but every entrance was still maxed. No one had left. An excellent sign.

Startled faces turned away from the windows toward Jake. Some of the paleontologists looked really concerned. More cynical FTL types started to smirk, as it dawned on everyone that the show was over. Protests erupted—"What? Oh, no. Go on. Finish up."—Swelling into a single chant—"*Encore, encore . . .*"

"Or we won't let you leave," warned a woman in the front row, lifting her glass. In an instant gratification society, no one wanted to be in suspense.

Jake shook his head. They could find out what happened in the downloaded data—look under Day 101.

Peg stepped out of the speed-of-light gate on hold for the guests of honor. Obviously undamaged and perfectly on cue. The reception room rocked with more shouting and handclapping. Real windows would have shaken.

Acting cool and devil-be-damned, Peg strode over to where Jake sat, kissing him on the cheek. Doubling the applause. They turned and acknowledged their immediate audience. And millions more plugged in throughout the system. They had done it. The biggest coup since faster-than-light was discovered.

With Peg at his side, Jake floated out into the sea of smiling faces. Shaking hands. Basking in adulation. He was at the zenith of his profession, without a clue about what to do. What miracle to pull off next. Jake had been far more prepared bellying up to the bar in the *Aleck Scott*'s saloon. Aboard the *Scott* he *knew* every gladhanding gent was likely to be a knave, all set to cheat him. That's why Jake loved the past. It was so thoroughly predictable.

Here, of course, half the faces were female, a thousand percent improvement over the *Aleck Scott*. But he was thoroughly and completely in love with Peg. And did not even *feel* like flirting. Jake was forced to play the bluff adventurer, eager to please, but totally obtuse. Which only made him more attractive.

There was the added dissonance of having talked to many of these people earlier in the "day"—before leaving for the Mesozoic. For Jake that morning was long gone, and a hell of a lot had happened. People he had seen briefly months ago acted like they had just been talking.

Fortunately Jake found he did not need to be charming. Or even coherent. Folks clapped him on the back, calling him a hero. Acting as if he had *invented* the Mesozoic. All he had really done was get there and back again.

Not everyone was in awe of him. Aside from sly congratulations, his superiors at FTL were lying low—basking in Jake's success. Nothing was said about his losing *Challenger*. No mention was made of how much *more* he might have brought back. But he knew that Faster-Than-Light was laughing up its collective sleeve. They were slick, sick fuckers.

Peg shot him a wink and a smile from across the room. She mingled easily with the crowd, making contacts, scheduling appointments as deftly as she threw Arkansas desperadoes, acting completely at ease with university historians, Feelie producers, museum directors—any sort of show business type.

That was fine by Jake. He had never wanted to wheel and deal. Not on that level anyway. He had worked like the devil, kept his nose semiclean, and shot up through the ranks of field agents. Promotion at FTL could be rapid, even dizzying, so long as a field agent did not drop out, go nuts, die, or disappear. His sole desire had been to pick and choose his assignments. Doing what he wanted, when he wanted.

Peg sauntered over. "Time to duck out and meet with the Smithsonian directors."

"What?" The party here in Paris was roaring along.

"There will be plenty of time for preening in front of your fans," Peg promised. "Hell Creek is in North America. If we let the first day go without dropping by, the Smithsonian will never forgive us."

A fate Jake could easily have lived with. They said their good-byes anyway, vanishing together through a gate.

It was still late afternoon in Washington. Jake found it moderately thrilling to realize the whole working day had been devoted to them. American paleontologists were hotly debating the details of what they had seen. There was an exhilarating silliness about it. Jake's scientific role was nebulous. He wasn't a paleontologist, or a chrono-physicist, or even a wormhole engineer—he was a field agent, a dubious, laymanlike, jack-of-all-trades. His main contribution to the success of the First Mesozoic Expedition had been piloting a dirigible (until

he crashed her) and playing Down-the-River with a pair
of smooth talking Missourians. Terribly necessary stuff,
but not easily translatable to folks who had not *been
there*. What could Jake add to the recordings, except to
swear they were real?

But it hardly mattered. These people still wanted him
there in the *flesh*, alongside Peg. In a 3V society, physical presence paid the ultimate compliment.

Jake was even invited to take part in paleontological
debates, before a museum board that had to have been
in office since the Late Pleistocene. A Montana field
paleontologist, a tough as bedrock old biddy, tried to pin
him down, asking if he favored, "the hot-blooded avian
model, or the bulk endotherm theory of dinosaur physiology."

Jake smiled at the notion of running a thermometer
up *T. rex*'s rectum just to check. "Dinosaurs are dinosaurs," he told her. To Jake, asking if they are more like
birds or reptiles was a lot like asking if Jenghiz Khan
was a better Baptist or Presbyterian.

His answer got a round of curious stares. As far as
Jake was concerned these people were reeling from
time shock—like Charlotte on the hovership. Whenever
a new period was opened up, history, archeology, or
paleontology was instantly revolutionized. After ages of
basing wild inferences on trivial clues, paleontologists
were being blasted by a hurricane of data, a tornado
that would turn their world unceremoniously upside
down. A junior researcher from the University of Paris
and a ne'er-do-well time traveler were now the leading
experts on the Uppermost Mesozoic. With more *practical* knowledge than all the universities combined. Old
debates were instantly outdated. Old battle lines oblit-
erated.

Which was why some people resented time travelers—tramping about in the past, stamping out perfectly
good arguments that had gone on for centuries. A lot of

folks had never forgiven FTL for showing that Moses was born an Egyptian, and Mohammed a Jew, or that Africans landed in the New World long before Leif the Lucky and Columbus. A vocal minority of tenured philosophers and religious fanatics denied that time travel even existed, claiming the whole thing was a hoax put on by FTL. Or with carefree consistency, they accused time travelers of mucking up the past, of changing things with their presence.

Fortunately Peg was in her chosen niche, respectful and unintimidating, pointing up new and profitable lines of research, assuring quarrelsome academics that there would be plenty left to fight over. At the same time she gently pushed her own pet project—opening up the Great Age of the Sauropods, by going straight to the Morrison formation Jurassic.

When they got back to Paris, the fete was still going on. In fact the mix was improving. Folks with business to attend to were filtering out, making room for time travel enthusiasts and the partying public—guys in gladiator costumes, biceps bulging with steroids, and young Parisian women, dressed like *fin de siècle* hookers with feather boas and fishnet stockings—all eager to celebrate.

But they they barely had time for a last bow before Peg was hurrying him off.

Leaving paleontology in free fall, they leaped the continents, going to LA, Level Seven, to have a late lunch with Tanya Larke herself. Having known her only from her Feelies, Jake had forgotten how old she had to be. In person, her skin had the hard angles and vague brittleness left by layers of biosculpt—traces of artificiality, even if the final product was perfect. When she was performing, computers softened the lines, making her forever young.

Tanya, too, was at the pinnacle of her profession, exuding confidence, not caring that one woman could not hope to live up to her many roles. She dealt in raw appeal. Whenever she spoke or gestured, Jake could feel her easy magnetism, the same current of strong restless energy you felt when you tuned into her—like during an action sequence, or when she made love.

She entertained them with tea and sushi, sitting on fresh tatami mats in a huge studio block. A virtual world all its own, set up to transmit near-infinite duplicates of any point in the known universe. And all possible permutations thereof.

Her private studio space was as big as the Sorbonne reception room, with even taller windows. The sole interior decoration was a giant slab-statue of a twin-headed snake-goddess, with a grinning skull dangling between her breasts. The view through the outsize windows was of Los Angeles. Not as the City of Angels was now, or had ever been. The scene was a 360-degree projection of LA as a northern Tenochtitlán, cut by canals and plied by flower boats, the outpost of an Aztec empire that never was.

White clay temples crowned the Hollywood hills, their altar smoke smudging the afternoon sky. Sunset Boulevard had become a broad open air market lined with shops and stalls—jammed with sweating porters, fat merchants, languid half-naked shoppers. Jungle entrepreneurs sold live monkeys in wicker cages. Mulholland was a great winding processional way, filled with feathered priestesses and Jaguar Warriors in spotted cloaks, chanting and singing their way toward the Hollywood Bowl, which had become a ball court. Beverly Hills was crosshatched with cornfields, and a haze of cookfires hung over the Wilshire District.

Closer at hand, Jake could see a tall pyramid, rising to window level. On its steps the final act of the Feast of Tezcatlipoca was taking place. An unblemished young man, the Sun-on-Earth, was bidding good-bye to his wives, four jade-necklaced temple prostitutes. He wore the feathered cloak and headdress of a war chief, and his chest rippled with muscles, but his eyes had the bright faraway look of a snake-charmed bird.

Tanya talked at hyperlight speed, emphasizing her points with sharp kinetic gestures, throwing her whole body into the conversation, saying to Jake, "I never *properly* thanked you for the work you did on Cleopatra." (Jake's Cleopatra interview had been the basis for a lavish, highly fictionalized Feelie, staring Tanya as Queen of the Nile, paramour to Caesar and Mark Anthony.) From the way she said it, Jake got the impression that "proper thanks" from Tanya Larke would beat a three-year lease on a harem.

"Your presentation was breathtaking," Tanya told them. "But dinosaurs are only backdrop. Splendid backdrop, to be sure. Lots of sizzle. But they lack . . ." Tanya groped for the right word . . .

Behind her, the Sun-on-Earth finished embracing his wives and mounted the pyramid, tobacco tube in hand, his neck garlanded with flowers. He paused at each level of the pyramid, to smash one of the clay pipes he had played during his year in office. When he mounted the final steps, reaching the top of the pyramid, his eyes were fixed on the sun above, no longer seeing what was happening in his last moments on Earth.

". . . Well. You know, the human touch." Tanya turned to Peg, laying a hand on her leg. "Which was why you two were so wonderful. I could feel the tension between you. That's what made it for me."

Peg smiled back. "So no more dinosaurs?"

"Heavens no. I've nothing against dinosaurs. Just don't forget to keep it human."

Black-faced priests with clotted blood in their hair seized the Sun-on-Earth, dragging him stumbling to the stone altar. Five of them held his head, wrists, and ankles. A sixth slashed at the naked, heaving breast with a long obsidian blade. In seconds the high priest had ripped the still-convulsing heart from the young demi-god's chest, holding it up to the sun.

"And Jake." Tanya reached out and touched him, too. Jake tore himself away from the human sacrifice in Aztec LA. The Feelie star kept a hand on each of them, as though she were completing a circuit, letting energy surge through them, like a living superconductor. "Don't give up on the historical stuff. Only be sure it has sizzle. How about Salome? Or Alexander the Great—he swung both ways, didn't he?"

Jake admitted he had not yet met Alexander of Macedon—but history had it that the would-be world conqueror was a staunch bisexual.

"There, see, something for everyone." Tanya gave Peg a wink, asking if they wanted more sushi. "I sliced and dressed it myself. Anytime you are in LA—*Mi casa es su casa.*"

Four hours later Jake found himself yawning through yet another lunch, this one in the Forbidden City. No 3V scenes this time, just green tea and centuries-old woodwork stained black with lacquer.

Chinese paleontologists plied him with questions. The Mongols were particularly persistent. Because of the Mesozoic land bridge, some of the closest analogs to Hell Creek carnivores were found in Mongolia's Nemegt formation. They pressed him to dredge up unrecorded details. Offering him help in searching his memory. "Should you require a brain scan, the best Tokyo facilities are being held open for you. *T. rex* and *Tyrannosaurus bataar* may actually be interbreeding subspecies."

Jake dredged up a polite refusal. The two huge carnivores could have been kissing cousins for all he cared—but no one was going to wring out his brain, especially not a Mongol. (After the Jenghiz Khan interview Jake had been accused of "defaming a historical character." Actually he had just let Jenghiz be Jenghiz, but the lovable old ogre was too much for some modern Mongols.)

He quizzed his compweb for the time in the Bahamas—10:00 P.M Monday, the day they arrived. In Bejing it was Tuesday already and nearly noon. He and Peg had been up since before dawn—1857. No amount of green tea was going to keep him going.

He signaled to Peg that it was time to run.

She was hard at work, deflecting polite suggestions down positive tracks—going full out, with the same eager, fanatic glint in her eye he had seen on that first day at Hell Creek. It took them over an hour to say their good-byes.

Outside the banquet hall Peg mentioned a breakfast meeting in Calcutta—"Just getting going." Somewhere in the great global city it was always morning, noon, or midnight, and every hour in between.

Jake shook his head, "No way, let's piss on the campfire and call it a day."

Peg looked shocked.

"No more," he insisted, feeling the whole weight of his first day at Home bearing down on him. "Besides, it's better for me to keep these academics at arm's length."

"Why?" Peg was entirely swept up in the academic dance—sharing her finds was second nature.

"FTL thinks I am too independent as is."

"Who cares what FTL thinks?" She dismissed his superiors with a negligent wave.

"I do. They are slick, slick mothers, and I need to stay on their good side."

"What do you mean?" English idioms did not always translate into Universal.

"When you have worked as closely with FTL as I have, you begin to suspect things."

"What things?"

"Just things . . ." It was an old story among STOP

teams and field agents, but not widely known to outsiders. Faster-than-Light gates are incredibly complicated—practically a new branch of physics. Nothing sub-light compared to them. Yet the breakthrough that produced it was too pat. Too big a leap to be believed. It was almost as if . . .

"But FTL needs us," Peg protested, nodding toward the Forbidden City's collection of pagoda-palaces—long ago turned over to scholars and museum curators. "It needs the academies, and the Feelies, and the . . ."

"Sure, mainly for the raw gigawatts"—gate technology required a planetary energy net. "But that doesn't mean they are not playing with us. Using us the way we used Twain and Bixby to get to New Orleans."

"So what? Right now we are bigger than FTL. Bigger than anyone. We made it to the Mesozoic."

Jake yawned again. "Well if I am that big, Bombay can wait."

"But the meeting's in Calcutta."

"Put the whole subcontinent on hold." He reached out to pull her closer. "I need to climb in bed. Preferably with you."

She resisted his pull, "But what about Charlotte?"

"Well OK, her too—but only if she enters into the spirit of it. She's got to drop that Southern belle pose, and promise not to snore afterward."

"No, you silly sex maniac. I just mean to look in on her. To make sure she's secure. There will be plenty of time to make love."

"Promise?"

"I swear to it."

He could see her mind was already elsewhere. As they headed for a speed-of-light gate a tiny robo-insect followed at a respectful distance; its plastic carapace kept changing color to blend with the Forbidden City's inlaid floors.

They kissed good-bye in predawn Paris, in a public

speed-of-light station. Peg did not have a gate in her apartment building. It was one of those old Paris apartments with narrow iron balconies, steel plumbing, and real windows. Jake was left standing alone in the Place de la Bastille. People poured past. Paris at night was still Paris. One of those parts of Megapolis that never seemed to sleep.

A second bug sat in the gutter, its audio-optic antenna locked on Jake.

He returned to North America, getting to Cis Luna Station by way of two little-used gates in the Dakotas. Jake had seen Cis Luna in a half dozen different centuries, including the late preatomic, when it was still called Grand Central—before they ripped up the rails and put in speed-of-light gates. He checked the time on the ancient clocks above the information kiosk. Nearly midnight. Monday. He was back in the same time zone as the Bahamas. Day one at Home was nearly over.

A wild-eyed, bulky young man was holding a sign up in front of the off-planet gates, haranguing people as they passed, yelling, "Stop—think about it. THERE IS NO SUCH THING AS A FREE LUNCH."

His sign read:

MAKE PEOPLE PAY!
Don't be a parasite!
Back to a natural economy:
—Free Food
—Free Housing
—Free Health Care
—Free Transport
Are all immoral!
They sap the will to work.

"Don't blame me," Jake muttered as he brushed past. "I've got a job."

"Good for you," the freemarketeer shot back, "but you'd be better off walking."

To Mars? Jake did not stop to argue, entering the gate marked SYRTIS MAJOR. This zealot would hardly approve of working for FTL. People who idealized the past usually hated time travel—it disturbed their prejudices to discover that the "good old days" were mostly dull and dirty.

Another bug scurried along in Jake's wake. As the stick-tight rushed to see which gate Jake took, the libertarian caught sight of the movement. He brought his heel down hard, crushing the tiny abomination.

Transit to Mars took twenty long minutes. The planet was nearing superior conjunction, and Jake had to route through Venus. Normally no one noticed time in transit. People stepped through a lightspeed planetary gate with no more worry than needing to remember to reset their watches.

But Jake's navmatrix and compweb made him conscious of every nanosecond. He found speed-of-light travel interminably tedious.

In transit he thought about Peg, wishing she were coming with him, missing her already. Until now he had had Peg almost to himself. In the Mesozoic it had been just the two of them. Now he was going to have to share her with the world. Just as well, maybe, the woman was a whirlwind, a tornado. More than he could handle at times.

Letting his compweb free-associate, he pictured their escape from the duckbills. He had been scared senseless, muttering Hail Marys as the hadrosaurs closed in about them, filling the air with their hoots. Great hulking bodies had ground closer, obliterating every escape route.

Peg's solution to the problem had been swift, concise, and to the point. She simply ordered her recorder to replay that morning's shot of *T. rex*.

The 3V image of the world's largest carnivore, appearing without warning in the midst of the dogwood thicket, set off a fifty-megaton zoological explosion. Hadrosaurs scattered in all directions. The rookery went into immediate meltdown, and the duckbills lost all interest in the two little bipeds they had been chasing. Jake wished he could have thought of that.

His admiration for her ingenuity was only slightly tarnished by her insane desire to hang around and "observe the hadrosaur reaction." For once Jake refused, hustling her to safety. It took the whole rest of Day 101 for him to recover.

Transit completed, Jake arrived at Syrtis Station to find a fifteen-foot-tall Green Martian greeting the throng from earth, waving a long sword, lance, and dirk in three of his four arms. Jake ignored the menacing apparition. Tars Tarkas was just a hologram. The Syrtis Major council used a fraction of the city's energy and computer budget to encourage tourism. More visitors meant a bigger overhead and transport allowance.

He took a speed-of-light gate to a public kiosk near to his apartment block. Remembering the advice of the fanatic at Cis Luna Station, Jake meant to walk the last hundred meters or so, to get his bearings. It was dark outside, after midnight—Syrtis time. Ornamental battlements frowned down on the glittering starlit surface of the Grand Canal.

When he reached his studio, Jake was perfectly primed to pack a pipe and bid the universe good-night. As he smoked, his mind slipped into the great gray emptiness of opium space, so like the blank 3V sensorium. His day had begun before dawn, 1857, in the Bermuda Triangle. Since then he had gone through two more time periods, taken an excursion into Tuesday, gone back to Monday—and now it was Tuesday again, on another planet. A fitting first day Home.

Thank heavens it was over. Putting away the pipe, he turned off the windows and went to sleep.

Despite the loss of the Cis Luna bug, the stick-tights had regained contact. The bug permanently assigned to Jake's studio clung to the fake Barsoomian facade above his door, waiting patiently throughout the long Martian night.

Beat the Pleistocene

The first day's dash through a dozen time zones, on three continents and two planets, set the pace for a tornado of debriefings, Feelie casts, scientific powwows and 3V seminars. Peg played the expert, dazzling everyone with her command of dinosaurs. Jake supplied the odd detail that Peg might have missed, or not been present for, but mostly he was just there to be *seen*—playing a stoic Tiger Tenzing to Peg's Lady Hillary.

On top of these came invitations to dinners, receptions, snap appearances, and breakfasts in bed—every sort of *soirée* or well-attended orgy on three planets. There was no hysteria, no one tried to rip Jake's clothes off (at least not over brunch), but everyone seemed bent on celebrating their trip. Every room Jake entered was crammed to capacity, every gate quickly maxed out. It was easy to forget that only a tiny fraction of the solar system's population gave a flying fuck about time travel—the people Jake met certainly did.

"Meeting the public" could be a mixed blessing. It meant dealing with the loonies that were inevitably attracted to time travel. Jake had not thought it possible to defame a dinosaur, but one tight-lipped young woman demanded to know why they had recorded *Albertosaurus megagracilis* carrying off that baby duckbill. "That was immoral," the woman declared.

"No, it was breakfast," Peg replied.

"All meat eating is immoral," the woman snapped back.

Peg tried to explain the problems involved with putting gorgosaurus on a meatless diet. The questioner was not assuaged. "A passive witness to murder is as guilty as the murderer."

Trying to to pry a struggling multiton herbivore out of the jaws of a huge carnosaur—armed with only a few *aikido* holds and a medikit—had no appeal for Peg. "We went to the Mesozoic to study dinosaurs. Not to teach them table manners."

Jake suggested the woman take her complaint to FTL. She could get a berth on the next expedition, and present her position to a hungry tyrannosaur.

The only person in the entire solar system (three major planets, and scores of moons and habitats) who did not seem to have time for him was Peg. Jake found it maddening to be always beside her, but hardly ever alone. When he managed to maneuver her back to her Paris apartment, he discovered Charlotte permanently installed. (Megapolis had tens of billions of rooms, leaving no need to double up—unless you liked it that way.)

Charlotte had discarded her gloves and parasol, but still dressed extravagantly in a hand-sewn gown, half lace, and ribbons. Holding her hand out for Jake to kiss, she told him, "Yew lied to me, suh."

"I lied to everyone," Jake protested, pressing his lips against her cool fingers.

"Yew never even hinted you came from here."

He straightened up, smiling, "I hinted—you just did not notice."

"Well, who would? Who would have believed?"

"No one," Jake admitted.

"Why, I can just step through a gate and be anywhere."

"Anywhere in Megapolis." All cities were one city.

But there was more to Terra than her cities—only the tiniest fraction of the planet was served by gates, but since that was the fraction most people *saw*, gates seemed to be everywhere.

"Even the Moon," Charlotte murmured.

Yep, even the Moon. Peg had invited him on a Lunar hike with her troop from Teen Lesbians. Jake had accepted, though tramping about in pressure suits while Peg played Pack Mother to a bunch of hyperactive teens was hardly the ideal date.

"And you can know everything. Any fact is at your fingertips—literally." Charlotte nodded toward Peg's 3V console. "Did you know that Armand gave up drinking?"

Jake said he had not heard that.

"Yes he did. He sobered up and got a commission, in the nineteenth Louisiana infantry, Breckinridge's division. He was killed at Chickamauga—that's in Georgia—stormin' a Yankee battery. I expected Daddy to be dead. But it is hard to think of Armand gone—we were just a few months apart, twins almost."

Charlotte shook her head, still showing signs of time shock. The Civil War and Emancipation Proclamation did not surprise her half so much as her brother's giving up whiskey and dying a hero. But drunk or sober, Armand could hardly have lived on for thousands of years. Everyone Charlotte ever knew or heard of was dead, as dead as the dinosaurs—along with their children and great-great-grandchildren.

Time shock turned some people psychotic. They never adjusted to everyone they knew being dead—or not yet born. Charlotte was tough, though; all she needed was time. That was all anyone needed.

But Jake wanted a special sort of time. Time with Peg—away from Charlotte. Away from academic conferences. Away from friendly Mongolians with four degrees who wanted to strain his brain for forgotten details.

He got her semialone during a vile little fete in their honor at Innocents, a *Danse Macabre* club just off the Rue St. Denis built by the faster-than-light set to resemble a medieval nunnery and charnel house. Mummified remains hung in wall niches. Cloister arches throbbed with 3V images. Death danced with rakehells, doctors, Sorbonne professors, troubadours, and pretty women. Skulls and bones lay scattered under the tables. Poets stood on top of chairs to read their verses, while a party of female impersonators in fourteenth century drag prepared to set fire to a nun.

Charlotte took one look and fled.

But Peg had lived all her life with bones. And Jake had seen the real thing in medieval Paris. (The club was built to match the recordings he brought back.) Kicking aside a set of thigh bones, they took the table reserved for them. They were late, and the buffet was badly picked over, looking like a famine tableau for the feast of the dead.

The stick-tight that followed Jake in curled up among the corpse beetles in the eye socket of a skull.

Half-listening to mediocre poetry, Jake leaned across the table. "Lets slip away afterward and brush up on our heavy breathing."

Peg wrinkled her nose. "In some public cubicle?"

"We could go to LA. Tanya Larke told us, '*Mi casa es su casa.*' We could turn off her human sacrifice tableau and have our own little orgy, in front of blank screens. I'll supply the wine."

"No. Tanya would want to join in, and she's not my type." The women Peg fell for tended to be young and pure—like Charlotte. Were they more than roommates? Jake had not thought to ask.

"We could go to my place on Mars," he suggested. Megapolis had become one big open gate to them, except when they needed to be alone. Jake was tired of riding this high-profile tidal wave.

She shook her head. "Mars would mean twenty minutes to get there—and twenty to get back. Besides, we can't make love all the time."

"Speak for yourself."

"Look, if you are feeling oversexed, give Tanya Larke a call. Or try that girl over there. She's been looking your way ever since we sat down."

Peg nodded at a young woman dressed in black, wearing a man's hose and doublet, with puffed and slashed sleeves, and a stiff white ruff at the neck. Long black hair framed fine bones in her face, and a wide full mouth. Her big, intense eyes were fixed on both of them.

"Come on," he insisted, "this time I was thinking of maybe doing something different."

"Really." Peg gave him an amused glance. "I didn't think there was a combination we had not tried."

"I was thinking of trying to have kids."

"Kids?" For once he surprised her.

"Sure, limited editions of us. You see them every so often." Universal contraception and interplanetary migration gave here-and-now humanity a fairly stable population—for the first time since the Late Neolithic. People had children only when they really wanted to. Jake warmed to his pitch—"Working for FTL is perfect for raising a family. We could spend six months in the past, and be back ten minutes after we left, the little terrors will never know we are gone."

Peg shook her head. "Perfect for you. I work in real time, remember? I am a researcher, with a good to excellent chance of making full professor before I am thirty. I have classes to put on, seminars to lead, theories to push—I can't do all that in the past."

Jake realized that he had assumed Peg would conform to his life, sharing his time trips with him. "Well, how about if you have them and I raise them?"

She laughed. "Tempting offer. Take nine months out of my life to get fat while throwing up, then turn my child over to you. I'll think about it."

Peg stared moodily off into space, as though she were considering Jake's proposition, then asked, "What about her?"

"What about who?"

She nodded toward the girl in black, who was still staring at them. A man came up, dressed as a harlequin-troubadour with bells on his coat and a lute across his back—as big and handsome as steroids and biosculpt could make him. He asked the girl in black to dance. The small figure in doublet and hose shrugged him off without even looking.

Jake sniffed at the mannish hose and broad-shouldered doublet. "She's probably a guy. Or some confused teenager with a crush on time travelers."

"Only one way to find out." Peg got up and asked the watcher in black if she wanted to dance. The on-looker's eyes opened wide, eagerly agreeing. Peg kicked off her shoes and they went at it, feet flying over the flagstone dance floor. Sometimes they danced alone, sometimes with the harlequin-troubadour. Jake had to admit they danced well, thoroughly enjoying the party—as he obviously was not.

That sour evening put him in the perfect mood to meet with his superiors. The following morning, Paris time, he left for Mother Africa. FTL's field headquarters was at the heart of a huge game preserve. Public entry was through an outdoor kiosk. For the first time since returning to Home Period, Jake was not followed by a bug. There was no need here.

Dawn mist hung over a nearby waterhole, ringed by the gray skeletal shapes of wait-a-bit thorn trees. Zebra-like quaggas were coming down to drink. Visitors were supposed to be impressed at seeing giant moas and great antlered Irish elk—it showed what a splendid job FTL was doing, restoring previously extinct species, exotic animals destroyed by human indifference.

There was probably more wilderness in the world now than at any time since the late preatomic. Megapolis soaked up excess population. On trips to the past Jake had seen a single timber company, or a few hundred goatherds, despoiling vast tracks of land. Both were unthinkable here-and-now. Thanks to 3V and speed-of-light gates, tens of thousands could be housed, fed, and amused in a single titanic apartment block. And just try to get them to go out and cut down a forest. Or tend a goat.

But FTL's pseudo-wilderness was wasted on Jake. Having seen the Mesozoic, it is hard to get excited over dodos and Caspian tigers.

Entering the low functional structure that served as FTL's terrestrial headquarters, he was confronted by a neatly groomed trio, two women and a man—balanced for age and race.

One woman was older, white-haired and European, with classic biosculpt features, designed to accent her broad mouth and big brown eyes. The other was her complete opposite, young, athletic, and African, with tribal tattoos on her cheeks. They gave their names as Juno and Anatha.

The man's name was Pole. He was a member of some mixed race, strikingly handsome, with skin like teak and bright laughing eyes.

Jake quizzed his compweb. Neither the names nor faces were on file. The panel was so courteous and good-looking, they might as well have been holograms.

This was an informal hearing. No charges. No hint of reprimand. Officially they were here to take statements about the loss of *Challenger*—for the benefit of future expeditions. He recalled Peg's parting encouragement, "Remember, we don't need them—they need us."

His inquisitors were polite but persistent. Why had he

agreed to head for South America? Didn't it make more sense to survey the northern hemisphere, before bucking the tropical storm belt? Jake must have known he was putting *Challenger* at risk. The two women, Juno and Anatha, gushed conciliation, taking Jake's ''side,'' offering him lots of time to respond to questions he did not want to answer, while Pole sat gravely smirking up his sleeve.

Jake reminded them that Mesozoic weather was supposed to be mild, with the tropic-to-subtropic gradient not nearly so steep. Besides, Peg was the expert. If she wanted to see sauropods—or flying saucers for that matter—his job was to find them, not invent reasons for refusing.

He had come hoping to plan new trips, not go over and over the last one. But the panel insisted on rehashing the crash. Asking why didn't you do this? Or that? No accusations of course. They all acted perfectly tactful and encouraging. Everyone *knew* Jake had done a heroic job, they just wanted to learn from his experience. The *Challenger* was equipped to circumnavigate the planet several times over. The crash cut everything short . . . ''We need to keep this from happening next time.''

Nonsense. Jake guessed this whole sanctimonious façade was nothing but an attempt by FTL to look good on the debriefing record. The only *next time* they cared about was a more formal inquiry. More than ever he was sure FTL had some private pipeline to the future. At least they could take little looks. These people talked like they already knew the outcome of the meeting. Their egos were not involved. They competed with each other at being friendly and conciliatory.

Flying blind, he tried to match their game, becoming a model of tact and understanding—without giving as much as a micron. The crash recordings were as they were—he had nothing to add to them, except to suggest bringing a backup airship next time. ''We can easily afford to double the commitment—it might mean ten times the data—*now that we have proved it is possible.*"

That was his way of reminding them that until *he* cracked the Hell Creek anomaly, the Uppermost Cretaceous had been one big crap shoot. Bigger expeditions were now feasible because *his* navmatrix held the map to the portal, the golden thread that marked a previous passage through the anomaly.

"Naturally there will be more expeditions," Anatha assured him.

Pole immediately agreed. "Hell Creek is a trove waiting to be tapped. But we need to learn as much as we can from your success. The Mesozoic is not going to go away."

In the meantime, Juno asked, could he please go over . . .

"Enough." Jake stood up. The Mesozoic might not go away, but he would. It was idiotic to keep making statements that could be used against him at a more formal hearing. He had made it clear he was eager to guide another, bigger team back to the Mesozoic.

They leaped to their feet, falling all over each other to let the testy hero have his way, putting the proper spin on things, proving FTL tried to be reasonable. Then came the studied afterthought. "Of course, we'll need to interface with your navmatrix to fix the Hell Creek gate coordinates."

This was the nub of this whole phony interview. If Jake allowed them to tap his navmatrix, the smiling friendly folks at FTL would have no need of him. Right now he was the hands-down choice to guide the next expedition. Without the portal map in his navmatrix, FTL would be back at square one, having to tackle the Hell Creek anomaly anew—knowing only that it *was* possible. Or at least it had been done once.

Juno assured him they only wanted to make sure the

information was not lost. "Another backup, nothing more." Her partners beamed.

They had deftly maneuvered Jake into giving that lecture about a second backup airship, letting him rattle on about the virtues of redundancy just to sound oh-so-reasonable now. One peek into his navmatrix, and all his bargaining potential was gone. Trapped by his own testimony, Jake had nothing to fall back on but icy good humor. "Put me at the head of the next team, and I'll walk them through the portal."

Eyebrows went up. Asking for the portal map was supposed to sound like a reasonable precaution. Anything could happen to Jake. There could be a portal slip next time out. He could stray off the path outside and be eaten by a pride of previously extinct Cape lions.

Freezing a smile on his face, Jake repeated his offer to lead the next team in, then he said his good-byes.

Jake left, heading for the kiosk by the waterhole with its wait-a-bit thorn trees, glad to escape the looking glass world of an "unofficial noninquiry." He'd have gotten a fairer hearing from that Helena jury.

Dodoes eyed him as he crossed the gardens. More than ever the place seemed like a gorgeous façade, an exotic Potemkin preserve, where the public could come to picnic in the living past. If FTL had a time tunnel into the future, you could bet it was not here.

So long as he watched his step, there was no way FTL could force the information out of him. Being a field agent was like belonging to Horace Bixby's true blue brotherhood of river pilots. Field agents did not own the portals, any more than Bixby owned the *Aleck Scott*—but they did own what was in their heads. There was no Pilot's Benevolent Association, like back in 1857, but the basic principle endured. River pilots made themselves indispensable by refusing to share their knowledge of the River—except among themselves. Field agents had a similar advantage. The time stream was every bit as uncharted as the antebellum Mississippi. Each new anomaly had to be mapped by a skilled operator. Cybernetic probes were notoriously useless. SuperChimps uniformly failed to come back.

Right now they had no excuse not to let him lead the next Hell Creek expedition. Jake was the man of the hour. Just the same, he was on a tightrope as tricky as any newly opened anomaly. If he gave FTL an angstrom of an excuse to refuse him the next run at Hell Creek, he could be accused of putting the team that did go through at risk.

Back in Paris he told Peg what had happened in the heart of Africa. She advised him not to worry. "We can easily whip up backing for a new expedition. To a paleontologist, every second of those recordings raised more questions than it answered. University departments are already begging us to go back. FTL has to fall in, or lose its lock on the past."

Jake doubted it would be so easy. "They did not look ready to fall for anything." In the cold light of a Paris day, he could see why FTL was being so cagey. Despite the loss of *Challenger*, he and Peg had been way too successful. The enthusiasm for more and bigger Mesozoic expeditions certainly threatened to break FTL's lock on the past. But if Jake could somehow be neutralized, or forced to turn over the Hell Creek map . . .

Peg raced ahead of him, busily planning an independent agency—"We'll call ourselves *Time Tours*. I'll line up the clients. You get ready to guide them through."

Jake nodded. Why not? He had given FTL two hundred percent—up front. If they wanted to dump him now, then fuck'em, he'd find another way.

Getting ready required another lightning round of vacuous amusements, parties, and happenings—some of them in places that made Innocents live up to its name. Jake's binge culminated in a nonstop twenty-four-hour gate-hopping Mardi Gras that followed Fat Tuesday around the globe, from Manila to Hong Kong, to Bombay, to Rio, to Awlins, to LA—wherever things were happening in Megapolis—staying a time zone or two ahead of Ash Wednesday. And ending in a Wednesday A.M. orgy for two on Tanya Larke's huge Theodora-sized floatabed. Jake found the Feelie star nearly as depraved and inventive in person as she was in 3V.

Tanya's personal quarters were spread around the planet, connected by a labyrinth of private gates. Workspace and offices were in the LA studio block, but her breakfast room was in a Mexican villa. The "play" room was part of a twenty-four-hour private club in Milan, opening onto ski slopes at one end and a beach-front cabana at the other. Her bath was a tropical waterfall, but the adjoining bedroom was in a low-g orbital habitat.

Life in Home Period could be a single seamless party if you let it. And Jake had a reputation to uphold—field agents on holiday were infamous for excess. Common prudence required that he prepare for a new and dangerous expedition by wringing every bit of partying out of his soul. Until his psyche rebelled in disgust and absolutely demanded serious work. Anything less might cost him vital concentration.

He recovered in time to meet Peg at her apartment, finding her brimming with happy enthusiasm. She had lined up backing for another run—"This will only be a warm-up, but it will be fun. Just a short hop. To Pleistocene California—sponsored by the Paige Museum and the Pacific Rim Universities."

"The Pleistocene?" Jake had a sick sense of disaster in the making. "Why would we want to go there?"

"Politics," Peg explained airily. "The mammalian paleontologists wanted a crack at one of their periods, so we settled on this Pleistocene trip to satisfy them. Then it's back to Hell Creek."

"But there are no portals into Pleistocene California."

"We're going to open one at Rancho La Brea."

Jake groaned, damning himself for ever trusting in academics.

"What's wrong?" she asked. "Everyone else was for it—even FTL liked the idea."

"I'll bet the bastards loved it." No wonder the FTL panel was so cagey about the crash. They must have known he was not headed back to Hell Creek. FTL had given up nothing by playing hard-to-get.

Peg did her best to soothe him. "But it only means going back thirty to forty thousand years, tops. That is nothing compared to the Cretaceous. The saving in energy cost is tremendous . . . ."

"Screw the energy costs." Once again, Jake found himself having to explain elementary wormhole theory to Peg. "Once an anomaly is mapped, it is a thousand percent more manageable. To get to the Pleistocene, I'll have to pioneer a whole new portal, always an iffy proposition. And FTL will use this as an excuse to pressure me to give up the map to the Hell Creek anomaly. I'll look totally irresponsible, hopping off to Rancho La Brea with the key to Hell Creek in my head."

Peg said she did not care much for the Pleistocene either, but she had done her best. "I'll look just as bad if we try to drop out now."

They had their first slam-bang argument since the Mesozoic. Fortunately Charlotte was there to play peacemaker, getting them to make up—and then make love. For an *Awlins belle*, Charlotte could be utterly practical at times.

Making love made Jake feel better, though he still did not like the Pleistocene detour. But the best way to silence FTL was to ace the assignment. A perfect run to Rancho La Brea would leave no excuse for holding off on Hell Creek—it was beat the Pleistocene or bust.

Rancho La Brea

"Saber-tooths, *Smilodon californicus*. Coming on fast." Jake triggered his recorder, speaking rapidly into the comlink. "Three, four, and more—probably a pride."

Morning air sizzled with tension. A hot dry Santa Ana wind whipped the grass tops. Raymond Chandler's "red wind," the stifling breeze off the desert that scorched the L.A. basin, prickling the skin and standing hair on end.

Watching the saber-tooths emerge from the tall bunchgrass, Jake felt the absolute awe that big dangerous cats always inspired. Part of the human love-hate relationship with large carnivores.

Without lowering his viewfinder, he tore a tab from the caffeine strip in his pocket, dropping it into the cup clamped between his knees. He felt the cup get hot. Its steaming caffeine smell sent a sharp wake-up call to every nerve not yet fully alert.

"Looks like better than a dozen," he decided, taking a sip. More big-toothed carnivores kept appearing out of the bunchgrass less than a hundred meters from where Jake knelt, hunched over his cup.

Meter-high grass gave a good deal of cover. Jake's corneal lenses let him count grass stalks on the Santa Monica foothills a couple of klicks away, yet the saber-tooths had been completely hidden from him until they began to lope forward, exposing tawny backs and long, terrible canines. Tall grass closed behind them, covering their tracks.

The lion-sized smilodons were not true cats. *Felidae* rather than *Felinae*. The upper canines of true cats tended to shrink during the course of evolution, but those of the saber-tooth grew longer, becoming flat curved blades with serrated edges. Beveled like the teeth of a tyrannosaur, their roots reached all the way back to the eye sockets.

Their whole bodies were thrust forward, adapted to use these twin daggers with maximum effect. Tremendous shoulder and neck muscles tapered down to slim hips and a bobbed tail. They killed by seizing their prey with brawny forelimbs and inflicting repeated jagged slashes with the upper canines, severing arteries and laming their victims.

Jake shifted his viewfinder toward the nearest water hole. The landscape hereabouts had changed drastically since the last time he was in L.A. Tanya Larke's pseudo-Aztec, City of the Angels had become bunchgrass savanna, dotted with live oaks, tall cypress, and small stands of juniper and coast pine. Dry summer heat drained the sumps and hollows, and animals gathered at the edge of tar pools slick with surface water. Humpless camels, long-horned bison, tiny antelope. Also wild horses as tall as Arabians, but more heavily built.

Jake picked through the herds, searching for people, calling a warning into the comlink. "This pride is headed smack for the water hole. Bearing two-two-zero from that big bent cypress."

Peg came on the link, "Our Lady of the Beasts is loose."

"Better rein her in." Jake had his viewfinder zoom in on the gathering at the water hole. Big bodies filled the field, flanks, legs, and shoulders, a shifting wall of flesh. Horns and antlers stuck out above. Heads that had been thrust snout first into the oily water looked up. A first cautious backing off began as the pseudo-cats got closer.

"She's not wearing a comlink."

"Shit." The senior academic on the mission had gone native with a vengeance. "Wave to her. Beat some drums. Get her attention before these cats mistake her for an antipasto."

"She's close to you. Try bearing zero-six-zero."

Jake swung the viewfinder, telling his navmatrix to mark the bearings. At zero-six-zero he kicked up the focus.

"Got her." He fixed on a small dark woman with kinked gray hair and heavy breasts, naked to the waist, dressed in a grass skirt and shell necklace. Intent on the scene at the water hole and completely ignoring the oncoming cats. Standing at an angle to their line of advance, she could not see them unless she looked away, over her left shoulder.

"Damn, I'm going to warn her." Jake let his recorder drop, to hang from the strap across his shoulder. Reaching into his bush jacket for his stunner, he set off at a run. As the only field agent in a big high-profile expedition, Jake was getting a crick in the neck from having to watch out for everyone and everything.

Grass tops whipped at his hips and chest. He could see the saber-tooths making their move ahead of him. Starting to run—heads down, ears back, and teeth bared. If they were bent on bringing down this SC Ph.D. in a grass skirt, there was little he could do to stop them. His sole hope was to get within stunner range, picking them off as they charged.

The scene at the water hole shifted into fast-forward. Horses and camels took off, stampeding for safety. Mini-antelope bounded into the brush. In a moment nothing was left at the bank but a family of great lumbering ground sloths, *Paramylodon*, ambling giants not much into running. The big grazing beasts stood two to three meters tall on their hind limbs, looking confused.

Seeing the herbivores scatter, the woman whipped her head around, searching for the cause.

Jake redoubled his efforts, waving and pointing toward the saber-tooths. His lenses were focused on the scene ahead. Trying to keep both the woman and the cats in sight, he did not see the grass part in front of him.

Suddenly he was treading on a black-tipped tail. With a hiss, snarl, and blur of motion, a huge spotted shape reared out of nowhere, rising from the grass like a great Aztec jaguar god. Twisting about, the tiger-sized beast sprang at him, fangs bared.

Jake just had time to give a startled shriek and squeeze off a shot before the snarling monster bowled him over. He hit the ground hard, scared and shaken, hanging on tight to the stunner.

Blue California sky whirled above him, framed by the grass tops. Sighting as best he could, Jake fired again, and again, but by now there was no need for further shots. A quarter ton of angry feline was lying atop his legs, sleeping peacefully.

This one was a true cat, a giant lionlike jaguar with a long tail and spotted pelt, bigger than the biggest African lion. The beast had been crouched in the grass, watching for an opening, when Jake came bounding up its back. Naturally it had resented the harebrained interruption.

Jake lay there for nearly a minute with the breath knocked out of him, happy to be alive and whole. Overhead, sundried stalks of needle grass bowed in the wind. He noted the long narrow leaves and purplish tinge. He could feel the huge feline on his legs. Its plush coat was softer than silk, astonishingly clean and sweet-smelling—in another time and place the fur would have brought a tidy fortune.

Eventually Jake remembered why he had run up this cat's tail in the first place. Heaving himself out from under the heavy panther, Jake looked up, frantic to see what was happening at the water hole.

What he saw beggared description. Saber-tooths were all over one of the ground sloths, clinging to its back, clawing at its flanks. The huge sloth was slow, but massively built, with great long forelimbs and terrible claws. The gigantic browser reared and bellowed, swatting at the tawny meat eaters, tossing a big hulking male teeth over tail.

The saber-tooth on the sloth's back refused to be shaken loose, stabbing again and again with its horrible canines. The sloth's matted hair and thick hide were augmented by a curious form of body armor, nodules of bone, dermal ossicles, buried beneath the skin. Normal teeth would have been turned back, but the smilodon's twin sabers were designed to stab past the toughest skin defenses, tearing into muscle and bone.

Another cat clamped onto the sloth's flank and pulled sideways, digging its claws into the turf, bringing up great lumps of grass as it tried to topple the behemoth. In seconds the giant *Paramylodon* was borne down by sheer ferocity, and weight of numbers. Pride members slashed at the sloth's broad underbelly, disemboweling the dying beast with their teeth.

One of the smaller sloths, hemmed in by the slaughter, ran squealing and splashing into the water hole, and could not get out—held tight by sticky tar lying beneath the surface of the sinkhole. Hip deep in the ooze, the young sloth stood bleating like a human baby, as the big pseudo-cats settled down to feed.

The SC professor in a necklace and grass skirt stood watching. Peg came up too, recording the meal from perilously close.

Jake sat back in the grass, grateful that it had all gone so well—for everyone but the ground sloths. Holding together a first-class expedition on his own was an incredible strain. He first had to feel his way through the newly opened portal, into a totally new period—never an easy task. And then ride herd on six senior professors representing four schools and nine departments, plus a gaggle of adventurous graduate students. FTL was supplying STOP backing, but nothing else—being scrupulously bent on making Jake's days as difficult as possible. He dearly missed the Mesozoic, when it had been just himself, Peg, and a world full of dinosaurs.

Peg had forseen none of this when she prepared this Pleistocene extravaganza. And now it made Jake increasingly nervous to see how close she was getting to the saber-tooths with her recorder. These pseudo-cats had only slight and intermittent contact with humans, so they could hardly be woman eaters. But Jake still did not trust smilodons—long saber-teeth, anchored deep in the skull, did not leave much room for brains. The pride might mistake Peg, or that SC professor, for a new sort of hairless sloth. Tempting morsels from the *à la carte* menu.

He raised the gain on his corneal lenses and microamps, trying to tell if the pride looked or sounded nervous. All he heard was sharp snarls and throaty growls as they fought over choice bits of sloth. A smilodon's tremendous overbite made eating a sloppy, grisly affair. The pseudo-cats would saw off bloody hunks of raw meat, work them past the huge canines, then swallow them whole.

Whenever Peg got too close, Jake could see the nearest cats' eyes widen and their shoulders bunch up—but as soon as she stepped back they started gorging themselves again. Unaware she was a vegetarian, the saber-tooths acted like Peg meant to snatch some of the raw, mangled ground sloth.

Satisfied, Jake turned back to the true cat as his feet. He had done a superb job of stunning the poor brute.

The great cat would be out until late in the afternoon, if it did not sleep the night. Getting out his medikit, Jake gave the jaguar a general antishock injection and put ointment on the animal's eyes, to keep the corneas from drying up in the hot morning wind. The beast's sleeping form felt warm to his touch, and solid as a steel log, massing maybe three hundred kilos. Jake wondered how he had ever lifted it off of him. Blind panic probably.

Peg sauntered over to see what he was up to. "*Panthera atrox*," she decided. "Did it attack you? They are not likely to be man-eaters."

"No," he admitted. "I tripped over it."

She gave her head a got-to-look-where-you-are-going shake. Peg was obviously in a jolly mood—with herbivores massing at the waterhole, and a carnivore kill, the morning had started off splendidly. She bent down and gave the giant panther a going-over, noting size and sex. "Maybe we could rig a sunshade, to keep him from dehydrating before he wakes up."

Jake scrounged some ultralight tent material and cut a couple of saplings. Spreading the tent fabric over the cat, they staked it down, using the saplings to make it into a lean-to, facing north, away from the hot LA sun.

By the time he was done the landscape had begun to fill up again. A pack of dire wolves appeared, their massive heads slung low, sniffing out the kill. *Canis dirus* was about the size of a timber wolf, but with big hulking shoulders, a massive low-slung head and bone-crushing teeth. Trailing the pack was a pair of coyotes.

The dire wolves loped forward, hoping for an easy meal. But the saber-tooth pride spit defiance, plainly in no mood to share. A snarling altercation ended with the wolves backing down.

They trotted round the tar pit, to see if they could get at the smaller sloth struggling in the mire. A couple of wolves ventured out, only to become trapped themselves. After some thrashing and splashing, one wolf made it back to shore. The other was held fast by the ooze—howling piteously.

All of this was happening half a klick from where Jake had attended lavish parties in twenty-first century Beverly Hills—between the Miracle Mile and Rodeo Drive.

Great condorlike vultures gathered, giant raptors with four-meter wingspans, attracted by the commotion. Circling the scene, they settled on the limbs of a large oak overlooking the tar pool. Soon there were several score of them, spilling out of the tree onto the ground. There they sat in orderly rows with wings folded—like a class of apprenticed undertakers on a field trip—patiently waiting for the saber-tooths to leave, or for the smaller sloth to stop struggling.

The smilodons showed no sign of leaving, settling down around the kill, resting in the heat of morning, hardly moving except to lick each other's chops, or give a toothy yawn. Very satisfied with themselves, some nuzzled each other on the neck, or just lay contentedly rump to rump.

Seeing this catlike affection, Jake settled down next to Peg, putting his arm around her, pulling her closer.

She looked over, smiling. "Shouldn't you be surveying the landscape?"

"Landscape looks fine," he replied. "In fact it looks darn romantic." He nuzzled her neck. Now that the cats had fed, he doubted there was any danger hereabouts. A pride ranged over twenty to forty square klicks. They might share their territory with a lone panther—who kept out other panthers—but the chances of seeing more saber-tooths was tolerably remote.

Peg made no move to shrug him off. "But what about the expedition?"

Jake kicked up the gain on his lenses. He saw professors with their heads together, rehashing the saber-tooth kill. Industrious grad students were gathering cat scats and antelope feces for diet analysis. Others were off hunting, having made their own throwing sticks, fire-hardened darts, and atlatli. The local animals in the area were astonishingly easy to kill, showing how little contact they had with humans. Jake had to see that every dart was radio-tagged and retrieved, since this type of going-native drove researchers nuts. Abandoned atlatl dart foreshafts were an early sign of humans in the Rancho La Brea area. Now no one could be sure who put them there.

Jake relaxed again. "They are leading the romantic life, drinking from gutskin bags, cooking gophers over the fire, or just lying together in the long grass—we could be doing the same."

Peg made a face. "Ugh, I hate gopher."

"No, I mean we could be making the grass tops sway." He patted the ground beside the sleeping panther.

Peg grinned. "Be serious."

"I am serious."

"I mean *serious*, serious."

"Really, try it." The flattened grass felt soft and warm beneath his fingers. A perfect bed.

She lay back, stretching out in the sun—"You're right—it is delicious."

Seconds later he was helping her get her shirt off. Just to let her skin breathe. Peg stood up, to loosen her pants, looking off toward the water hole. Half-naked, with grass stems in her hair, she was a stunning sight. "You're sure you want to do this?" she asked. "Animals are starting to come back."

"I'm sure." Jake looked over his shoulder toward the water hole. Herbivores had begun to drift back, coming from upwind, unable to see or smell the saber-tooths basking in the tall grass. More of the humpless camels—*Camelops hesternus*—came up, followed by a pair of tiny tapir and a sizable herd of the long-horned bison.

They seemed to be moving pretty purposefully. Drawn by the water. Or maybe spooked by something downwind.

Suddenly he saw Peg go tense with excitement, her pants half-off. ''Look! Mammoths!''

Jake turned up his corneal lenses. They were mammoths all right, towering over the bison. Emperor mammoths, three or four meters at the shoulder, swinging their huge heads and colossal curving tusks—the first they had sighted. He reached up to help Peg with her pants.

''Wait,'' she insisted. ''There's something strange about this.''

She was right. Trust Peg to spot the odd or out-of-place. The mixed herds were moving much too purposefully. Animals in the wilds were most active at dawn and dusk—but now it was getting close to noon, not a time to be moving briskly. It just Jake's luck to have a freak migration trample on his attempted nookie. Like that triceratops herd at Hell Creek.

''Maybe they are just thirsty,'' Jake suggested. ''Those smilodons are fed, and animals hereabouts have no reason to fear us.'' Humans were still so rare in North America that animals had no fear of man-the-hunter.

Peg struggled back into her shirt. ''Or maybe it's a storm. The sky to the east is darkening.''

A gray smudge was spreading along the eastern horizon, its top frayed by the wind. Jake zoomed in with his lenses, seeing a sooty curtain creeping slowly closer, driving animals before it. The freak migration was explained.

''Fire,'' he whispered. Alarms sounded in his compweb.

Peg turned to look at him. ''Really?''

''You betcha.'' Suddenly he had much more to think about than getting Peg prone and pantsless. ''A big fire, moving fast.''

Faster than Jake would have thought possible. Savanna grass fires were usually stately monsters, taking days or even weeks to arrive. This one was roaring toward them, whipped along by the Santa Ana. "We better get everyone together," he told her. "And start thinking about firebreaks."

Breaking in on the seminar at the water hole, they sent frantic calls out on the comlink—drop your fieldwork and feces samples and get back to camp.

By late afternoon the entire colloquium was at the water hole, swapping options and taking nervous looks at the eastern horizon. A tremendous pall of smoke reared thousands of meters into the sky, blocking the sun and bathing the landscape in an eerie end-of-the-world twilight. The thin crescent moon became a crimson sickle.

The SC prof who had gone native whispered a pair of lines from Revelation 6:12:

> . . . *and behold, the sun became black as sackcloth,*
> *and the moon became like blood . . .*

Everything that crept and crawled was fleeing before the flames. Clouds of insects came sailing in on the searing wind. Sleepy saber-tooths looked up, as flakes of ash fell like snow around the water hole. The fire was some way off, but Jake saw blackened oak leaves—their veins and spikes easily recognizable—fluttering down from the tops of the smoke cloud several klicks above them.

"We're going to have to set backfires," he declared.

Peg was first to volunteer, followed by the SC prof and several of the more athletic graduate students. Jake explained how he wanted to start a ring of small fires around the water hole, to burn away the grass. "We can huddle behind that firebreak when the main blaze arrives." Small grass fires might be tricky, especially in a roaring Santa Ana, but anything was better than being overrun by a raging firestorm.

They fanned out in a 270-degree arc around the water hole. Jake took the center position, walking directly up-wind into the stinging smoke. His compweb counted meters. Peg was on his left. The SC prof was on his right. But he soon lost sight of both of them in the weird fiery half-light.

Animals were everywhere. He saw quail and California turkey, also a pair of magpies and a big La Brea owl. The blazing firefront seemed to flare and recede before him. The fire was ridge-walking, dimming as it moved down into dips in the landscape, then flaring up again when it reached the top of the next ridge. Tiny antelope milled nervously; so did camels and bison. A herd of peccaries dashed squealing past him, headed the other way. He saw the pair of coyotes that had come with the dire wolves, busily snapping up grasshoppers flushed by the flames.

When his compweb told him he had come far enough, Jake took out an igniter and knelt, nervously pulling up handfuls of dry stalks, making a little tent for his back-fire to catch in. Twisting the fuse on the igniter, he shoved it into the bed of grass.

Then he stood up. The hot blast from the big fire hit him full in the face, like the flash from an open-hearth furnace. Fed by the flames, the Santa Ana was rising to hurricane force.

He sprinted thirty meters to the right and left, repeating the procedure. As he set the third fire he saw a new pride of saber-tooths emerging from the smoke, driven out of their home territory by the fire. They glided right past a group of those stocky Arabians, all thought of horsemeat driven from their minds. Hopefully none of the animals would get trapped between his little back-fires and the main inferno—though that seemed hardly likely. The grass fires he was starting should break the front of the main fire, creating a wide burnt space where animals could shelter.

He dashed back to the water hole to do a head count.

Minutes after he had arrived, the others had all checked in. Predictably, Peg was the last to appear, retreating slowly before the flames, panning her recorder. The water hole was now ringed on three sides with a red band of backfires, flaring against the dense back cloud from the main blaze.

He put everyone to work clearing brush and tramping down grass, so when the backfires arrived they would have little to feed on. When an adequate area had been cleared, he studied his handiwork, thinking, ''That should hold it.''

Minutes ticked by, and he watched the backfires merge, slowly marching toward the water hole. It amazed him to think that just a few hours before his main problem had been trying to get Peg to lie down in the long grass.

Academics were already arguing over how to make the best use of the fire in their research, plotting possible rates of regrowth, wondering which species profited from the lack of grass cover.

A biblical plague of small rodents poured past, pocket mice, ground squirrels and kangaroo rats, driven out of their dens by the flames. Clearly the coyotes and horned owls were going to have a banquet. But the grass eaters and larger carnivores were likely to suffer from such devastation at the bottom of the food chain.

The backfires licked at the base of some live oaks a hundred or so meters upwind. Then the impossible happened. The protective ring of fire burst into a roaring wall of flame, blotting out the main fire.

''What's happening?'' Peg demanded, putting down her recorder.

Jake's jaw dropped. What the hell *was* happening? The small backfires should have burned past the trees, keeping the oaks from feeding the larger conflagration. Instead, flames raced up the trunks, somehow feeding on thick bark and green wood. Live oaks virtually exploded. A tall cypress burst into a pillar of fire, shooting sparks like a Roman candle.

Jake yelled for everyone to start pulling up grass.

Professors dropped their debates, weeding for all they were worth, tossing bunches of grass into the water hole, until matted islands of turf floated on the greasy water. The backfires had become a howling inferno, every bit as bad as the main blaze. The only hope was to scratch out a bare area around the water hole—it was that, or retreat onto the open prairie, running before the fire.

The smilodons were up now, pacing nervously. The small ground sloth had been suffering silently in the mire. Now it began to bleat again, pleading piteously. The pall of smoke grew denser. Jerking out a handful of grass, Jake looked up, trying to gauge how long they had before the fire wall arrived.

Dark shapes appeared, denser and blacker than the smoke around them. He switched his corneal lenses to infrared, letting him make out cool outlines against the heat from the fires. What he saw nearly knocked him over.

"The mammoths," he shrieked. "They're stampeding."

Giant shapes burst out of the smoke. Only Jake's warning kept several profs and a graduate student from being mashed into the grass roots. The smilodons quickly decamped. Scholars scrambled for cover behind the live oak on which the vultures had gathered. Huge hairy elephants thundered past, trampling everything in their path.

Peg and a pair of students managed to drag some of the equipment into the shelter of the vulture tree, but the SC professor was moaning that her recordings were being crushed—hardly Jake's prime concern, trapped between panicked mammoths and the treacherous tar pool.

Oily water lapped at his feet. Jake could hear the little ground sloth screaming in the mire behind him. Fire had swiftly enveloped all open lines of retreat. The low rise where the sleeping panther lay was a mass of flames. Jake saw the fireproof tent material rise up, whipped aloft by the heat, pulling out the tent stakes and sailing away like some great demented bat. The stunned panther he and Peg had labored to save was incinerated in his sleep.

Above the roar of the fire and the screams of the sloth, Jake made out a familiar mechanical beat. Fine-tuning his microamps, he recognized the whap-whap of rotor blades. Ash whirled madly about, sucked sideways by a tornado of grit and smoke. A huge reverberating bulk descended almost on top of them. STOP was cutting this pickup frighteningly close.

A door opened in the hovership, and a helmeted head poked out. Hands reached down. A cheery voice came on the comlink, ''All aboard what's comin' aboard.''

Backwash from the rotors whipped the fire into an uncontrolled frenzy, fanning embers in the grass, igniting the entire campsite. A position that had been hopeless was now unbearable. In the mad scramble to get to safety, Jake hung back, to give the others a chance— full professors and graduate students first. Peg started to heave equipment aboard.

Two figures in flameproof suits hopped out. One grabbed Peg and hoisted her up. She struggled aboard, still holding tight to her recorder.

The second one hustled Jake toward the hovership.

Nearly blinded by the blast of smoke and fire from the propwash, Jake lunged for the entry port. Peg reached down for him. He took hold of her hands in an acrobat's grip, hand to wrist, and she heaved him up.

Jake rolled aboard, as STOP team members sprayed him with fire retardant foam. Smoke poured through the open entry port. Gasping like a landed flounder, Jake saw two fire-suited figures step over him. The deck heaved sideways as the hovership took off. Through the open door he watched the water hole drop away as the vulture tree burst into flames.

Peg was on her knees beside him, her face blackened. Foam bubbles clung to her hair and eyebrows. "Where's my recorder?" she demanded, searching the deck with her hands.

Jake blinked and looked about.

"My recorder." She rose up, looking wildly about. "I set it down to pull you aboard. Did you bump it coming in?"

Jake hadn't bumped anything but the deck. He did a quick survey and head count. The entire expedition was there, looking stunned and gasping from the smoke. But none of the samples, none of the specimens, and not a single recorder had made it aboard.

He looked past Peg at the open port. Going back was impossible. They were better than a thousand meters up, and the whole of Rancho La Brea was swept by sheets of flame. Surface pools of tar had caught fire, blazing like great fiery patches in the wider sea of smoke and fire. The door slammed shut.

An oversolicitous female meditech bent down to ask if he was hurt. He nearly shoved her off him. Hurt? Hardly. But he *was* hopping mad, cursing the bastards at FTL. "No. I'm fine—really fine. Just give me a goddamn specimen bag."

"A specimen bag?"

"Yes, damn it. Give me a pair of them, and a steel scalpel."

The meditech produced a pair of plastic bags and a razor-edged scalpel from her kit, handing them to Jake.

Struggling to a sitting position, he started scraping ash, mud, and grass stems off his pant cuff. Putting the purplish blond stems and black ash carefully into the bags, he looked significantly at Peg and the puzzled meditech.

"These samples came right off my clothes," he told them. "You are my witnesses."

They both nodded dumbly.

Jake sealed the bags, then made them thumbprint the seals. It was all they had to show for the first trip to the Pleistocene.

Red Planet

"An accelerant." Jake laid the specimen bag containing charred grass and ashes on Peg's low black antique table.

Peg stared at the little bit of the Pleistocene in her Paris apartment. "How do you know?"

"The way those backfires burst out of control was utterly unnatural. So I had some lab people look this over. They detected a petroleum-based fluid accelerant. The whole area around the campsite must have been sprayed with it."

She nodded. It had been way too neat, the fire blazing out of control, and their STOP backup arriving in time to save everything but the data. "But how?"

Jake grimaced. Had he possessed the foresight of a paramecium, he would have seen this coming. "Those academics insisted on having STOP backup. That made it simple. Someone at STOP gave FTL the portal map. FTL sent in a team, timed to arrive a day or two ahead of us. They sprayed the area and set a delayed igniter to kick off the fire. Then STOP came thundering to the rescue, making sure we got out with nothing but our lives."

Such split second timing had been impossible in the Mesozoic—but the Pleistocene was practically next door, a few thousand years before the historical periods.

Peg fingered the bag. "If we can prove it . . ."

"I have proved it—to my satisfaction. Proving it to your academic friends will be more tricky. FTL picked their accelerant carefully."

"What did they use?"

"Fine droplets of petroleum distillate. Not just any petroleum, either. It perfectly matches tar taken from the Rancho La Brea pits." FTL had centuries of experience at covering its tracks.

Peg looked glumly at the specimen bag.

They could well imagine what a fine time professors would have with that—studies and counterstudies, arguing over whether the tiny tar droplets were a natural phenomenon or an engineered disaster. It would take an entire new Pleistocene expedition. Maybe several. And still not everyone would be happy.

Jake reeled off his pet theory, about FTL having a pipeline to tomorrow. "We can only build gates that go backwards, but there could also be a gate or two originating in the future, and opening here. It would explain a lot, if the organization here-and-now were being fed information from the future—not all the time, but often enough to make a difference."

"How far in the future?"

"Who knows? A week, a month, a millennium. Far enough to stay one jump ahead. I think they *knew* that whoever came back from the Mesozoic would be too big to handle. So they set us up. To take away our aura of being 'the first.' "

Some slick suckers. He could picture the planning. Keep the breakthrough team small—a first time paleontologist and a senior field agent with an insubordinate streak. "They baited us into trying to go it alone, with a rigged disaster waiting to happen in the Pleistocene."

Not for nothing did field agents joke that FTL stood for Fuck The Locals. The fire had burned everything, leaving hardly a nanosecond of material to show for the vast expense of sending an entire graduate seminar tens of thousands of years into the past. No DNA scans, no chromosome samples, no additions to the world's stock of previously extinct species. *Time Tours* had put a huge black hole in the energy budgets of half a dozen university departments. The biggest boosters of the Pleistocene disaster were now pleading for FTL to pick up the pieces. *Time Tours* had about as much future as *T. rex*.

It won no points for Jake to point out that *he* had been against Rancho La Brea from the start. *He* had wanted to go straight back to Hell Creek, rather than tackling a totally new period—with all the shocks that entailed.

Peg got up and paced, still going over possibilities for academic support. Jake refused to listen, sickened by how neatly he had been ambushed by her academic accomplices.

Leaping up, he seized Peg by the elbows, trying to stop her gyrations around the apartment. "Give it up. Look, I'm going back to Mars. Come with me. I have a friend in Chryse, a real Tars Tarkas who will lend us a pleasure boat. We can ply the canals together, and let past and future go hang."

She twisted angrily out of his grasp, not at all ready to play Dejah Thoris to his John Carter. "No. I won't let them do this to me—or to you."

"They've already done it. To both of us." Jake knew all too well there was no undoing the past.

Peg got madder, goaded by his inaction. "We have to put together another expedition or *Time Tours* is finished."

"*Time Tours* is finished. It was a silly idea from the start. I just want to get on with my life." Some life.

"Then get on with it without me."

The argument that followed was one that even Charlotte could not patch up, though she managed to keep them from breaking things. The last Jake saw of Peg she was stalking off to attend a face-to-face conference.

Fine, let the profs have her.

He tried taking his case to Tanya Larke. But this time he got no hand-rolled sushi, much less an invitation to her private labyrinth and a romp in the big low-g float-abed. Tanya dealt totally in image, and Jake's image at the moment was mud.

"I like you, Jake," Tanya told him, sitting cross-legged on her tatami mat. "I really do. You know that—I don't fuck just anyone."

For once she sounded her age, worldly wise, without a sexy catch in her voice. Almost matronly, as though he were an errant schoolboy. "I can only work with what you bring me. Bring me something with sizzle, and I'll back you against FTL and all the university depart-ments on the planet."

"Dinosaurs have it," he protested. "You said so. The key to the Hell Creek anomaly is still in my head."

"Dinosaurs had it, but they lost it. They've been dead for a million years, at least. What sizzled was you and Peg. You were a gung ho pair of talented overachievers, acting like the planet owed you a living. Now you can-not understand why the crowd has turned. I know what that is like."

She nodded toward her tall studio windows—now showing the bottom of a coral lagoon, brilliant blue-yellow fish darting through sunlight and sea grass. "Why do you think I ran that Aztec sacrifice for you? Keep the miracles coming, or they feed you to the crocs. Bring me something new. Something with guts and sex appeal."

"How am I supposed to bring you something new when I'm grounded?"

"That's up to you. But don't waste any time, we live in a lightspeed society with the collective attention span of a gnat."

Stuck in the present—stranded in real time—there

was nothing for Jake to do but go home to Mars.

FTL had long ago dropped him from its rotation, citing his "instability." At the time he had hardly cared; he and Peg had been headed for the Pleistocene—a new period and new triumphs. Now FTL's judgment had been roundly confirmed. They had even taken back his corneal lenses, and the microamps from his middle ears—but the thing FTL most wanted, the map to the Hell Creek anomaly, was still safe in his compweb.

At Cis Luna station he took the gate marked HELLAS. No bugs bothered to follow him.

Minutes later he emerged on the Hellas beachfront, along with a horde of Terrans who had come millions of kilometers to see the Avenue of Quays, a pseudo-Barsoomian boulevard-cum-canal, with its pleasure barges and submerged palaces.

Hellas was ancient, one of the first settlements, nestled in the tremendous natural depression containing the Sea of Hellas. Underground rivers connected it to the canal net. As terraforming progressed, Hellas was continually swallowed by her sea. Half-sunken buildings and ramped porticoes marched straight into thin rippling wavelets, their upper floors serving as piers. Windsurfers cut back and forth between towers farther out, sailing over a sunken city. Old Hellas—the original settlement—was completely submerged, a sea bottom metropolis that could only be reached by submarines or speed-of-light gates.

When Jake was a boy, Sandi had lived up in the hills, kilometers from the sea. Now she was a short walk from speed-of-light gates along the beachfront. Her place had not changed—it was an old-style home atop a ten-meter entrance-pillar. All the homes in her development had been built well off the ground, to delay the inevitable day when the Sea of Hellas would submerge them. They looked like high-tech mushrooms, towering over red-grass sward and flowered walkways.

He had not seen Sandi in years, not professionally at least, but she, too, had hardly changed. Sandi was a typical Hellene (here everyone said "Hellene"—never the vulgar "Hellot") with Afro-Scandinavian features and a touch of something Oriental. Her short-cropped hair was steel gray, and the lines in her face had deepened. But her body was still strong and taut from constant exercise—she considered that important. "It's my instrument," she had told him during his first therapy session.

Jake had not expected *that* sort of session, but before he knew it they were making love. The bed was right there in her office, always neatly made, with the pillow fluffed and sheets turned back. From it you could look out her high windows (glass ones, not 3V) over the flat sheet of blue water, and see hills rising up to encircle the sea like the rimwall of a giant crater.

The sex was gentle at first, and underplayed, then more urgent, and by the time they were done immensely satisfying. (This was Sandi's chosen profession, which she took as seriously as Jake had taken time travel. Microelectronics in the bed did the rest.) After a session with Sandi, he often wondered why he went looking for other women.

"Because you are supposed to," she told him. "If you could not go out and find someone else, I would not be doing my job."

Lying next to her, a hand on her thin hip, Jake thought about how he had been making to love to Sandi, off and on, ever since he was a teenager. Sandi was the first woman he had ever slept with. Sometimes he felt like she would be the last.

"Nonsense"—she shook her head—"there will be others. You are just going through a hard time."

"How did you know?"

"How could I not know?" She stroked his cheek, "You are news, big news. I could barely tune into a 3V cast without witnessing the ups and downs of my most famous patient. Coming back from the Mesozoic alive, and carrying on a very public affair with your expedition partner. Then disaster in the Pleistocene—dropped from the FTL rotation. Now you are back on Mars without Peg. Want to talk?''

He lay back, staring at himself in the mirrored ceiling.

"You don't really have to be here. My professional evaluation is that you are basically healthy—or I would have hauled you in for treatment. But I don't like to see my patients only when they are totally strung out. That makes for a strange relationship.''

Jake did not bother to respond. He did not have to. Sandi's bed was hardwired for everything from heartbeat to brain waves. Sex therapists made love on a surface as sensitive as a surgeon's table.

Sandi ignored his silence. "It's been flattering. People at parties and conferences have been giving me *that look*. Everyone's aching to ask, 'What is Jake Bento like in bed.' I give them the knowing 'doctor-patient' smile—but secretly I feared you might never have time for me. The 3Vs of Peg are astonishing. Dashing around after dinosaurs—she made me feel old.''

"I used to think you were old," Jake admitted. In their first get-acquainted sessions, he had been a boy in the throes of puberty, sitting in this same home-office, staring out the window at the far-off sea, talking about peer group relations and genital hygiene—but all the time wondering when he was going to make love to this strange *older* woman. "Now I've caught up with you."

She smirked. "That bad, eh?"

Jake nodded.

"Like it or not, being mired in the past is an occupational hazard with you.''

He stared mulishly up at his nude reflection in the mirror. "Because I work for FTL?" Used to work for FTL.

"Not really. I saw it long before you worked for FTL.

I remember when you first came here, seeing you stare out the window, I thought right away, 'this boy is a real handful.' The type who falls head over heels for his therapist. I knew if I wasn't careful, I'd never be rid of you.''

"And here I am, back in your hardwired bed."

She stroked the back of his neck. "You have a stubborn, out-of-date romantic streak in you, which is why you have done so well with FTL."

"I'm out of their rotation, remember?"

"You'll find a way back. You won't be happy until you do. That romantic streak is incurable. You're stuck with it. That's why you keep going back. Most patients quit sleeping with their therapists once they've found real relationships. But here you are, the same stubborn boy—a little older, maybe wiser."

He reached over, tracing the lines on her face with his finger. "And you put up with it so well."

"It's my job." She kissed him good-bye.

Jake followed up the session with an aimless walk along the Hellas beachfront. It was southern hemisphere summer. Hellenes went nearly naked, dressed in the traditional kilt and harness, with red, black, yellow, and white skin tones. Terrans came in all styles, from beachcombing wear to tourists' tinsel wigs.

It amazed him to see life still streaming by. He had lost everything. Peg. His job. His ability to visit the past. Even parts of his extended anatomy—the ultrasharp sight and hearing he had come to think of as his own. Lost it all—yet tourists still yakked. His breath went in and out. One foot went in front of the other, as though nothing had happened.

A slender Martian woman separated from the crowd, a red-haired Llana of Gathol in full regalia. She wore ruby sandals and a jeweled tiara—with nothing in between but two silk swatches held in place by diamond clasps and a clever imagination. He pictured her as Peg, though she was just another scantily clad princess.

She smiled. Like an idiot, he smiled back, letting her make eye contact. The princess went immediately into a breathless pitch. "Do you suffer from guilt?"

"Never," Jake assured her, wishing he had not smiled.

"Are you nagged by the feeling that there is more to life than having a good time?"

"Not lately." Jake tried to dodge around her, but she sidestepped agilely, keeping in front of him.

"Afraid of death?"

"I'd pretty much welcome it at the moment," he admitted. "So long as it's not overly messy."

Despite her victim's attempts to dodge, the computer-perfect princess kept to her pitch. "Bothered by transcendental impulses? There is no need to suffer. Free yourself from false prophets and misquoted messiahs. At Elysium Mons we treat all forms of religious addiction including Islam, Judaism, Buddhism, Hinduism, Taoism, Scientology, and every known form of Christianity . . ."

Jake stepped right through her. The friendly talkative sex princess vanished. God, now he was trying to pick up holograms on the street. Tourist towns like Hellas let public service announcements wander about, so long as they kept in costume and only spoke when approached.

Jake left Hellas by the nearest speed-of-light gate.

He had put in for employment, but there was no danger of his finding work anytime soon. In an economy of overabundance, jobs were the scarcest commodity. Megapolis supplied food, housing, hospitalization, 3V entertainment, and universal sex therapy. Anything more you had to work for—and work hard. If you did not like living in an apartment block—build yourself a house. If you wanted more from life than lazing about, find yourself a job. Plum positions—like forestry or performing arts—were incredibly competitive.

While waiting for his name to work its way to the top

of a file, Jake cruised the canals in his buddy's hand-built traveling barge. The boat had an upholstered cabin and a single-handed schooner rig, solar-assisted.

Prevailing winds carried him west and north from Chryse, toward the Boreal Sea. On the days when the wind was not right, he would lie on deck studying the towering Martian clouds, three times as tall as clouds on earth. Emotional inertia set in. Having gone from phenomenon to failure, Jake felt himself turning stale, drifting without purpose or direction.

Bored with dodging icebergs on the Boreal Sea, he sailed down the Gulf of Utopia, returning to the canal net, crossing Elysium and the Amazonis Planitia. Glaciers gleamed down from Nix Olympus, reminding him of Peg. He docked on the edge of a newly opened robo-farm in northern Arcadia, tended by autocombines and smart tractors. Huge dozers were grinding up the landscape, crushing red-gold rocks into dust, then spraying the dust with the bacteria and nutrients needed to turn dust into soil.

Damned hardy bacteria, he decided. It was northern hemisphere winter and bitterly cold. Orange rocks poked up through a thin layer of frost. The winter sky was deep blue, almost black. Dust and spray from the dozers gave it a greasy look.

In the middle distance he made out a lone horse and rider coming over the winter landscape. A strange sight, dozens of kilometers from the nearest gate. Jake wished he had his corneal lenses. As the horse drew closer, he could see it was a big thoroughbred bay.

On the bay's back was Peg, riding pretty as you please, over the frozen soil-to-be of subarctic Mars.

Hallucination was his first thought, brought on by heartache and a thin air. Sandi warned him this would happen if he kept living in the past, replaying scenes through his compweb. But this hallucination kept coming, riding right up to where he was sitting. Her big bay blew clouds of hot breath in the dry frigid air.

Jake shook off his disbelief. "What in the hell are you doing here?"

"I got us a new expedition."

"Where? When?" He half expected her to vanish like that hologram princess.

She did a cheerful dismount instead. "We're going back to the Cretaceous. Back to Hell Creek. As soon as the team's assembled."

Jake jumped up. He was more than ready to go. For over a month he had been pining for Peg, reliving odd moments in the Mesozoic; now here she was in the flesh, inviting him to go back. But where was the catch? He forced himself to ask sensible questions. "What sort of budget? How big a team?"

She gave an angelic shrug. "Six people. Two dinosaur experts—I'm one of them. Also a mammalogist, an ornithologist, a paleobotanist, and a stupendous budget. FTL is handling the details."

"FTL?" That sounded bad. "Why did they give in?"

"They did not actually give in." Peg acted evasive. "Everyone wants to get back to the Mesozoic. Paleontologists are desperate for more data. FTL wants dinosaurs for its African game park. And the key to it all is right here." She reached out, tracing the arc of his temple with her finger.

It seemed so long as he had the map to the Hell Creek portal in his head, life would never be lonely. "So I'm back in the rotation as a field agent?" She had said six people, and named five scientists. Jake assumed the last slot was his.

"No, the agent-in-charge is an FTL exec named Kotor."

"Then what am I?" Jake saw trouble already.

"Transport. You are needed to get the team in and out."

"Is that all?" What a lame excuse for an assignment.

Peg looked embarrassed. "It was the best I could do, after the mess we made of the Pleistocene."

The mess we made? Hardly. FTL had done that, or so Jake supposed. "Do I at least get my field equipment back?"

"FTL says you won't be needing it."

Fat chance. This had all the makings of another high-profile disaster. He'd be going in absolutely cold. Totally under the thumb of FTL. With no corneal lenses. No microamps. None of his favorite crutches. It sounded like a brilliant scheme to bury him somewhere in the Latest Cretaceous, beneath layers of Hell Creek Sandstone and Bearpaw Shale.

"So will you do it?" Peg kept shifting from foot to foot, grinning, anxious to get going, full of the old fire. She was not going to let danger and disadvantage hold her back.

He looked her over carefully. Confound it, despite disaster and disappointment, he still liked what he saw. "What about us?" he demanded.

Peg looked puzzled. "What do you mean?"

"I mean where are *we*?" Were they going to get back together?

"On Mars." She smirked. "But I'm going back to Hell Creek. So if there is going to be any *us*, you'll have to come with me."

Jake shook his head. "Better a short life but a merry one." FTL would just have to be dealt with.

BACK TO THE MESOZOIC

Those who learn from history are still doomed to repeat it.

—Jake Bento

Bird-watching

"Good morning, Mesozoic!" Jake took big breaths of steaming air, savoring the hot peat smell of rotting forest floor. No rock music rattled in his head. FTL had him on a tight leash, refusing to return his microamps or corneal lenses. He was strictly transport—*el burro*.

But it was great to be back. He had negotiated the Hell Creek Portal for the third time, *with no nasty shocks*. Another notch on the navmatrix. A new world record—plus a personal best.

Not that the Uppermost Cretaceous looked the same. The little billabong shaded by flowering trees (where he had first seen Peg naked) was gone, replaced by pine bog, fallen trees, and fern brake, towered over by tall, tall trees—*Sequoia giganteum*. A tree fit for dinosaurs.

The Mesozoic was big, ten thousand times as long as all of human history. Each time he left Home Period Jake's navmatrix blazed a new trail—similar but not equal to the last one. Temporal anomalies opened out like four-dimensional fans, widening as they went back, narrowing to nothing near their point-instant of origin. Only return journeys could be near exact. Jake's chance of hitting the same point-instant in the Cretaceous on the second shot was like randomly picking a planet in the nearer spiral arm and having it be Earth. He had not even tried. Instead he pushed the envelope, going back a bit farther, exploring more of the anomaly—expanding the portal.

Nobody complained. Kotor, the FTL team leader, had adopted a defensive position, his shock-rifle out, aiming to take on the Mesozoic single-handed. Dressed in Martian kilt and harness, he had tiger-striped green-and-black skin toning and an aura of pure bullshit.

The senior scientist, a big bluff paleobotanist named Hooker, was down on his knees, running ferns through his fingers. The rest of the team looked about in rapt amazement. Moments before they had been standing in Montana badlands beneath a towering sky—now they stood knee deep in ferns and horsetails. Flat white light filtered down from tiny blue patches between the trunks of giant redwoods.

Third in command was Tomi, a mammalogist from Alpha C, looking like a forest sprite, or a piece of living art. She had razor-straight bangs, lively blue eyes, and skin like translucent ivory, stretched over a body trim enough to have been turned on a lathe—the eugenically pure creation of a custom-made world. Seeing her standing small and blond among the men, a passing tyrannosaur would have concluded they came from separate species.

Those were the team leaders. The lesser half of the expedition was headed by Chepe, a carnivore expert, one of the jovial Mongolians who wanted to wring out Jake's brain. His bush outfit matched Hooker's, all pockets and zip flaps. Peg was at the bottom of the scientific crew, along with Rima the staff ornithologist—an Afro-Australian with an impudent air.

FTL had picked the team to maximize public impact. Leaving aside Jake (who was strictly adjunct) exactly half the team were women—and a third were offworlders—precisely mirroring Home Period's population. Every Earth continent was represented, excepting Antarctica and South America. (In contrast the First Moon

Expedition had been very poorly picked—three white guys from North America in a little boxy capsule.)

Kotor, their man-on-the-scene, was Martian, from an Old Settler family. His ancestors had came over on the *Lowell*, when speed-of-light gates were still science fiction. (Jake's parents had been Brazilian.) Kotor wore the traditional kilt and tooled leather harness over a wrestler's body—making Jake's Lakota buckskins look mighty shabby. Plainly, Jake was meant to play Tonto to Kotor's *kemosabe*. But months spent in the Mesozoic had to count for something. Even FTL could not finesse that.

This expedition structure made splendid media sense, but it meant the team leaders were a temporal bureaucrat and a plant biologist. They aimed to bring back a dinosaur, yet the highest-ranking vertebrate biologist was Tomi—an offworlder specializing in small mammals, who never tackled anything more sinister than a chipmunk. Peg, the only dinosaur expert who had experienced them in anything but 3V, rated no better than fifth. Jake himself was dead last in the lineup, right behind Rima the Bird Girl.

On the south side of the clearing, a huge sequoia had come down, undermined by groundwater. The falling titan took out a grove of smaller trees, opening a hole in the canopy. Tomi peered up into sunlight streaming through soggy air. "Look, a pterodactyl!"

Rima swiftly corrected her, pointing out that this was the Upper Maastrichtian of the Latest Late Cretaceous. True pterodactyls had not been seen since the Jurassic, some seventy million years away. Tomi had more chance of spotting a scramjet.

Tomi looked contrite, "So what was it?"

"A bird. Birds are about to inherit the earth." Rima always talked about dinosaurs as though they were a sideshow.

"Here, I'll show you." She vaulted atop a log, then

climbed onto the side of the fallen goliath on the south end of the clearing. Jake had liked Rima from the first. Her stubborn, insubordinate streak made her a natural ally. Tomi followed Rima up the log. So did Peg, who had already begun to shuck her clothes, glorying in the strong young Mesozoic sun. Possums scurried out of their path.

As the female half of his expedition headed up the pile of timbers, Kotor called out, "You should have protection."

"Certainly." Peg signaled to Jake from halfway up the side of the fallen sequoia. He rummaged through his silver rucksack, produced a hand-sized black canister, tossing it to her.

"What was that?" Kotor was required to be suspicious of Jake's every action.

"Bug bomb," Jake replied. Ultrasonic bug repellant.

Kotor had clearly been thinking of something with more stopping power, but did not stoop to argue, jumping on the chance to reprimand Jake. "Equipment is to be logged and checked before being disbursed."

"It was." Jake tapped his head with a crooked finger. FTL had not taken away his memory banks.

If Kotor were not a sworn enemy, Jake could have pitied him, having to ride herd on a bunch of headstrong scientists sixty million years from civilization. Snapping a light climbing line about his waist, he scrambled up after the women. Deprived of fixed duties, Jake aimed to please himself.

Rather than go trailing after the lower half of his team, Kotor told Hooker to stop fondling the ferns and take charge of the unauthorized expedition into the trees.

Meters above the ground, with his moccasins slung around his neck, Jake used bare toes to cling to the rough surface of the logs. He had seen the same bark prints pressed into Montana bedrock. The women were just ahead of him, standing single file in slanting lanes of light. Peg was talking mammals with Tomi. Beyond them he saw a great blue bowl of sky, edged by standing trees.

Rima was right. The hole in the canopy was a great open aviary, a big bird feeder alive with insects—huge dragonflies, magnificently colored day moths, and biting flies. Light, air, and rotting vegetation drew clouds of insects. Birds came from klicks away to feed. Rima pointed out waxwings and flycatchers wheeling overhead, along with insect-eating hawks. Mesozoic bugs were big enough to draw falcons.

Peg triggered the bug bomb and set it down. The insect cloud retreated.

"Unbelievable," Tomi breathed excitedly, bending down, trying to coax a possum closer.

The gap in the greenery gave Jake a glimpse at just how much this part of the Mesozoic had changed. The Hell Creek floodplain had become a low, swampy delta covered with pine jungle. Silvery channels stretched toward the Mississippi Seaway, which was nearer and larger than last time. Stands of magnolia, oak, and tupelo stood among groves of giant pines.

Kotor came on the comlink, advising utmost caution. Jake thumbed down his receiver.

Hooker caught up with them, saying he had ID'ed a dozen species of saprophytes, lichens, and hanging moss. Tomi looked up from her possums. "I never expected it would be so big and noisy." The Mesozoic never seemed to shut up. Insects hummed. Wings beat. The forest wall a dozen meters away was filled with bass rumbles, unexplained crunchings and crashings.

"And so old." Tomi gave up trying to make friends with the marsupials.

"Old?" Peg looked puzzled. By now she had seen a sizable chunk of the past, from St. Louie to Rancho La Brea—but the Mesozoic was always new to her.

"Sure. There's nothing like this in Alpha C." Tomi

painted a stark picture of bubble colonies and orbital habitats, a system still being terraformed—and making a slow go of it. "Everything's spanking new and in your face. This is all old and distant."

Rima snorted. "I'll show you how new this place is." Stretching out on her stomach, she pointed along the log. "See that flat shimmering. That's a biggish pond where the fallen redwoods dammed a stream." Rima had a rock-hard grip on reality. Transported sixty million years to a world where Montana was a hot, wet delta, she was already pointing out odd bits of topography.

Tomi said she saw it, too. So did Peg and Hooker. Through the shadows in the trees Jake spotted the pond surrounded by a fern meadow. A couple of long crocodilian shapes lay in the water. He tried to take a closer look—but his eyes would not cooperate. Without corneal lenses he could not get zoom close-ups.

"The birds wheeling above that pond are a sort of freshwater frigate bird," Rima told them. "Their descendants will fly over seas yet unborn, but right now they are afraid to leave the land."

Rima talked like the Mesozoic brimmed with potential. "But the Tertiary is when birds really take off— with types seen nowhere else. Diatrymids. Bathornithids. Phorusrhacids. Three-meter-tall meat eaters. Giant seagoing penguins. Half-ton ostriches. Condors the size of pterosaurs. All they need is for a cosmic mountain to come along and give the world a whack, getting rid of these pesky dinosaurs."

A curtain of rain swept over them, drenching everyone. In less than a minute the downpour was replaced by shafts of sunlight steaming through cloud breaks shot with tiny shimmering rainbows.

"What dinosaurs?" Tomi looked over the wet pine jungle. Vine leaves gleamed like glossy green mirrors, throwing back the light. "We've seen birds, possums, butterflies—everything but dinosaurs. It's like they are already extinct.''

Peg raised an eyebrow. ''You want to see dinosaurs?''

Tomi nodded excitedly. Hooker did too. ''It's what we came for. As soon was we establish base camp, I'm gonna hunt one up.'' Even a plant biologist could get the dinosaur bug. Down below, Chepe was industriously doing an equipment check. Kotor paced nervously, staring up at his wayward team.

Casually Peg helped Tomi to her feet. ''Watch this.'' Jake grinned at what was going to happen. What was the sense of being in the Mesozoic if it was not *fun*? They had not come sixty-odd million years just to look serious and work their recorders. He picked up the bug bomb, handing it to Peg.

She cocked her arm back, and let fly. Tossing a perfect tight spiral, she banged the canister off a dusty green patch between two big branches. ''Hey, you dumb duckbill,'' she yelled, ''look at us.''

A yellow-crested hadrosaur head rose up, looking them over with one unblinking red-ringed eye. The beast's mouth was full of pine branches. Its head was higher than the log pile.

Hooker swore aloud. Tomi gasped. Kotor called over the comlink, demanding to know what was happening.

For twenty minutes they had been standing a dozen meters from a dinosaur, but only Jake and Peg had noticed. To anyone who had never *been there*, it is hard to convey how a dinosaur's sheer size becomes splendid camouflage in dense cover. The hadrosaur had to be about twelve meters long and two stories tall, but the trees and brush broke its outline into irregular patches of mud-spattered hide—each puzzle piece the color of whatever the hadrosaur had last been wallowing in.

The duckbill stared at the handful of strange mammals, its huge intestines continuing to rumble, churning and crushing hundreds of kilos of leaves and branches.

Then the hadrosaur went nonchalantly back to feeding—its head disappearing below the level of the log. But if she had cared to, Peg could have strolled out along the tree trunk and touched the titanic scaly back.

Torosaurus

"Big aren't they?"

Hooker summed up what everyone who had *seen* the hadrosaur had to be thinking. Jake could see it sinking into this cocksure team just what a colossal undertaking it was to bring back an adult dinosaur or two. And they had to do it alone. No STOP backup. No second chances. If things went amiss in the Mesozoic, no one in the future had a hope of finding them, much less bringing back the pieces. So far only Jake had successfully navigated the portal. If something happened to him (Heaven forbid!), Kotor could no doubt get the expedition Home. Otherwise, there was no going back for help or advice.

Kotor climbed up to look at the hadrosaur.

Jake called for Chepe to come up. The Mongol thanked him, but kept unpacking. Chepe was a carnivore man, and took his calling seriously. He soon had the boggy clearing overflowing with equipment. Dual reactors. Energy fencing. Even an autodoc. Inflatable shelters sucked in air, wringing it out and cooling it off. FTL meant to make this the definitive Mesozoic expedition.

Normally Jake would have given Chepe a hand. But his mission profile no longer called for that—it did not call for much of anything. Knowing Peg would prefer to sleep outside, he set up their shelter-half on a semisolid patch in the lee of the fallen timbers. Then he conspired with Hooker to produce some five-alarm vegetarian chili for an impromptu team party, the traditional "we made it" celebration. Tomi taught Peg and Rima some new fling dance steps from Alpha C—while Jake, Hooker, and Chepe entertained themselves with a wicked combination of hot sake and straight bourbon.

Kotor kept to himself, already feeling the weight of command, having a rambunctious team to maneuver— millions of years from the home office. A situation Jake always enjoyed, but the time bureaucrat plainly found unnerving.

It rained waterfalls the next morning. That did not stop Peg and Tomi from tramping about along the tops of fallen logs, exploring the strange vertical landscape. Jake went with them, finding the cool oceanic downpour an improvement over the first day's muggy heat and clouds of flies.

During a break in the rain, Jake climbed a hundred-meter sequoia to get a look at their surroundings. Large purple day moths and little white butterflies fluttered atop the uppermost canopy. A washed-out sun shone down on a swampy green delta—a ripe delirium of tall trees, rotting logs, strangling vines, gleaming waterways and dizzying heat.

Pines held the islands in place. Mangroves waded on stilt roots into the channels, turning them into a weird watery morass teaming with aquatic toothed birds, giant flightless insects, tiny tree crabs, and climbing lungfish—not to mention the well-known megafauna.

From his pine top Jake spotted a dinosaur, an elephant-sized *Torosaurus*, built like triceratops, but with a longer backward-sweeping frill.

"The largest known head of any land animal," Peg told him over the comlink. "We have to get a closer look."

They caught up with the dinosaur as it crossed a flat

marshy channel to get to a brush-covered island. Or maybe *Torosaurus* was on the mainland, and they were on an island. The maze of streams and tree trunks made it impossible to tell.

Tomi was awestruck. "How can it maneuver that huge head in this tangle?"

"I'll show you." Peg motioned them down the log to the edge of the stream. "Ceratopsians are even better suited to delta country than the duckbills—their feet are bigger, and that horned beak can shear through tough woody limbs and cycad fronds. It keeps its head low and eats its way along."

Crouching behind a big root ball, Peg tested the breeze, finding they were directly upwind of the dinosaur. "Watch, it will smell us."

Jake's compweb estimated wind speed and clicked off seconds. Exactly when their scent would have reached it, the torosaur looked up, gave a suspicious snort, and headed deeper into the brush, slicing and dicing the vegetation with its powerful shearing beak and close-packed teeth. Maybe it did not like what it smelled.

Peg insisted they cross over after it.

As Jake stripped to swim the stream a slash of rain came down the channel, blotting out the far bank. Coiling his climbing line around one shoulder, he gave the free end to Tomi to hold. Then he climbed off the log-jam, letting his bare feet sink into the bottom muck. Warm water gurgled against his hips, driven by an invisible black current, its dark surface pocked by drops of rain.

Letting go of the logs, he took a couple of tentative steps. The bottom vanished. Jake floundered about in midstream, only Tomi's firm grip on the line keeping him from being carried seaward. The current had not bothered *Torosaurus*—but it swung Jake back to the bank, a rope's length downstream from where he had started.

He gave another try, kicking off from the bank, thrashing for all he was worth—hoping he did not tempt the crocs. This time he was able to touch bottom on the far side. Using the taut rope to keep from being swept off his feet, he struggled up onto the island.

For the first time since leaving camp, Jake stood on solid ground, instead of swamp bog and fallen logs. It was only an overgrown mudbank, but definitely *terra firma*. He secured the line to a log, then Peg and Tomi pulled themselves across.

Of course they had lost *Torosaurus*. In the time it took to bridge the channel—and put on Jake's water ballet—*Torosaurus* had mown down the mud ferns, disappearing into the greenery. Another dinosaur that got away.

But Peg was not about to give in. The trail was easy to follow, and they set off after the torosaur, pushing through a screen of fronds and creepers. Rain gave way to sudden sunlight, and they entered a lush clearing choked with lady ferns and club moss. Fat honeycombs hung from the surrounding trees. Bees buzzed in the warm honey-scented air.

Peg motioned for a halt. Putting a finger to her lips, she pointed at the far side of the glade.

Jake's unassisted eyes strained to pick out what Peg had seen. The wet tangle of vines and leaves formed a sparkling green tapestry, as transparent as armor plate. The torosaur could be in spitting distance, but he could not see it. He cursed FTL for taking away his corneal lenses.

Then he saw it. At about head level a face stared at him from amid the luxurious undergrowth on the far side of the fern sward. It was not a torosaur. It was a sharp carnosaur face, with a long snout, bulging jaw muscles, and two forward-looking eyes. Grim, pointed teeth curved down from beneath its lipless upper jaw.

Tomi stirred nervously, reaching for the stunner

tucked under her armpit. Peg stayed her with a touch. "What is it?" Tomi whispered.

"*Nanotyrannus lancensis*," Peg replied. "And there is more than one. Don't do anything to excite them."

Little tyrannosaurs. A pack of them. Jake stood stock still. He had nothing to defend himself with, not even a neural stunner—he was strictly transport. Peg was the expert. Tomi was the team leader on the spot. He had to trust in them.

The nanotyrannosaur entered the clearing, looking as wary as Jake. The beast was not much taller than him, but massed over half a ton, with a half-meter head full of saw-blade teeth—a truly rapacious predator twice as big as a Bengal tiger. A second carnosaur followed the first one into the clearing. Then another. And another.

"Don't act like prey," Peg advised. "Remember, we are not what they eat." Jake did not think they looked overly picky. The buzzing and whirring in the sun-drenched clearing seemed to rise up, filling the silence between them and the toothy carnosaurs.

Kotor came on the comlink, with a location check. Jake listened to Hooker, Chepe, and Rima check in.

Sweat trickled down the line of Jake's jaw, tickling his neck. Tomi's hand stayed clamped to her holstered stunner. How good a shot was she? Would her stunner even stop them? Jake hated to have to find out.

Kotor acknowledged the responses, then called for Tomi and Peg to report. No one answered. He turned up the volume. Where were they? What were they up to?

The lead nanotyrannosaur cocked its head. Almost as though it could *hear* Kotor's calls through some sort of Mesozoic ESP. Then it made its decision. Turning delicately on three-toed feet, the carnosaur stalked off in the direction *Torosaurus* had taken. The others waited to see what action the humans took.

Jake, Peg, and Tomi did not move a micron. Kotor was having a seizure on the comlink.

The remaining carnosaurs turned, following their leader into the tangle. Tomi put in a breathless call to Kotor. Jake could practically hear her heart racing between each word. Everything was fine—just a bit twitchy. They were returning to base camp.

That night there was no party, just tense excited comparisons of the day's discoveries. Hooker had seen more hadrosaurs and a tanklike ankylosaur. Rima had doubled the number of known bird species in the Uppermost Cretaceous. Chepe disputed Peg's identification of the carnosaur pack, "So-called *Nanotyrannus* is not a true species. What you saw was either a pack of immature tyrannosaurs, or small albertosaurs, similar to those found in Mongolia's Dabasu formation."

Peg insisted they were a long way from the Gobi. "Their coloring was nothing like an adult *T. rex*. These were grayish brown, not black and tan."

"Perhaps they darken as they mature. Did you get a good look at the teeth?" Peg admitted she hadn't. "I thought not." Chepe gave her a grandfatherly smile, implying Peg had been panicked in her identification. "We won't *really* know if they were juveniles until we look at their ossification and cranial sutures."

Jake took no part in the debate. As far as he was concerned they were still suffering from time shock, arguing about bone sutures when the living, breathing Mesozoic lay right outside the shelter. They had just had a brush with a band of hideously deadly meat eaters, more dangerous than *T. rex*, because they were more apt to see Jake as a decent meal. Whether they were juvenile delinquent tyrannosaurs or stunted gorgosaurs, he was delighted not to have gotten a closer look at their teeth.

He sneaked a glance at Kotor. The whole Second Mesozoic Expedition was wandering about with no clear notion of what to do next. As much as Jake despised FTL, Kotor was the agent in charge, the fellow who was supposed to give this scientific fracas some direction.

But Kotor did not even seem to be *listening*. Lost in a frenzy of private concentration—the team leader seemed to be frantically searching for a sign from a future that no longer existed.

Finally he spoke, "It is time to commence phase six."

Conversation was replaced by puzzled attentiveness. Phase six? Jake wondered what had happened to phases one through five. He listened to Kotor prattle on about their "success" so far. Phase one turned out to be leaving Home period. Phase two was their trip through nineteenth century North America to get to Hell Creek. Phases three and four were used up entering and exiting the portal. Chepe had accomplished phase five by setting up base camp. "Phase six will be to bring back an adult hadrosaur."

Everyone interrupted in unison. What about the surveys? They had two reactor-cum-dirigibles and a whole world to explore. If they snagged a dinosaur and took it back through the portal, the odds against returning to this point-instant were astronomical. It would likely be lost forever. Chepe wanted to know why it had to be a hadrosaur? Why not an albertosaur or a *T. rex*? Even Peg, the herbivore expert, did not want to just shanghai a duckbill and go Home. "What about the birds?" demanded Rima. "And mammals," added Tomi.

Kotor smiled heavily. "This is why we have *two* field agents—to ensure we could both bring a dinosaur Home, and carry on with our surveys."

Here it came, the fast shuffle. Kotor now had the portal map in his head—all that mattered to FTL. So Jake was going to be sent Home, nursemaiding a kidnapped duckbill. Jake objected strenuously: it made no sense to discard their backup with the expedition barely underway. Trying to shove a live dinosaur through the Hell Creek portal should be the last thing they did—not the first. FTL was going at things ass-backwards just to eject him from the Mesozoic.

But Kotor had his arguments smoothly in hand. Returning with a dinosaur was the main goal of the expedition, and should be accomplished first. He reminded them that the First Mesozoic Expedition "failed to conform to the expected timetable." A pointed way of saying Jake had fucked up once before, flying off on a South American junket before basic ground work had been completed. And the First Pleistocene Expedition had fared even worse. Not this time, thank you.

Chepe cut in, still pushing his absurd notion of waylaying a full-grown carnosaur, claiming, "A predator would be easier to trap and simple to maintain—they are not so fussy. Get them hungry and they will eat. So long as it's flesh."

Needled and outmaneuvered, Jake sat fuming, listening to them discuss the notion as if it made sense.

He felt like a right idiot for agreeing to FTL's conditions, but the chain of command was explicit. Kotor was in charge. Jake had no grounds—aside from common sense—to try to stage a *coup d'état* and take over the expedition. Everyone was here because FTL had picked them. So long as FTL got its duckbills up front, the scientists would make their surveys.

Kotor concluded by saying the survey team itself might return with more dinosaurs—maybe even *Tyrannosaurus bataar*. His sop to Chepe.

Why not promise an ultrasaur as well? Unable to take Kotor's bullshit a nanosecond longer, Jake got up and stalked off.

Leaving the air-conditioned comfort of the base camp shelter was like stepping into a dark, noisy steam cooker. The Mesozoic night throbbed with clicks, hoots, shrieks, and chirps. A hot cacophony that reminded Jake what an alien world they were in—if only the Mesozoic were on another planet, people might take it more seriously.

He slogged through the clearing toward his lean-to. The moon was rising, shrinking as it climbed through

thin layers of mist. Fireflies winked at each other—
blinking out a primordial come-on in Mesozoic Morse
code, "Let's fuck. Let's . . ."

Peg called out, "Wait."

Jake turned and waited. The heady scent of night-
blooming magnolias reminded him of the Old South. So
did Peg, looking lovely as ever bathed in white moonlight, wearing nothing but a worried look.

She came walking up shaking her head. "Too bad."

"Too bad, nothing. This is a fucking four-alarm disaster."

"What do you mean?" Peg looked puzzled and concerned. Jake had said it half in English. Universal did
not have words to match his bitterness. It was an overly
polite language, designed to keep the peace on a
crowded planet.

"This expedition is balanced on a microscalpel, and
Kotor's big concern is getting rid of me." He should
have been flattered—FTL had put JAKE BENTO at the top
of the file. Instead he was outraged. FTL was putting
everyone at risk to score points in some weird endgame
with him.

"It is not that bad," Peg protested.

"It's worse," he insisted. "Kotor is going to get people killed. If by some miracle this hadrosaur hunt suc-
ceeds, come back with me." Once he was gone,
anything could happen. Jake and some dumb duckbill
might be the sole survivors of the Second Mesozoic Expedition. He pictured himself spending the rest of his
life searching the Uppermost Cretaceous for Peg.

Peg folded her arms, hugging her bare shoulders despite the muggy heat. "I can't do that. I've spent my
life training for this. I can't give up up just because the
going is rough . . ."

Rough was not the word for it. Things were headed
for a crack-up at a record clip, but he was the only one
with enough sense of self-preservation to see it.

She shook her head. "Jake, you're not the entire expedition."

But he *was* the one that mattered most. The focus of the moment—even FTL knew that. He made that point forcefully to Peg.

Fat lot of good it did him. She turned and went back to the base camp shelter. Her professionalism was on the line. She had come to offer sympathy, not to get dragged into male gamesmanship.

Jake stood alone in the hot clearing. Clouds shone silver-gray around the moon, but the forest floor was black.

At first light he lay in the little half shelter he had set out, dreading the dawn. Gunmetal sky began to blush pink. The rest of the expedition filed out of the base camp shelter, looking hopelessly chipper in the soft gray shadows. Peg carried a silver rucksack.

He listened to the hollow tonk of shock-rifles being assembled. Kotor had divided the expedition into two teams. Hooker headed one team, with Tomi and Chepe under him; Kotor headed the second, taking Peg and Rima with him. Hooker and Kotor had the shock-rifles. Chepe and Tomi carried neural stunners. Peg and Rima were armed only with recorders. Mercifully, Kotor gave Jake no role in the operation.

There was a plan of sorts, based on Peg's success with her 3V recorder at the hadrosaur rookery. Hooker would open out the energy fence into a funnel, then Kotor's team would use the recorders to project a pack of 3V carnosaurs, stampeding the local duckbills. Hooker's team would stun the terrified hadrosaurs atop the portal (so no one had to drag six-ton sleeping duckbills over soggy ground). Jake would immediately take the stunned dinosaurs through the anomaly into nineteenth century Montana—bidding the Mesozoic a permanent good-bye. A STOP team with heavy lifters would be waiting to whisk the duckbills through the Bermuda Triangle into Home Period.

Neat. Efficient. Nearly foolproof. On the surface everything seemed "in control." Kotor's team had the recorders. Hooker had the mobile firepower. Each team had a shock-rifle able to bring down anything in the Upper Cretaceous.

Kotor summed up his instructions, punctuating each sentence with short finger jabs, acting awfully tough for someone named after an old folks' resort on the Adriatic.

Peg waved as her team set out.

Jake had recorded some of history's all-time disasters—from the Fall of Rome to the Battle of Antietam— they all began by piling complacency atop over-confidence. Rome had stood for a thousand years. Lee's Army of Northern Virginia could flow like wildfire and strike like a lightning. Neither survived the ultimate test.

Kotor's initial miscalculation was thinking that Jake would sit still while Peg went into harm's way. He rigged a relay so his compweb could respond to Kotor's signals as if he were at the portal, then he strapped on a pair of heavy trail boots and headed off, homing in on the comlink calls.

The hadrosaurs Hooker had seen the day before had been grazing downstream from the fern meadow beyond the big pile of timbers. There the water and forest blended into one gnarled morass. Jake ran along the tops of fallen logs, crossing over streams and skirting patches of bog. Calls came over the comlink. Kotor had located the hadrosaurs. Hooker's team was opening the energy fence, while Kotor prepared to herd the duckbills into position.

Jake stepped up the pace, plunging into a patch of swamp. Ignoring crocodile nests and jagged snags, he scrambled over mangrove roots, jumping from tree to tree. His navmatrix promised firmer ground ahead.

It was not yet clear what Jake could *do* in case of trouble. Without his microamps and corneal lenses, he felt deaf and blind. His only weapon was the bowie knife he had picked up at the St. Louie docks—"The Fifth Ace"—tucked into his right boot top. But he was absolutely determined to "be there."

Hooker came on the comlink, saying he had the fence open and could hear the duckbills coming.

Paying attention to the comlink instead of his feet, Jake tripped on a mangrove root, splashing into the muck, sinking to his armpits in stinking ooze that sloshed like liquid cement. Seizing a gnarled wrist of branch, he hauled himself out. Even without corneal lenses he could see a great overgrown fern glade ahead. Scrambling from root to tussock, he made it to solid ground, homing in on Hooker's signal.

And ran right into *Nanotyrannus lancensis*.

The kodiak-sized killer entered the fern glade from the far end. Jake froze. The toothy carnivore stared at him. Jake stared back. Alone. Unarmed. With nothing to confound or confuse the beast, he played back Peg's advice. "Don't act like prey. You are not what they eat."

Jake glared as hard as he could. Most hunters were at least semibinocular, so Jake's two forward-looking eyes were his best defense. They brought the beast up short. *Nanotyrannus* cocked its head, puzzled by this foolhardy biped.

The leaves to the carnosaur's left shivered. Another nanotyrannosaur poked its head out of the brush. Followed by another. Time to retreat. Staring hard at the nearest carnosaur, Jake stepped carefully backward.

The nearest nanotyrannosaur took a three-toed step forward.

Not good. Jake reversed direction, taking a step forward.

The nanotyrannosaur reared back, not sure it wanted to play this game.

An agonized shriek came over the comlink. Followed immediately by a loud and repeated MAYDAY.

Jake recognized Chepe's accent. Hooker's team was in trouble—but Jake had troubles of his own. Sliding slowly backward, he tried to reach the wall of cycads behind him, without turning around, or seeming to be in any hurry.

The nearest *Nanotyrannus* gave him that cool slantendicular look, like it was wondering what Jake was up to.

There was no time to explain. Another shriek came over the comlink, louder than the first. Keeping his eyes fixed on the killer, Jake continued to edge backward. As soon as ferns and cycads closed around him, he spun about, sprinting through the undergrowth. His compweb fixed the location of Hooker's team, bearing one-five-zero—two hundred meters to the southeast.

Jake set a Mesozoic record for the two-hundred-meter dash, galloping through pine bog and bracken, legs aching, ears straining, wishing he had his microamps to warn him of what was ahead.

Chepe stayed on the link, repeating his MAYDAY like a Mongolian mantra.

Suddenly the morass opened up, giving way to low ferns and mudflats. Tomi was just ahead of him, standing knee deep in ferns, her stunner in her hand, tears streaming down her cheek. Jake pulled up short, gasping, "What's happened?"

"Over there," she motioned with her stunner. He looked to where Tomi was pointing. Someone was down, wriggling in the mud. Horrid hoots and grunts came from the brush beyond.

Jake stepped out onto the mud, meaning to help whoever was hurt. A menacing snort came from the undergrowth, sharp and heavy as a cleaver.

"Don't!" Tomi grabbed at him.

Her words set off an explosion in the brush. Birds burst into flight, sending shock waves through the tree-tops. Jake looked back at her. "Why? What is it?"

"*Torosaurus*," Tomi shouted.

As she said it, vegetation parted and the great horned beast itself burst out of the underbrush, grunting in anger. Bathed in the green light falling through the canopy, it swung its huge frilled head about, looking for something to gore. Three massive horns cut the wet air, turning toward Jake and Tomi.

Tomi, Can You Hear Me?

"Help me!" The agonized cry came in English, followed by a piercing inarticulate shriek. It was Hooker who was down. And in terrible pain, forgetting his Universal. Likely to die unless Jake could get him to an autodoc.

But between Jake and Hooker stood the elephant-sized *Torosaurus*, three meters tall at the shoulder and thoroughly aggravated. Its long brow horns swept back and forth at about head level. Short thick forelegs raked the mud. Stepping into the clearing would be suicide.

Jake turned to Tomi. "I'll work my way around. Try to keep the torosaur looking this way."

Tomi nodded, wide-eyed. Reaching into her pack, she produced a pressurized bag of plasma with an IV needle attached, tossing it to him sidearm.

Taking that as an okay, Jake set off into the brush. He had no weapon, aside from "The Fifth Ace" in his boot top. Nor did he have much chance of dodging trouble. The torosaur could gallop at twice his speed through the worst sort of tangle. And irate grunts from several directions told Jake that the torosaur had touchy companions lurking in the scrub. They were on the fringes of an angry herd.

As he slid through the undergrowth his compweb poured questions into the comlink. Where was Peg?

Where was Kotor? Where were the shock-rifles? And where were the damned duckbills they were supposed to be stampeding? What in the hell had happened?

One question was answered at once. He nearly stepped on Chepe crouched behind a low mossy berm, clutching his stunner.

"My weapon won't even slow it," the Mongol complained. No surprise. Stunners were designed for human-sized targets in the historic periods, where elephantine horned monsters were not much of a problem.

"Where's Hooker's rifle?" Jake desperately hoped to equalize the contest.

Chepe motioned toward the clearing. Halfway between Hooker and the torosaur Jake spotted a gleam of metal. The shock-rifle.

Shit. "Get Kotor," Jake demanded. The FTL man had the other rifle.

"We've been trying," Chepe explained.

Peg came on the comlink. Jake was elated just to hear her voice. "Rima and I are a hundred meters west of you—headed your way."

He told her about the torosaur, then asked, "Where's Kotor?" And more importantly his rifle.

"We've lost him," Peg admitted.

At a more relaxed moment Jake would have relished the news—now it just added to his troubles.

"And the rifle?" It was too much to hope that Peg had it.

"He took it with him."

Bastard. Jake turned to Chepe. "We have to do this the hard way."

The carnivore expert smiled grimly, showing some of the old Jenghiz Khan grit. Mongols never expected life to be easy. "You see to Dr. Hooker—I'll go for the rifle."

Tomi came on the comlink. "I'll move to cover you."

Jake almost said, "No." But Tomi outranked both of

them. If she wanted to be a heroine, he lacked the authority to stop her.

Edging as close as he could to where Hooker lay moaning, Jake waited for Chepe to break cover. He could see daubs of mud getting up and scurrying about, becoming ground-dwelling insects intent on avoiding the torosaur's feet.

Chepe burst from the brush, sprinting for the shock-rifle.

Torosaurus turned toward the movement, snorting indignantly.

Taking that as his cue, Jake leaped up and dashed for Hooker, hoping two targets would confuse the torosaur.

It worked. The dinosaur hesitated, not sure whom to stomp first.

Sliding in next to Hooker, Jake administered an immediate antibiotic-anesthetic. The man's legs were a mess, and he had been gored in the shoulder. But an autodoc could save him—If he could get Hooker to it.

Jake looked up. *Torosaurus* had made its choice.

It was Chepe. But the carnivore expert had beaten the beast to the shock-rifle. Chepe scooped up the weapon, turned, and took a firing stance as the horned nightmare bore down on him.

"Shoot," Jake and Tomi shouted the word together.

But Chepe did not shoot. Instead he stood staring over his sights as the torosaur raced toward him.

He was still standing there, aiming the shock-rifle when the dinosaur slammed into him. *Torosaurus* hooked his huge head sideways, sending Chepe halfway across the clearing to land with a wet splat in the mud.

Aghast, Jake had no time to wonder what had happened. Giving a satisfied snort, *Torosaurus* turned on its clawed toes and bore down on him, determined to do evil.

Running was pointless. In parts of the past, Jake's ability to dodge and weave were the stuff of legend, but he could not have outrun the torosaur on a clean track with a wind at his back. Trying to slog through sucking mud with Hooker slung over his shoulder was hopeless. He let Hooker drop, and dashed sideways, arms windmilling, trying to draw the torosaur away from the wounded botanist.

He succeeded. *Torosaurus* went for the moving target. Jake feinted left, then ducked right, managing to get a twist of brush between them—a young magnolia growing in the right spot at the wrong time.

The torosaur bellowed and came on, shattering the little tree into twigs and leaves. Jake tried to backpedal on the slick mud, slipped, and landed on his butt instead. Prone and helpless, he saw a movement out the corner of his eye.

Tomi came running up. Shouting and firing her useless stunner, she tried to distract the beast. And she did. The torosaur turned with the grace of a greyhound, once more choosing the moving target.

Bouncing to his feet, Jake made a mad dash for the shock-rifle lying in the mud a few meters from the fallen Chepe. He reached the rifle just as the torosaur took a swing at Tomi. She dodged nimbly aside, giving Jake the extra second he needed.

He felt for the safety. It was off—the rifle was ready to fire. Jake spun about, yelling for Tomi to duck.

Too late. The torosaur took another swipe. This time the right horn caught Tomi just above the hip, sending her spinning in a spray of blood. She hit hard, bounced, then lay still.

Seeing Tomi go sailing, Jake shouted, half in anguish, half to draw the torosaur's attention. "You big horned bastard," he yelled, "come get me."

Torosaurus was delighted to oblige. The huge beast turned and launched itself at Jake—the only human left standing—in a head-down, tail-up charge.

Jake leveled the shock-rifle. As the great frilled head

grew huge in the sights, he fought to ignore the horns, aiming just above the flaring nostrils. There, behind layers of horn, flesh, and skull was the small bone box shielding the beast's brain. A single solid hit would knock the torosaur snout first into the dirt.

At fifteen meters his compweb urged him to fire. He could not miss. Jake slowly squeezed the firing stud.

Nothing happened. He hit the safety and squeezed again. Nothing. Now he knew why Chepe had not fired. Being slammed about and thrown in the mud had somehow jammed the shock-rifle—something FTL swore would never happen.

He stood horrified, still aiming the useless rifle. Nothing was going to stop the torosaur. Muddy clods flew from the beast's clawed feet as it cut the distance between them at a ground-eating gallop. His compweb reeled off the closing distance. Ten meters. Then five. Then two . . .

At the last moment he threw himself sideways, rolling in under the horns, trying to stay free of the great clawed toes.

The torosaur snorted and swung at him, so close Jake could feel the dinosaur's steaming breath. Fortunately the short nose horn pointed up and away, and the long brow horns hit the mud beyond him. Jake kicked at the huge head, hitting next to the nostril. It was like kicking bedrock. The big beast did not seem to feel it.

Jake kicked again, trying desperately to miss the limb-cutting jaws. Muscles stretched between the long frill and the coronoid process on the lower jaw produced tremendous shearing power—easily able to take off a foot.

Torosaurus lowered its massive head and tried to butt Jake into the mud. The largest head of any land animal bludgeoned the ground to get at him, backed by six tons of bone and muscle (assuming the beast had been watching its weight). Jake did not try to resist. Seizing a long smooth brow horn with his left hand, he pulled himself up. Hooking one leg over the nose horn, he braced his other foot against the frill, struggling to avoid the terrible limb-shearing teeth.

The torosaur reared back, with Jake clinging to its face. Knowing he could not hold on for long, Jake reached down and drew "The Fifth Ace" from his boot top. The torosaur's yellow eye glared at him, as if he were a twig that had gotten foolishly lodged just above its jaws.

Jake drove the Arkansas toothpick into the angry yellow eye.

The torosaur hooted in rage, throwing its head sideways. Jake went flying across the clearing to land in a tangled heap at the edge of the thicket. Stunned and aching, Jake tried to burrow into the mud and ferns, as the beast circled to its blind side, looking for him. His compweb claimed there were no bones broken, but his legs felt like lead. Getting up was not an immediate option.

The torosaur ceased circling, lifting its beaked nose. Snorting and sniffing, it made a slow, one-eyed survey of the clearing, plainly bent on finding Jake, then mashing him flat.

Suddenly a silver streak sailed through the clearing, hitting the torosaur just above its good eye. It was a heat-reflective rucksack. The dinosaur turned on the rucksack, stamping it repeatedly, then tossing it with its horns, trying to kill the hated human scent.

Jake had no idea who had thrown the rucksack. Hooker was half-dead. Chepe and Tomi were both down. But it was a godsend. Rolling to one side, he wormed his way into the brush.

Peg was waiting. She was kneeling, recorder in hand—no longer carrying the silver rucksack she had left camp with. Rima was there too, dragging Tomi into the ferns. There was no sign of Kotor, or his shock-rifle.

Right then, Jake did not care. He was overwhelmingly relieved to see Peg unhurt, and to have gotten out of the clearing alive—in roughly that order. Life was precious, but Peg was priceless. Who else would have known just *what* to throw at an enraged torosaur?

He lay alongside her in the low ferns, his chest heaving, watching *Torosaurus* shred the last of the rucksack. When the rucksack and its contents were ground to pieces, the torosaur turned on the groaning Hooker, taking a few moments to methodically stomp the paleobotonist into the mud. Then the beast lumbered back into the brush, disappearing the way it had come.

For a moment everything seemed still, then the steady hum of Mesozoic noontime rose up to fill the silence. Jake struggled to his feet.

The scene the torosaur left behind beggared belief. The clearing looked like center ring in Hell, churned to muck and littered with shattered cycad fronds, shreds of the rucksack, and bloody bits of Hooker's tailored jungle jacket. A torn sleeve in one spot, a zip flap in another. Chepe lay at the far edge making a horrible keening sound, with white bone poking from his shin. Flies buzzed about his wound, but he was insanely lucky to have survived.

Rima bent over Tomi from Alpha C, medikit in hand, repeating again and again, "Tomi, can you hear me?"

Tomi's flawless body had a big ragged hole above her left hip. Gleaming intestines protruded from the wound, and she had lost more blood than Jake thought she had in her. But she was breathing. Her lips moved, and in a moment she was talking. Her first words were, "Where's Hooker?"

Jake nodded grimly toward the clearing. Hooker was beyond help, so completely smashed it would have taken a team of expert coroners to tell if the big paleobotonist was faceup or facedown.

"Then I am in command," Tomi whispered. "Until

Kotor comes back.'' She had a wound that would have made a combat medic queasy, but she was still ready to take charge. FTL team leaders were picked for single-mindedness.

Jake stared across Tomi at Peg, who was working hard to close the hideous wound with a pair of butterfly clamps. "Where the hell *is* Kotor?"

Peg shrugged. "He vanished the moment the torosaurs appeared. I don't want to say . . . ."

"Then I will." Rima's anger came out smooth and even. "He ran. I was right beside him when the torosaurs broke cover. He was gone like that." She slapped her hand and clicked her tongue to show how fast Kotor took off.

"What happened?" Jake wondered aloud. They both talked like there were several torosaurs—but he had seen only one. Though that one had done more than enough.

"Kotor had a lock on a small herd of hadrosaurs," Peg explained. "Mostly females. Perfectly positioned. Ready to be chased onto the portal. But there was a knot of torosaurs in among them. Kotor did not see them. Nobody did."

Jake could fill in the rest. Horned ceratopsians were nothing like duckbills. They were tough and hideously well armed. When they saw the 3V tyrannosaurs they did not spook, they fought.

Tomi tried to struggle upright. Slipping in and out of consciousness, she seemed in no shape to give sensible orders, but it was not up to Jake to take over—both Peg and Rima outranked him. "See to Chepe," Tomi insisted, then collapsed again.

Chepe lay across clearing, still keening horribly. Peg was busy with the butterfly clamps, so Jake asked Rima for her medikit. "And any plasma Tomi can spare."

Rima did not answer.

Jake had his hand out, expecting the medikit and plasma. When he did not get them, he looked questioningly at Rima. She was looking past him, eyes wide, lips parted, as if she were about to shout—but had thought better of it.

He spun about, thinking to see *Torosaurus* returning. But what he saw was worse, much worse. "We're fully fucked," he whispered.

Silent as noon shadows, the *Nanotyrannus* pack entered the clearing. You would never expect that half-ton carnosaurs could slink so quietly, but they did. Even the insects fell silent. The whole Mesozoic seemed to draw breath—making Chepe's high-pitched moans sound all the louder. The four carnosaurs stood surveying the carnage in the clearing with toothy grins on their faces.

Nanotyrannus Lancensis

A nightmarish situation. Given a couple of minutes, they could have collected themselves and beat a retreat behind the energy fencing. Mourning the death of Hooker, and wondering what the hell happened to Kotor—but otherwise semi-intact. Previous encounters with *Nanotyrannus* had been benign, because humans behaved calmly and carefully. But calm, careful behavior did not include lying about, moaning, and bleeding.

Jake frantically quizzed his augmented memory for the stunners—current locations. Tomi's was lying wherever it had landed when she was gored and thrown. (His compweb offered a locus of point-probabilities.) The other was in Chepe's holster. Jake urged the Mongol to get his gun out—"Fast!"

Chepe answered with a groan.

Sweating in the fever heat, Jake watched Chepe fumble at his shoulder holster as the minikillers fanned out into the clearing.

They studied Hooker's remains, then turned on Chepe—who at last had his stunner out. He fired at the closest one. The carnosaur staggered to a stop, its head cocked, but did not go down. A stunner was light for this sort of work.

The remaining nanotyrannosaurs did not seem to notice their companion's incapacity. A healthy boom and blast might have put the carnosaurs on their best behavior—but all the stunner did was hum. The next expedition needed sound effect stunners.

Sensing a meal, a couple of the hungry theropods closed in on Chepe from opposite angles.

"Watch out!" Jake shouted into the comlink."Two more coming. One at 280. The other at 140."

Chepe lurched around, freezing the one coming in over his shoulder.

"Now the one at 140," Jake yelled. Chepe rolled back, swinging his stunner around.

The *Nanotyrannus* struck at the movement, its jaws catching Chepe's arm just beneath the wrist. He screamed in agony as the beast bit down. Struggling in the saw-toothed vise, Chepe refused to give in, making a left-handed grab for the stunner, clinched in his half-severed right hand.

He missed, unable to get past the beast's snout.

Chepe tried again. The wary carnosaur jerked its head back. Chepe shrieked as the movement pulled him half to his feet. His right hand fell free, still clutching the stunner.

The fourth carnosaur grabbed him on the thigh, pulling the other way. Chepe collapsed in shock. Twisting in opposite directions, the two carnosaurs tore him apart, then proceeded to feed on the carnivore expert.

Now there were two stunners lying in the clearing. The nearest had Chepe's hand attached. Jake was not tempted to go for either of them. Not in the wake of such a gruesome demonstration of the weapon's weakness. Unless Kotor showed up with the second shock-rifle, they were as defenseless as Christians in the Colosseum.

The carnosaurs Chepe had fired on quickly shook off the effects, looking distrustful but alert. Neither wanted anything more to do with Chepe. They turned instead to look at Tomi, lying in Rima's bloodstained lap—seeming to like what they saw.

"Get her up," Peg ordered. Tomi was technically in charge, but Jake did not wait for the command to come through channels. He helped hoist Tomi up, supporting her under one shoulder while Rima took the other. To lie in the mud and bleed was to die.

Peg tore off the remains of Tomi's tunic, working her pants off with it. The red wound and plastic sutures stood out against her startlingly white body.

Balling up the bloody clothing, Peg turned to confront the minityrannosaurs. She took two calm steps toward them, and the carnosaurs stopped, cocking their heads to see what she would do. Throwing hard, Peg tossed the ball of clothing past their noses into the clearing.

Taken aback, one snarled in surprise, but the second leaped on the bundle. A moment later they were fighting over it, ripping the bloody fabric to shreds.

"Now, while they're distracted." Peg gave a backhand wave, signaling Jake and Rima to get moving. Supporting Tomi between them, they slid back into the thicket, abandoning what was left of their teammates to the theropod pack. Jake had learned long ago to cut his loses—Hooker and Chepe were as dead as chivalry, but Tomi might still be saved. Peg stayed to cover their retreat.

Jake's navmatrix laid out a shortest available route to base camp, skirting deep streams and sucking bogs. Rima was strong and Tomi massed next to nothing, so they made splendid time. The slurping, bone-cracking sound of carnosaurs feeding was soon lost in the Mesozoic hum and bustle.

He worried about Peg. She always knew what to do, but anyone can make a slip—being a carnivore specialist had not saved Chepe. But getting Tomi to safety was the best help he could give Peg. He was having to deal with way too many things already. FTL had fucked up on a stupendous scale, leaving it up to Jake to tackle torosaurs and help carry off the wounded.

In no time Peg was on the comlink, chatting with Rima. Dodging horns and staring down carnosaurs had not suppressed the scientist in Peg—she insisted on *learning* from the experience. "Those grunts given off by the torosaurs were not just angry articulations. I think they were warning the rest of the herd away."

Rima agreed. "Their behavior is a lot like flocking in birds." She was as hopeless as Peg, blithely discussing flocking behavior while they crossed croc-filled creeks, trying not to get blood in the water.

Peg caught up with them at the energy fence. She was securing it behind them when a call came in from Kotor. He was hurt.

"That's nice," Jake muttered. He was in the mood to call it a day, leaving Kotor on the wrong side of the invisible fence, hopefully decorating a *Torosaurus* horn. A tempting prospect. But there was Kotor's shock-rifle to consider—their only remaining weapon able to keep a dinosaur at bay.

Tomi had swooned from the shock of being carried, putting Peg in nominal command. She took stock. They were safely behind the fencing. Two of them could easily get Tomi to the autodoc. "One of us should go for Kotor," she decided.

Jake grinned. "Let it be me."

She gave him a worried look. "All right, but we need him alive. Don't hurt him."

"No more than I have to."

Peg grimaced, handing him the remaining medikit. He gave a casual salute and headed off, leaving Peg and Rima to get Tomi back to camp.

By back-feeding the comlink signal into his navmatrix, Jake got a location fix. Kotor was only a couple of klicks away. Which was good. Jake could no longer move as quickly as he needed to. Being hammered by that torosaur had taken the bounce out of him. Liberal use of the medikit masked the pain and fatigue, but his steps were no longer sure. His thighs felt stiff, ready to buckle, and his legs could not be trusted on uncertain footing.

Heat also took its toll. Sweat soaked his buckskins, and clouds of tiny flies swarmed about his head, trying to drink the salty perspiration around his eyes and at the corners of his mouth. He tore off his jacket, tying it about his waist. Then he set off a bug bomb, suspending the canister about his neck from a plastic loop.

The flies retreated, leaving him with just the muck and marsh to deal with.

Kotor had picked a perfect place to lose himself. Here the delta fanned out under a dense pine canopy, full of deep shadows and bottomless bogs. Great rafts of floating vegetation choked the waterways, masking channels that got bigger and more croc-infested as they neared the sea. Trees had to send roots up through the muck to breathe, some as sharp as *punji* stakes.

Jake stopped atop a log to rest. He saw a thescelosaur amble down a narrow game trail toward the water. This so-called "wonder lizard" was a quick long-tailed plant eater, twice the size of Jake and colored a brilliant pink and black. The Cretaceous equivalent of an antelope.

There was a slight shimmer in the water. The plant eater turned to flee.

A six-meter-long croc burst from the water in a fountain of spray. The monster must have massed more than a ton but it moved with blinding speed, seizing the startled herbivore by the leg. The horrified thescelosaur kicked and shrieked, hopping about as the croc hauled it backward toward the water. In a matter of seconds the croc disappeared, pulling the struggling dinosaur after it. Muddy ripples closed over the spot.

After that little show Jake kept up a steady pace. It was plainly unhealthy to linger.

He caught up with Kotor on the far side of marshy island, covered with horsetails. The expedition leader was sitting on a pine log slanting down into the water. It was clear why he had not gone any farther. Here the salt marsh and bog mire ended abruptly, butting onto a Mesozoic Ganges, more than a kilometer wide and swarming with crocs. The only way to cross would have been on their scaly backs.

Kotor looked dizzy and disoriented, sitting head down, half-retching. His black-and-green skin toning had run together, becoming a gray-green smear. The John Carter of Mars kilt was torn in several places. When he finished trying to vomit, Kotor straightened up, staring in horror at his hand.

Jake stepped up onto the log. First things first. "Where's the shock-rifle?" he demanded.

Kotor looked dumbly up.

"The shock-rifle. Where is it?"

"I lost it."

Jake sighed. "Where?"

"Back there." Kotor waved with his left hand. "I dropped it fording a channel."

Jake shook his head. "You sorry sucker." So much for getting something useful out of the man. Jake's main motive for coming was blown.

Kotor held up his right hand, a deep slash ran from palm to index finger. "I've been hurt. I tore it on a water root."

Jake thought of Tomi headed for the autodoc, with a hole in her side the size of a torosaur horn. And never a complaint. Not to mention Hooker, mashed flat because of Kotor's mistakes. Or Chepe, gored and thrown by a torosaur, then torn apart by carnivores. "You got zero to bitch about."

"I need medical assistance," Kotor insisted, still whining about his hand. "You're supposed to help me."

There was an even longer gash on his left leg, which he did not seem to have noticed.

Jake shook his head, making himself comfortable on the log, reaching down and drawing "The Fifth Ace" from his boot top. "I'm not *supposed* to do anything. Strictly transport, remember?"

Kotor looked shocked. His eyes went even wider when he saw the knife. "What are you doing?"

"We're going to have a private conference, just you, me, and this log."

Kotor scrambled up one-handed, looking for a way off the log. But he was backed against the river, where the fallen pine trunk bent down into the sluggish current. Several scaly-backed floating snags lay within jumping distance, but they weren't tree trunks.

Jake examined the edge on his blade. "Take your choice. Me or the crocs. You'll find me just a millimeter more reasonable." Jake had no plans to eat him.

"What do you want?" Kotor looked like he might prefer the crocs.

"Answers. Straight, truthful answers."

Kotor said nothing.

"Otherwise . . ." Jake tossed the bowie into the air, letting the blade tumble in the sunlight. His compweb computed the arc, and he neatly caught the knife as it came down.

Kotor slumped back down on the log. "I never wanted to be here."

"Then what the hell did you come for?" There were thousands, maybe millions who would have happily taken Kotor's place—weird as that was—just to walk through this hot watery landscape with its carnivorous insects and irritable megafauna.

"I was ordered to come." Kotor made it sound like being sentenced to a prison asteroid.

Jake took out the medikit, setting it to transmit EKG,

EEG, and skin response readings to his compweb. He tossed it to Kotor. "Strap this on."

Kotor complied gratefully, not caring that the medikit now functioned as a lie detector.

"So, who ordered you to come here?"

"The uppermost level at FTL."

"In Home Period? Or from farther in the future?"

Kotor did not answer. He did not have to—the medikit answered for him. Kotor knew—or at least believed—that the orders came from somewhere beyond Home.

"Why?"

Kotor shrugged. "I was ordered to keep you in check."

"Why me?" Jake wondered if he would ever make sense out of this. He always naturally assumed he was important, but not *that* important.

"Because it's essential to them."

"Essential to the future?"

Kotor nodded. "Essential to the near future at least."

"How so?"

"FTL is going to lose its monopoly on time travel. And you are a key part of that. We cannot stop it, but we at least hoped to delay it."

"What about the others, the ones from the future?"

"They don't care about the monopoly. All they wanted was for us to establish the portals for them. The shits. They know *everything*, but they don't tell us. They show up when they feel like it. Giving orders. Dropping hints. But mainly leaving us in the dark."

Jake recognized FTL's boxes inside boxes security system. The leaders from "farther along" protected themselves by keeping their Home Period stooges purposefully ignorant. Just like Jake had glibly lied to friend and foe alike aboard the *Aleck Scott*. Who cared what you told the locals?

But that need to deceive meant they were somehow vulnerable. And wary of Jake.

"No one even told me what I was supposed to do *exactly*." Kotor was back to whining. "It was all just dumped on me . . ."

And he failed spectacularly. All of this was the pitiful truth, according to the medikit. Jake shook his head in disbelief. Wasn't the Mesozoic dangerous enough? It was absolute madness to send in a team divided against itself. But that was what "they" wanted. Someone in the future planned to profit from the farce.

He told Kotor to listen up. "This has all got to stop."

"What do you mean?" The man looked miserable, trapped between a failed expedition and a river full of crocs. The Mesozoic was supposed to be glamorous and exciting, not hot, sticky, and dangerous.

"You've got to forget about your orders and start making a job of this, or else . . ."

"Or else what?"

"Or else I feed you to the crocs." Tanya Larke's favorite fate for the inept and unlucky.

Kotor looked aghast. "That's murder."

"Not technically," Jake explained. Logically there could be no such thing as murder sixty million years beyond the most liberal statute of limitations. Montana would not have a functioning legal system until the Indians arrived, none of whom cared a plugged buffalo for Kotor. Sitting Bull was Jake's *friend*, and the Crows were always glad to see He-Who-Walks-Through-Winters. Kotor was some Martian they had never met.

"You wouldn't." Kotor said it, but the medikit showed that even he did not believe it. He thought Jake was capable of just about anything.

"I can't afford to keep watch on you. Too distracting." Jake stopped toying with the knife, holding it between them in the fencer's grip. He was not overly skilled with edged weapons, but Kotor could not know that. There was no lie detector on Jake. "Right now you're a dangerous liability—a threat to everyone's safety. Just ask Chepe and Hooker."

Kotor brightened. "You mean they survived?"

"Nope, they were both gored and trampled, then eaten. Which sort of makes my point."

Kotor slumped back into apathy, acting too pitiful to be killed.

"You've got to promise to take orders and not make trouble. Or you don't leave this log alive."

"But, I'm the expedition leader."

"Not anymore."

"You can't just take over." The medikit indicated this protest was purely rhetorical.

"I don't intend to." Jake had never seen himself as a team leader. Not here at least—the Mesozoic was millions of years away from his prime turf.

"Then who is going to lead?" Kotor looked genuinely mystified.

"Peg is." Unless Tomi made a miracle recovery. This answer relaxed Kotor—the medikit readings fell back to normal.

"But that means no more lame attempts to get rid of me." Peg would not put up with it.

Kotor nodded. The medikit said he meant it.

Jake asked if Kotor knew *where* the portal was that connected Home Period to the future. Kotor shook his head again. He honestly did not know. Jake insisted that the medikit stay strapped around the FTL man's arm—in case Kotor suddenly remembered where his duty lay. Then he let him off the log. The deposed team leader acted absurdly thankful.

"Just don't make me sorry I'm doing this," Jake advised.

When they got back to base camp Peg gave them an "I'm-glad-you-boys-worked-it-out" grin. Tomi was in the autodoc on life support—safe enough so long as her condition remained stable. Even a STOP team or a Home Period MedCenter would not be able to do much more for her. But if she took a downturn, a surgical trauma team would have to go to work. To have that backup she had to go through the Hell Creek portal, then be transferred to Home Period.

Kotor was everyone's choice to take Tomi through. He had had more than enough of the Mesozoic, and no one here would miss him much. "All we need is a dinosaur to send with them," Peg concluded.

Jake assumed this was a grisly joke. When he found out she was dead serious, he hauled her aside for a private conference atop the pile of fallen redwoods. Birds flocked above them, diving at the insects.

Peg's face and hands were slashed by cycad fronds. Tears had cut rivulets through the dust on her cheeks, but she was still full of fight. "We're staying, aren't we?"

She did not make it sound like a question. "We've got twice the equipment this time, and two reactors. It's our chance to do the job we were meant to do." The way Peg saw it, losing two-thirds of the team—half dead, and half *hors de combat*—was hardly an excuse to turn back. Magellan's first circumnavigation began with five ships and 265 crewmen—only one ship and eighteen men finished the expedition. Which made the Mesozoic look like an outing in the park, spotting birds and dodging torosaurs.

All Jake had to come back with was, "What about Rima?" Was she willing to stay?

Peg smirked. She and the team ornithologist were birds of a feather. Rima hated the Mesozoic. She despised dinosaurs, and could not wait to see them slam-dunked. She thought the whole expedition was misdirected, and should have been aimed at the Tertiary. But that did not mean she wanted to go Home. What would Rima say when she got back? That the Upper

Maastrichtian of the latest Late Cretaceous was just too tough? No way. Not if Rima wanted a shot at the First Tertiary Expedition. Like Tanya Larke said, "Keep the miracles coming."

"Okay." Jake nodded. He, Peg, and Rima would be staying. Kotor would be taking Tomi back.

Peg smiled. "So this is our only chance to send something back before we return ourselves. What's it going to be?"

Right. What should they send back? An admission that things were going badly? Condolences to Chepe and Hooker's friends and relations? A sampling of fern spores and tree snails? None of these would make it—not if you meant to keep the miracles coming. Only a dinosaur would do.

Time's Fool

Peg had a plan. Or rather, Peg and Rima had a plan. Rima was the one who pointed out that the torosaur's movements mimicked flocking behavior in birds. Despite her disdain for dinosaurs (or because of it), she had cogent observations to make. While Jake was running down Kotor, Rima and Peg had analyzed and synthesized the torosaur calls. Instead of trying to stampede dinosaurs onto the portal, they thought they could coax them onto it.

Everything had to be done in a hurry, to give Tomi the swiftest possible trip Home. Rima was ransacking the veterinary supplies, which included hypodermic darts for collecting blood samples on the hoof, and a two-year supply of bird tranquilizer for gathering specimens. Peg figured she could calculate the proper dose for a torosaur. "But first we have to find them."

That was going to be Jake's job. He felt like time's fool for agreeing, but he owed it to Peg. She had saved him from a fate worse than sobriety. And not for the first time, either.

But by the time they got to the gap in the energy fence, he felt barely ready for what lay ahead. His legs began to shake. His body was at the point of betraying him. Bullying Kotor had put him in an upbeat mood, but he still had not gotten over the gut-wrenching violence in the clearing.

Peg stood at the gap in the fence, holding her recorder—a light piece for taking down torosaurs, but all they had until the hypos were ready.

"I'm scared," he admitted. And shaken. And exhausted.

"Perfectly natural," Peg assured him. "But we can't put this off."

Jake nodded glumly. They could not chance Tomi's taking a turn for the worse. He thought about sitting in the hovership, coming back from the first expedition, sipping Irish coffee and wondering why he ever left Home. An excellent question.

"Okay, but you have to admit I was right."

Peg looked puzzled. "Right about what?"

"About Kotor's hadrosaur hunt. A first magnitude disaster, and I saw it coming."

"Well of course." Peg acted like that was obvious.

"Not good enough."

Peg rolled her eyes.

"Let's hear it," he insisted.

"Jake was right," she recited. "Absolutely right."

"That's better," he perked up. "Let's go."

Peg shed her clothes, to slip through the brush more easily. For a moment she stood framed by the energy fence pylons, looking like a red-haired forest nymph, then she vanished into the green wall a meter away.

Jake stripped down to his leggings and followed, using "The Fifth Ace" to cut through a living net of creepers and strangler vine. The torosaurs had retreated into the ugliest cover they could find, a green claustrophobic tangle fit to turn back hungry tyrannosaurs. Here a sudden horned charge would be unstoppable.

Visibility fell to zero, a few centimeters at best. Peg was a rustle of leaves ahead. Or an occasional patch of tanned skin. He caught her when she knelt to examine a dinosaur dropping, inspecting the slick drying surface of the dung.

"It's fresh," she beamed. Whatever monster had made this bowel movement had not gone far.

They set off again. Rain shook the treetops. Water crashed through the foliage in wet parallel lines, ricocheting off leaves to splash in Jake's face. He took it as a good omen. Fresh rain would lay their scent, and the rattle of leaves would cover their approach. Jake had been on all sorts of hunts—everything from turning over rocks looking for dinner, to full dress affairs with dogs, beaters, drunken gamekeepers, and debauched Middle East monarchs. This was the wildest yet.

The rain ceased, cut off in mid-sentence. He saw a clearing ahead. At the end of a long leafy tunnel, saw-toothed dinosaur flies buzzed through bars of light and shadow, a sure sign that something big was nearby. Jake stole forward over the soft ground, trying not to give off warning tremors, his ears tuned for the splintering of brush that meant another torosaur charge. He cursed the uncanny silence of huge beasts in heavy brush. Sometimes all you could hear was their digestion.

Peg was just ahead, crouched behind a snarl of bush. She held one hand low and behind her, signaling caution. Jake scanned the green patchwork for several seconds, seeing nothing. Silver drops gleamed on giant spiderwebs, giving the glade a chaotic sinister beauty.

Peg grabbed him and pointed.

He stared harder, willing his eyes to see. Rising above the tangle ahead was the big upward-sweeping frill of a torosaur. Peg pointed left and right. He saw a hip here, a shoulder there, then the regular swaying of a tail. They were on the edge of the herd. A few more meters and he would be barging in among them.

Jake made the hand sign for retreat, and they pulled back into the brush. He mouthed the words, "What now?"

Peg tapped the recorder, signing for him to keep an eye on them while she went to work. Jake nodded, watching for movement in the herd. The torosaurs seemed to be over their nervousness, having gone back to demolishing greenery.

The first snort from Peg's recorder was so real that Jake jumped—afraid he had a *Torosaurus* in his hip pocket. A frown from Peg calmed him.

The herd looked up. The nearest beast began casting about to see who was calling. Peg played her recorder again. This time the herd started to move, shifting their way. Two huge brutes silently broke cover right in front of Jake.

Time to pull back. Keeping a firm grip on Peg he retreated downwind, angling toward the gap in the energy fence. According to his navmatrix they had less than a klick to go, but the retreat had to be smooth and steady. Kotor had shown what happened when you provoked a stampede.

The gap in the fence got nearer. Five hundred meters and they were there. Jake glanced at Peg, an arm's length away, coolly working her recorder, calling in the herd.

Looking back the way they were headed, he nearly had a heart attack. Staring down at him through the leaves and vines was a familiar eye and half a face.

Jake did not have to see the rest of the monster to know who was watching them. The slab-sided head, the boxy, muscled cheek, the slanting teeth were all unmistakable. *T. rex* was looking over his shoulder. The huge theropod was crouched a few meters away, eyeing Jake carefully. By drawing the torosaurs upwind, he and Peg had created a perfect predator ambush. They were caught between the king of carnosaurs and the advancing horns of the torosaurs.

How to break this to Peg? Reaching out slowly—so

as not to alarm the tyrannosaur—he squeezed her shoulder.

"What?" she whispered. "The torosaurs are getting closer."

"Stop the recorder," he hissed.

Peg shut down the recorder and half turned, giving him a puzzled glance. Jake rolled his eyes to indicate the huge head looking down at them.

"*Merde!*" It was the first time he had heard Peg use the word, except to describe dinosaur droppings. She reached out and grabbed the waistband of his leggings, pulling him sideways, crosswind and away from the tyrannosaur.

Jake silently complied. The tyrannosaur watched them go, not about to ruin its ambush by snapping up a pair of mammals. *T. rex* was not a possum hunter.

As soon as ferns and creepers closed around them, they huddled. History was about to repeat itself with devastating effect. Kotor had shown how torosaurs reacted to sham tyrannosaur attacks. Nature was about to replicate the experiment with the real thing.

"What do we do?" Peg whispered. For the first time she sounded at a loss.

"Get Rima," Jake hissed.

Hearing her name, Rima came on the comlink. "The hypos were ready. Do you have a target?"

"We're up to our asses in targets, but you got to be patient."

"We don't have long," Peg reminded him. "That tyrannosaur has heard and smelled those torosaurs. If they don't keep moving downwind, she'll slip upwind toward them." One quick glance, and Peg had sexed the tyrannosaur and put herself in its place.

Jake nodded. The huge carnosaur counted on taking the torosaurs by surprise, getting in a good spine-snapping grab behind the frill. Or maybe flipping one on its side and going for the neck. Either way they had seconds to work with, then this bit of the Mesozoic was going to erupt. It would be like a meteor had hit.

"There's one way out," he whispered. "You and Rima angle the energy fence to the northwest. Keep drawing the torosaurs toward the gap. I'll get the dart gun and keep Her Highness out of your hair."

"Are you sure?" Peg demanded. "You've never even worked one of those hypodermic rifles."

"It's my job," Jake hissed back. He might be low man on the expedition, but he had his place—thank you. Peg was there because she knew dinosaurs. He was there to make things happen—with a minimum of hassle. (Some joke there.) Serving meals. Crashing airships. Transporting people through space and time. Winning at poker and deflowering virgins. Whatever it took. If he had to stop a hungry tyrannosaur in her tracks—sobeit.

Leaves shivered, and something touched his shoulder. Jake suppressed a startled scream. It was Rima.

Following the debate on the comlink, the ornithologist had wriggled through the brush to deliver the dart-rifle. She cocked an eyebrow. "Are you *sure* you're in condition for this?"

Jake took a couple of quick breaths to slow his heart. "Of course. As soon as I've got nothing but a seven-ton carnosaur to deal with, I'll calm right down."

Rima broke open the hypodermic gun. "This is not a shock-rifle. Use it like one and you're dead." Shock-rifles were designed to give massive paralytic shocks to the nervous system. "All this does is deliver a hypodermic dart at high speed." She showed him the dart, a big two-handed hypodermic, designed for elephant control. "I double-dosed these for quick effect—but it's got to get into her. A bad angle or a mass of bone will make it bounce right off." Trust Rima to see the cheery side.

She slid a hypo into the chamber and three more into a tubular magazine slung under the barrel. "This way you won't stick yourself trying to reload—a dose that would cool her will kill you. Pump this slide to bring up a fresh hypo and prime the next shot."

Gingerly Jake turned the rifle over in his hands, noting the vital parts. The trigger tucked beneath the chamber. The slide pump riding on the magazine. A thumb safety just above the grip.

"Go for the arteries in the throat," Rima advised. "Or a chest shot, as close to the heart as possible. An intramuscular hit on the hip, or a belly shot, and you'll wish it was a miss. She'll be picking you out of her teeth before she gets drowsy."

So much for just sneaking up and spiking her in the tail. All the advantages seemed to be on the side of *T. rex*. Jake had just seen half the expedition laid out by a single enraged torosaur. The brute he was going after *ate* torosaurs on a regular basis.

Peg pulled him aside. "One more thing."

"What now?" Jake wondered. He had more than enough to worry about.

She took his head between her hands, giving him a lingering kiss that turned his mouth inside out. When she was done, she whispered. "Try to come back alive. I'll make it worth your while."

Just the encouragement he needed.

Too bad there was no time for more.

Ducking beneath branches and sliding between log piles, Jake went over the workings of the rifle, finding way too many moving parts. The Mesozoic had proved too tough for an electrostatic shock-rifle. How much faith could he have in this jury-rigged dart gun?

Deciding he already had too many things to think about, he tore a thong from his fringed leggings, using it to tie down the trigger. Now as soon as he pressed the safety the gun would fire. And fire again every time he worked the slide. So long as he kept his thumb on the safety, all he had to do was point and pump—the rifle would do the rest. Or so he hoped.

Working his navmatrix backward, he crawled soundlessly on hands and knees through the disorienting thicket. Ground slid and squished beneath him. Pulse pounded in his temples. Unaided ears strained for the swish of leaves that might betray a seven-ton carnosaur headed his way.

Without his microamps and corneal lenses, he had no particular edge over the tyrannosaur and its tickbird sentinels. His sole advantage was that even the most paranoid tyrannosaur could hardly believe any mid-sized mammal would be daft enough to do this. Too bad the idiotic woman who had wanted to put tyrannosaurids on a meatless diet could not see him. She'd be so proud.

His first warning came from the twitter of tickbirds, tiny scavengers who attached themselves to large carnosaurs—picking their hosts' teeth and alerting them to movements in the brush.

His next warning was coming nose-to-toenail with a giant three-clawed foot resting comfortably in the muck. A pillarlike leg disappeared into the tangle overhead. He was practically under the bloody beast, but he had not seen it until he nearly bumped into it. It amazed him that something so huge and scary could be so unobtrusive.

Peg came on the comlink, saying the torosaurs had started to move toward the gap. Had he found the *T. rex* yet?

Jake swore silently. What was the point of telling Peg he was close enough to give the brute a pedicure? Instead he started to work around to the front. There was no way to get a good angle on the neck or chest without putting himself in range of those meter-wide jaws.

Worming forward, he tried not to startle the monster. Half a minute, and he would be in position. Jake eased the dart-rifle around, getting ready to shoot.

Suddenly, something went terribly wrong. Maybe it was a leaf tremor, or a whiff of his strange scent. Or maybe the tickbirds. Or the torosaurs moving away.

Whatever it was, it set off the tyrannosaur. Bush above him seemed to expand, then explode. Tall ferns parted, and a second spring steel leg came crashing down next to him, shaking the earth as it struck.

Another nanosecond and the tyrannosaur was towering above him, unbelievably huge, an awesome fleshy avalanche in overdrive, aimed at Peg, Rima, and the gap in the energy fence. Jake's compweb warned him he had less than two seconds to shoot in. Already the tyrannosaur was moving too fast for him to catch up—if she did not casually crush him as she brushed past.

Jake jammed the dart-rifle at the tyrannosaur's big corded neck, pressing down on the safety. The dart gun fired. He slammed the pump back, and the gun fired again. He was getting off a third shot when the titanic beast bowled him over. Muddy ground flipped up, slapping Jake senseless.

By the time he awoke, seconds had passed, and things had calmed considerably. Sunlight streamed through a rent in the canopy above. Carrion flies buzzed about him, trying to tell if he was ready to eat.

Slowly he sat up, shaking off leaves and dirt. A big bruise ran down his side from ribs to hip. Otherwise, his compweb pronounced him semi-intact. Using the dart-rifle as a crutch, he struggled to his feet.

The tyrannosaur was long gone.

Jake checked the gun. A single dart remained in the magazine. Grimly he pumped the slide to get it into the chamber. Seeing a great wide thoroughfare torn through the thicket, he followed it, calling to Peg over the comlink—telling her there was a tyrannosaur headed her way.

Peg came on, sounding pleased and chipper, saying they had the torosaurs. "Four of them are in the pen. Three females and a male. But we have not spotted your tyrannosaur."

Jake acknowledged with a soft "Never mind."

Lying on the trail in front of him was the tip end of a reptilian tail. The tail's owner had to be in the green jumble just ahead.

Cautiously following the tail, Jake found a giant carnosaur attached to it. Edging past the huge hips, legs, and chest, he knelt down to examine the neck. Buried just below the base of the lower jaw was one of his darts. From the look of things, the first one he had fired. A centimeter more to the left and the dart would have struck bone, bouncing off in some useless direction.

The tyrannosaur's head was flung back in repose, baring the target area, but he saw no sign of the other darts. Just as Jake had thought, he had flinched as the carnosaur bore down on him, pulling his shots. Sitting himself down on a big exposed root, he whistled softly at what had to be an amazing bit of shooting. Who else could claim to have missed the world's largest land carnivore *twice* at point-blank range?

He was still sitting beside the sleeping titan when Peg came to get the dart gun.

She and Rima took down the torosaurs—an awesome, fantastic spectacle that Jake could just barely watch. They constricted the energy fence, forcing the penned dinosaurs on top of the portal. The torosaurs acted like caged hornets, hooting, howling, and charging the fence, until Peg and Rima knocked them out with a few well-aimed shots from atop the pile of timbers. Jake sat nursing his injured side, awed at the sudden stillness once they were asleep.

FTL had its torosaurs. They might have had a *T. rex*, too, but both reactors working together could not produce enough traction to move the comatose monster.

Jake clapped Kotor on the back, saying, "See you on the other side." Thanks to nonsimultaneity, Jake could spend as much time as he wanted in the Mesozoic and still get to the nineteenth century minutes after Kotor.

He aimed to be there before the torosaurs were packed in the hoverships. Ready to rub FTL's face in the fact that he and Peg had succeeded. Again.

Tomi emerged from the autodoc, groggy and bandaged, taking a final pained look at the Mesozoic. She said her goodbyes, then vanished into the portal with Kotor and the torosaurs. The Second Mesozoic Expedition had sent back four live specimens and its walking wounded.

Jake lay down on the safe side of the energy fence, slipping into a much-needed coma, while Peg and Rima went to check on the the tyrannosaur, making sure she did not drown in the muck.

Days later, they rode one of the twin reactors down to the river, to the spot where Jake had caught up with Kotor. Once they were out of the trees and under the scalding sun, Jake told the reactor to take a drink. In a matter of hours, they had a new airship. Rima christened her *Challenger II*, and they loaded her with the autodoc and most of the portable equipment—including such psychic essentials as Jake's lucky two of spades, and his autographed copy of *Life on the Mississippi*.

Then Jake took her aloft. Standing on the forebridge with the windows open, he watched insects buzz about the slowly ascending airship. Peg stood next to him. Rima leaned out a lounge window, recording their ascent.

A giant dragonfly with half-meter wings did a lazy split S right in front of him, diving after a Dracula-sized mosquito. An insect-eating hawk power-dived hard on the dragonfly's tail, turning the hunter into the hunted. The Mesozoic never seemed to let up.

Peg looked out over the Cretaceous, relaxed and satisfied, her elbows resting on the open window. At five-hundred meters the whole circuit of the immense green delta shimmered beneath them. A great pine swamp, cut by brown river channels, and edged on three sides by the sandy shoreline of the Mississippi Seaway. She looked to Jake. "This is how to keep me happy."

"Really? Remember what happened last time I flew you about."

She smiled. "Not flying, silly. That's just a way of getting there. I want to go places and see things."

"And that will keep you happy?" He had wondered what the secret was.

"*Yew betcha!*" Peg had picked up that English phrase from Sitting Bull. She leaned over and kissed him hard, a lingering tongue-twisting kiss that blanked his memory banks. A kiss that made Jake want to take her anywhere, and do anything, even stand up to tyrannosaurs—if they absolutely could not be avoided.

"But I want it all," she warned him. "Not just the *motherfucking* Mesozoic, but the Paleozoic, too. Maybe even the Precambrian. And beyond the stars."

A reasonable request. Jake looked toward the thin blue line where air, land, and sea merged, asking. "So what do you want to see now?"

Her eyes sparkled. "Everything."

"Sure *enuff*." He smiled back at her, mixing Universal and English. Why not? They had all the time in the world.

THE CONTINUATION
OF THE FABULOUS
INCARNATIONS OF IMMORTALITY
SERIES

PIERS ANTHONY

FOR LOVE OF EVIL
75285-9/ $5.99 US/ $7.99 Can

AND ETERNITY
75286-7/ $5.99 US/ $7.99 Can

RETURN TO AMBER...
THE ONE *REAL* WORLD, OF WHICH
ALL OTHERS, INCLUDING EARTH,
ARE BUT SHADOWS

The Classic Amber Series

NINE PRINCES IN AMBER 01430-0/$4.99 US/$6.99 Can

THE GUNS OF AVALON 00083-0/$5.99 US/$7.99 Can

SIGN OF THE UNICORN 00031-9/$5.99 US/$7.99 Can

THE HAND OF OBERON 01664-8/$5.99 US/$7.99 Can

THE COURTS OF CHAOS 47175-2/$4.99 US/$6.99 Can

BLOOD OF AMBER 89636-2/$4.99 US/$6.99 Can

TRUMPS OF DOOM 89635-4/$4.99 US/$6.99 Can

SIGN OF CHAOS 89637-0/$4.99 US/$5.99 Can

KNIGHT OF SHADOWS 75501-7/$5.99 US/$7.99 Can

PRINCE OF CHAOS 75502-5/$5.99 US/$7.99 Can

Magic...Mystery...Revelations
Welcome to
THE FANTASTICAL
WORLD OF AMBER!

ROGER ZELAZNY'S
VISUAL GUIDE to
CASTLE
AMBER

by Roger Zelazny and Neil Randall
75566-1/ $10.00 US/ $12.00 Can
AN AVON TRADE PAPERBACK

Tour Castle Amber—
through vivid illustrations, detailed floor plans,
cutaway drawings, and page after page
of never-before-revealed information!